She knew this would happen.

Tamara shook her head. “You don’t need a good jockey. You need a good legal team.”

Nathan grimaced, blue eyes haunted. “There are few people who want to hitch their reputation to Blackwell Stables nowadays.”

Tamara was tempted to say, “*That’s not my problem.*” Nathan had, after all, severed contact with Tamara and had her fired when she desperately needed his vote of confidence. Without it, no one in the Paducah area had been willing to give her a chance as a race jockey, not even the trainer she’d worked for.

He blackballed me. I should walk away.

But there were his soulful blue eyes. She’d always been a sucker for them.

When was the last time Nathan smiled?

Tamara licked her lips, trying not to worry about him. She had her own problems. “Let’s be honest, Nathan. You don’t want to hire me.”

Dear Reader,

Are you a Big E Blackwell fan? I hope so because this old cowboy recently turned over a leaf from a new branch of the Blackwells and decided mending family fences was important again. This time, he's in Kentucky, trying to heal a tragic rift his cousin made with his five sons many moons ago.

Nathan Blackwell—one of those sons—is at an all-time low. In the past two years, he's buried his wife, had to sell off most of his race horse breeding stock and put down his most promising colt. When Big E Blackwell, the cowboy he barely remembers, shows up wanting Nathan to return home to help save the Blackwell Racing Stables, his family's legacy, this single dad's first response is a hard pass. But Big E is persuasive. He even convinces Nathan to hire jockey Tamara Vaughn, a woman he's tangled with in the past and has sworn to keep out of his future. There will be a rough track ahead for that pair.

I hope you enjoy this installment of The Bluegrass Blackwells. Slip on your boots, grab your hat, and saddle up for another visit with the Blackwell family!

Happy reading!

Melinda

A COWBOY TO REMEMBER

MELINDA CURTIS

Harlequin
HEARTWARMING

Harlequin® HEARTWARMING™

Recycling programs for this product may not exist in your area.

ISBN-13: 978-1-335-60517-7

A Cowboy to Remember

For questions and comments about the quality of this book, please contact us at CustomerService@Harlequin.com.

Harlequin Enterprises ULC
22 Adelaide St. West, 41st Floor
Toronto, Ontario M5H 4E3, Canada
www.Harlequin.com

HarperCollins Publishers
Macken House, 39/40 Mayor Street Upper,
Dublin 1, D01 C9W8, Ireland
www.HarperCollins.com

Printed in U.S.A.

1 2 3 4 5 6 7 8 9 10 HDC 28 27 26 25

Melinda Curtis is the *USA TODAY* bestselling author of lighthearted, contemporary romance. In addition to the Blackwell series, Harlequin also publishes her current miniseries, The Cowboy Academy, about foster brothers. Look for the TV movie—*Love in Harmony Valley*—based on her book, *Dandelion Wishes*. Between books, Melinda spends time with her husband remodeling their home by swinging a hammer, grouting tile and wielding a paintbrush.

Brenda Novak says *Season of Change* "found a place on my keeper shelf."

Books by Melinda Curtis

Harlequin Heartwarming

The Cowboy Academy

A Cowboy's Fourth of July
A Cowboy Christmas Carol
A Cowboy for the Twins
The Rodeo Star's Reunion
Cowboy Santa
The Cowboy's Wedding Proposal
Country Fair Cowboy
The Christmas Cowboy
Winning the Bull Rider's Heart

The Blackwell Belles

A Cowboy Never Forgets

Visit the Author Profile page
at Harlequin.com for more titles.

To Carol Ross, Cari Lynn Webb, Amy Vastine and Anna J. Stewart for always being willing to saddle up and take another ride on the trail forged by Big E Blackwell.

PROLOGUE

Paducah, Kentucky
September 1

ELIAS "BIG E" BLACKWELL parked his motor home behind a black truck on a narrow, unpaved driveway and took stock of the small, white farmhouse and overgrown pasture that was owned by his dead cousin's youngest son—Nathan Blackwell.

The farmhouse was in need of repair and a little TLC. White paint was peeling on the south side of the house. A rain gutter hung loose over the front porch, a string of Christmas lights sagging beneath it. The first-story windows were open and lacking screens. Small flower beds flanked either side of the stairs to the front door. They were filled with weeds.

Nathan, widowed two years now, was in need of assistance.

That's a good sign.

Since Big E was here to broker a reconciliation between Nathan and his dead father, a truce that would have Nathan returning to his childhood home—Blackwell Stables, hundreds of miles away from Paducah in Gold Finch, Kentucky.

Big E lumbered out of the motor home into the September midday heat, setting his black cowboy hat on the sparse white hair atop his head. He took another look around, his inspection underscored by a symphony of cicadas.

The barn was small, perhaps only able to hold eight horses. Cottonwood and walnut trees bordered the pasture. A small fort had been built in one tree. A rope swing hung from another. There was a gray colt grazing in the large pasture. He had the fine lines and long legs of a thoroughbred. A chestnut quarter horse with a white blaze on his nose moseyed out from under a tree for a closer look at Big E.

"Dad! Come watch me!" a childish male voice called from inside the farmhouse.

"Zeke, wait for Dad." There was something slightly different about the second young voice, although Big E couldn't quite put his finger on it. "Dad, come quick! Zeke found trouble."

"T.J., you're not the boss of me." That sounded like the first youngster's voice.

Big E smiled. There was mischief afoot.

He hurried to the front porch stairs. He was close enough now to hear the pounding of authoritative footsteps inside the house.

"*Wheeeee!*" Something of substance—*Zeke?*—crash-landed on the other side of the front door.

And then the air was filled with a howl of pain, "*Ow-woo!*"

"I told you to wait for Dad," T.J. said in that slighter voice, this time with a superior tone.

A tall man in blue jeans and a red T-shirt hurried past one of the open front windows, a man Big E assumed was Nathan. "Zeke, what did you…? Are you okay?"

"Ow, Dad. My wrist hurts so bad." Zeke's voice was teary now. "No, no, no! Don't touch it!"

Big E was tempted to open the door and offer his assistance. Instead, he moved to the screenless window and shamelessly peeked inside.

Two boys of about five sat on a rug in the foyer. Their T-shirts were dirt smudged. Their blue basketball shorts wrinkled. Their sandy brown hair uncombed.

One boy clutched his wrist to his chest, most likely Zeke, given the snatches of conversation Big E had heard. The other had an Itoldyouso smirk on his face, most likely T.J.

Big E smiled to himself. He was learning a lot about those young cowboys just by watching. He imagined they had a roguish nature, the same as him.

"Let me see." Nathan knelt next to Zeke, carefully taking his right wrist and examining the already puffy appendage. Nathan bore a slight resemblance to his father, Big E's dead cousin Walter. It was there in his thick, sandy brown hair and the stoic set to his jaw. Nathan still wore his wedding ring on his left hand, a detail that gave rise to all kinds of questions on Big E's part. "It's either sprained or broken, Zeke. Wouldn't swell up like this otherwise." Nathan sounded defeated, as if this was just another in a long string of setbacks.

Big E longed to help Nathan. The question was: *how?*

"*Ow, ow, ow.*" Tears spilled over Zeke's cheeks. "Not another cast, Dad. I just got one off my foot. *Please.*"

"Can't promise that, Zeke," Nathan said matter-of-factly. "We're going to need to load up and head to the urgent care clinic."

"I can give you a ride," Big E offered, bending to fit his head in the open front window, bumping the crown of his black cowboy hat on the sash.

The three Blackwells inside turned toward him, surprised expressions on their faces. The resemblance to each other was strong.

"I'm family," Big E quickly assured them, introducing himself with a smile. "Nathan, your father and I were cousins." Although not particularly close ones and not of the same age. Walter had been a generation younger than Big E. "We lost touch over the years. But I met you, Nathan. I met you when you were very young."

"Can't say as I remember. And you being related doesn't explain why you're here now." Nathan opened the front door. "Boys, get your boots on."

"Your father made me executor of his will." Big E eased out of the window, keeping an eye on happenings inside while holding that nonthreatening smile on his face. From what he'd heard, there was just cause Nathan and his brothers hadn't shown up for their father's funeral. By all accounts, Walter had been a distant father after his wife died. Big E had to tread carefully with Nathan if he was to convince him to return home. "The reason I'm here is that you haven't been answering the phone. Your brother Asher and I have tried calling. Blackwell Stables are in a spot of trouble. We could use your help."

"I don't answer my phone." Nathan tugged on his boots, plopped a cowboy hat on his head and then grabbed his wallet and a set of keys from a small table near the door. "I don't check voicemail, either. And as you can see—" he gestured at nothing in particular "—I'm busy with my own...*business*."

"Someone's gonna have to help me put on my socks and boots." Zeke was trying hard not to cry again. Given his grimace and urgent sniffs, his wrist was clearly hurting. And hurting bad.

"And I can't put my boots on because I don't have clean socks," T.J. lamented, holding up a pair of blue cowboy boots. He was the smaller twin.

"What's left of your socks are in the dryer, T.J." Nathan turned to Big E. "Socks that match, don't have holes *and* are clean are a rare commodity around here." Then he turned away. "Okay, boys.

Put on your boots without any socks and let's go. The wait at urgent care is bound to be long." Nathan bent to help Zeke, steadying him while he slipped his feet into a pair of scuffed black cowboy boots.

Meanwhile, Big E took in the bed pillow directly at the base of the stairs. "Did you try to slide down the banister, Zeke?"

"I did." Zeke's blue eyes lit up. "Overshot my pillow."

"By a mile," T.J. added with a lofty grin. "I told him it was a bad idea. He should have listened to me. *I'm* supposed to keep him out of trouble."

Zeke scoffed. "It was your idea."

"Was not."

"Was too."

"Was—"

"*Boys!*" Nathan rolled his eyes, shooing them out of the door, then following them to the porch. "Now isn't a good time for a family reunion, Elias."

"Call me Big E, please." Only his wife and sister used his given name and only when they were angry with him. "But I disagree. Now *is* the right time for family to come together." In Big E's opinion, there was never a wrong time. He trailed the trio down the porch stairs. "You look like you could use a little help with…things." The house, his small racehorse breeding operation, and most of all, those boys.

Nathan frowned. "Is this about the racing ban imposed on Blackwell Stables? I can't do anything to help. Sovereign's Pride tested positive for performance-enhancing drugs and now Blackwell Stables can't race their three-year-olds as a result."

He'd heard? Maybe Nathan isn't as isolated from family as he claimed.

The twins were noticeably quiet, soaking up the adult conversation around them as if they hadn't heard much about their family.

Shame, that.

"Not to mention..." Nathan scrubbed a hand around the back of his neck before fixing Big E with a cool stare. "That was what? Nearly two months ago? Why ask for my help now?"

"Because new information has come to light. News that could lift the racing suspension."

Nathan scoffed. "What information?"

"We identified a suspect behind the doping." Big E drew a deep breath before launching into the tale. "A man by the name of Elliot James was the assistant manager of Blackwell Stables. We suspect he doped Sovereign's Pride before his last race." Anger seeped into his words. Big E couldn't abide folks who mistreated their animals, much less folks who stabbed you in the back. "We found the same type of drug and syringes in Elliot's room at Blackwell Stables...*after* Elliot died in an odd car accident, cause unknown. Now, we can say for certain that Pride was targeted. That *Blackwells* were targeted." But Elliot's death complicated matters. The local sheriff wanted to investigate Elliot's crash and the horse doping via legal channels. And that took time. Time that Big E didn't feel they had if Blackwell Stables was to be saved. They were bleeding money like water through a leaky bucket. "I won't rest until whoever is behind the doping is under lock and key."

"I'm no lawman," Nathan said, striding toward that black truck Big E had parked his motor home behind. "Don't see why you need me."

"You know a large operation like your father's takes a team to manage properly," Big E said calmly, refusing to get frustrated. "Asher is good at finances. And you… Well, you're experienced in horse farm management, regardless of your current circumstances."

"*My current circumstances*…" Nathan turned and faced Big E, a hard look in his blue eyes. "You need to move your rig, *Elias*. Now." He pointed at the motor home blocking his exit. "We've got our own problems. Don't need my dad's state of affairs dragging us down further, even if it's Asher who's asking."

"Who's Asher?" T.J. asked, wide-eyed and severely interested.

"And Savvy… Soggy… And *Pride*?" Zeke added, giving up on trying to pronounce the word *Sovereign*. "You mentioned him racing. He didn't die, did he?" His lower lip thrust out.

"No, Pride is very much alive," Big E assured him, not mentioning the three-year-old was suffering long-term effects from the drug. "And Asher is your father's older brother. One of your uncles."

"You met Asher at Mom's funeral," Nathan said to his boys, although he continued to frown darkly. Whatever had driven him away from family, Big E vowed to fix.

"*Our* racehorse died," Zeke told Big E, looking more upset about that than about his injured wrist.

"*After* he won a race," T.J. added proudly.

Nathan made a noise that sounded like a growl but otherwise said nothing.

"But we've still got Pest." Zeke pointed to the gray colt in the pasture. "He's two."

"Pest is fast," T.J. added, chest out, fairly bursting with pride now. "He could win races…if Dad let us race him."

"You haven't run your two-year-old?" Big E studied the fine-looking gray. "Why not?"

Nathan met Big E's inquisitive gaze with silence, chin raised.

There's more than a lack of funds holding Nathan back.

Big E's heart went out to the man. His kin. Then and there, he vowed to try to help Nathan get back on his feet.

Just as soon as he helps me get Blackwell Stables back on theirs.

Because that would give Nathan the opportunity to reconnect with family and to learn it was all right to ask for help when help was needed.

Nathan tipped the brim of his straw cowboy hat back. "Are you going to move your rig?"

"Yep. I'll drive you to urgent care," Big E told Nathan with a reassuring smile and a tone that discouraged argument. "That'll give us time to talk more about your return to Gold Finch. Your family needs you. And whatever problems you have getting your horse breeding operation back up and running, we'll work on solving them, too. Together."

Nathan wasn't an easy sell. In fact, he was a pessimistic cowboy, of a mind that things were bad here but would be worse in Gold Finch.

But Big E was used to hardheaded Blackwell men. He got his way in the end.

By the time Zeke's sprained wrist was wrapped and resting in a sling, Nathan had agreed to return with Big E to Gold Finch, Kentucky.

And he'd agreed to take that fine-looking gray thoroughbred with them.

CHAPTER ONE

Gold Finch, Kentucky
A few days later...

THE TWINS WERE unusually quiet in the back seat of Nathan's truck as he drove through the ornate gates of Blackwell Stables. They were quiet as Nathan drove between miles of green pastures and the state-of-the-art stable buildings came into view. They were quiet as Nathan turned onto a private road, passed through a nondescript wrought iron gate and parked in the horseshoe-shaped driveway in front of the rambling, one-story house he'd once called home.

Nathan exited just as quietly, moving toward the rear door to let the boys out.

The heat and humidity of September pressed down on him, as heavy as the memories pressing forward from the back of his mind. He tried to only let the good memories resurface—the living room window where Mom used to put a fresh pine Christmas tree, the thick, tall hedge he'd cut through to reach the racetrack, the lawn where he and his brothers played football on holidays.

But one darker memory slipped through: *You don't add any value here, Nathan.*

Nothing like a good old dose of fatherly "love" to keep things real.

Nathan's mouth went dry. His father was the reason Nathan hadn't wanted to come home. He found fault in all his sons.

In the trailer attached to Nathan's truck, a horse whinnied, high-pitched. Then another in a lower register. Blaze and Pest were eager to get out. Almost as eager as the twins.

"This can't be the Blackwell Stables." Zeke stood on the truck's rear running board, looking around the property where Nathan had grown up, his injured wrist half out of the sling, his straw cowboy hat askew. "It's *huge*."

"It *is* the Blackwell Stables. This is where I grew up," Nathan assured his son, lowering Zeke to the circular drive. He adjusted Zeke's sling to better support his wrist.

T.J. hopped down from the same rear truck door Zeke had, head on the swivel. "If this is the Blackwell Stables and you're part owner, we must be rich."

His boys glanced at each other, then tossed their cowboy hats into the air, whooping and dancing about. "*We're rich! We're rich!*"

"Hey." Nathan made the calm-down gesture with

his hands, waiting for the twins to stop celebrating. "I hate to burst your bubble but we're just as poor as we were before." If only because Blackwell Stables hadn't recovered from the recent doping scandal. And in fact, if Big E was to be believed, the operation was spiraling toward bankruptcy.

The boys drooped.

"I really wanted to be rich," Zeke grumbled, scuffing his boot on the driveway pavement.

"If we're not rich, why did we come?" T.J. dusted off his cowboy hat and then Zeke's before plopping them on their heads.

"I told you…" Nathan summoned his patience. "If we chip in and help here, we'll have the money to rebuild our place." And get a leg up from rock bottom.

Understanding dawned in T.J.'s eyes. "And then we can make our farm look like this."

"Because we'll be rich like these Blackwells." Zeke's triumphant laughter rippled through the air. "We can even build our own racetrack."

"Take a breath, boys. Horse breeders don't need racetracks," Nathan reminded them. And they'd never have a property that equaled the grandeur of the Blackwell Stables.

This facility was next level, used primarily to train racehorses, both owned by Blackwell Stables and horse owners lacking training facilities. When Nathan had lived here, they'd also had a small breeding program, primarily Blackwell stallions to Blackwell brood mares. He wondered if they still did.

There were barns here. Plural. The largest for colts and a smaller one for fillies. Not to mention, there was a collection of circular horse walkers and stations for bathing horses. Plus, pastures. Lots and lots of expansive, grassy pastures where a horse could rest in the shade of a cottonwood tree or run, tail high, to his heart's content. Most of the horse buildings were hidden behind a small copse of evergreen trees that separated the main house from the working horse farm. A tall hedge that encircled most of the racetrack was located at the far end of the house lawn.

Blackwell Stables hadn't changed much except…

There weren't nearly as many horses as there used to be in the pastures they'd passed on the drive in. Even though it was midafternoon, a slow time for any training operation, the main stable buildings had looked deserted. Nathan finally realized Big E wasn't exaggerating when he said the place was in trouble, having lost much of their contracted training business after Pride was doped.

"Nathan!" Asher burst from the front door of the ranch house they'd grown up in, plopping a brown cowboy hat on his head. His older brother quickly reached Nathan and encompassed him in a bear hug.

Despite Asher's casual attire—charcoal jeans

and an orange polo shirt—his embrace was stiff, tense.

A result of picking up the broken pieces here after Dad died?

Nathan didn't know.

Asher released Nathan, giving him a once-over, presumably taking in his faded blue jeans and the roll in the collar of his worn red button-down, possibly under the correct impression that Nathan had fallen on hard times. "You've grown up so much, little brother." His gaze drifted toward the twins behind Nathan. "And I still can't believe you're a father."

He thought of Asher's visit when his wife had passed, but to be honest, he could recall very little, awash in grief. He also thought of Dylan's funeral when Nathan was just twenty-three. Now thirty, Nathan rubbed a spot on his chest over his heart, trying to find something less grim to speak of. "So… I look old? Yes, I do. Fatherhood—" *and widowhood* "—will do that to a man. I discovered my first gray whisker the other day."

"Things here might give you more gray hairs than your boys do." Asher reintroduced himself to the twins and shook their hands as if they were business associates, not his nephews.

They were joined by a tall, familiar-looking blonde woman with a welcoming smile and cookie tin in her arms. Asher introduced her as his fiancée, Kelley, a woman Nathan had gone to high school with twelve years ago but hadn't been close to. Kelley wasn't horse folk. Never had been. And didn't appear to be now. Today, she wore leggings, a fluttery green blouse and sneakers.

"I know being back here is awkward, Nathan," Kelley said in a warm voice, hugging Nathan as if they were family, not acquaintances. "But we're incredibly glad you came. I've been cooking food daily for what little staff we have left. You won't have to worry about being fed." Kelley hadn't changed in one respect. She was still the same superorganized woman Nathan remembered from high school. "And I prepared some bedrooms for you and the boys to stay in."

"Thank you but..." *There's no way I'm staying in that house.* There were too many memories of his father in it. Nathan took a moment to watch Big E pull up in that large, lumbering motor home of his before adding, "Given I'll be running operations, we'll be sleeping over at the stables."

"The stables?" Kelley turned to Asher, as if expecting him to argue.

But Asher only stared at Nathan, nodding slowly. "By all means, do what's best for you, Nathan."

Of course, Asher would understand Nathan's need to distance himself from the past. Even before Dylan died, Asher had been the target of Dad's censure more than any of the other Blackwell brothers combined. But as Nathan's older brothers left

Gold Finch, and Nathan, behind, Dad's mood had darkened.

You don't add any value here, Nathan.

He hoped that wasn't the case today.

"Zeke!" T.J. nudged his twin with his elbow, practically dancing with excitement. "Did you hear Dad? We're sleeping in the stables!"

"Cool!" Zeke grinned at everyone. "Dad never lets us do that at home."

"We don't sleep in our barn because we don't have bedrooms above our horse stalls," Nathan explained patiently. The two largest horse barns here had staff housing on the second floor.

"Your boys look just like you, Nathan." Asher lifted T.J.'s cowboy hat and tousled his light brown hair before setting it back on his head. "I bet they find trouble as easily as you did." He gestured toward Zeke's sling.

You have no idea.

"They promised to be on their best behavior." Nathan drew his kids to his side, giving them a playful hug that had them squirming for space and freedom. "Right, boys?"

They nodded, rolling their big blue eyes.

"Childhood promises are as solid as butter on a hot stove." Big E walked toward them with the same purposeful stride that Nathan's father used to have. He had an opinion on everything and always spoke with authority. "I'd rather T.J. and Zeke promise to be careful than to behave." He fixed a stare on each of the twins in turn. "You'll be careful, won't you?"

"Cross my heart," Zeke said, doing just that, not fooling Nathan.

"I'll keep him out of trouble," T.J. said solemnly, not fooling Nathan, either.

"I'm so glad you and the boys came," Asher admitted while Kelley slipped the twins each a cookie from that tin she carried. "It's a big ask to put your life on hold for several months."

Several months?

"Hold on…" Nathan's head started to pound. "I'm just here for a week. Two at the most. The boys are supposed to start kindergarten soon."

Asher frowned. "But—"

"Nathan." Big E entered the fray, even-keeled as always, although the old cowboy carefully avoided Nathan's gaze. "Asher thought coming here when I needed him to would be a quick visit, also. The fact of the matter is…we're going to need you more than a handful of days."

The sly old dog didn't tell me that. I just assumed...

Nathan pressed his lips together, feeling boxed into a corner of a too-small stall.

"Like it or not, brother," Asher began in a deliberate tone. "You've got a stake here. You can help protect your investment or—"

"Why don't you enroll the boys in school here?"

Kelley interrupted, laying a hand on Asher's arm and giving Nathan a friendly smile as she did so.

After a moment, Asher nodded. "That's a great compromise."

The couple was in sync, enviously so, reminding Nathan of what he'd lost when his wife died.

Hang on. I can't get distracted. They're united in getting me to stay.

Nathan frowned.

Kelley handed the twins each another cookie from that tin of hers. "You'd like to make new friends here in Gold Finch, wouldn't you, boys?"

"Nope. We're best friends." Zeke ate half his cookie in one bite.

"Dad says we don't need anyone else," T.J. added before nibbling on his cookie.

"*You don't need anyone else?*" Asher muttered to Nathan. "Picked that line up from Dad, did you?"

Nathan nodded. And not happily. He hadn't realized that's where his oft-repeated saying came from until now. He thought he'd shed the past when he left town. How quickly it boomeranged back now that he'd returned.

"As I understand it, school starts Monday. You can enroll them tomorrow." That was Big E, taking charge the way he had the day he'd shown up at Nathan's. "It might do the twins good to go to school during the day while you're working." Ignoring Nathan's frown, the old cowboy turned to Kelley. "Given the heat, I could do with some refreshment and these men could do with some privacy, I think."

"I just made a pitcher of lemonade." Kelley handed the cookie tin to Big E, then she extended her hands to Zeke and T.J., which, amazingly, they took.

"Do you have double-chocolate fudge cake?" T.J. asked.

"It's our favorite," Zeke added.

Double-chocolate fudge cake.

Nathan couldn't think of that dessert without thinking about Tamara Vaughn, the woman who'd provided them with that cake before every ride she'd taken on Frostfire Wind. For luck, she'd said. He rubbed his suddenly tense chest, not wanting to think about the female jockey and the horse they'd lost during a race.

Kelley, Big E and the twins disappeared inside the main house, leaving Nathan and Asher alone.

"Just like old times. I'm doing what I'm told." Nathan headed for the back of the horse trailer, trying to look for a silver lining. "Where do you want me to keep our horses?"

Asher followed him. "Let's put them in the hay barn pasture." That was where they'd kept their horses as kids. "Do you remember how Mom used to make us ride around there in our Halloween costumes?"

"Oh, yeah." Nathan paused at the trailer door, sparing his older brother a brief smile. "I remember the time you dressed in camouflage gear and pretended you were protecting the world from a zombie apocalypse." The zombies being any of the other five Blackwell brothers. "You were deadly with a squirt gun."

"I'd forgotten about that." Asher chuckled. "I always remember the time we dressed as green ogres. Mom had a different snack for every lap we rode around the pasture. Gummy worms. Peeled grapes that were supposed to be eyeballs. Sugar cookies frosted to look like brains." He paused, giving Nathan a searching look. "Did Marilee dress the kids up for Halloween?"

"Did she ever." Nathan felt something inside of him ease. No one talked to him about his dead wife anymore, as if it was taboo. "Let's see. One year the boys were Frankenstein and his monster. Then ghost pirates. Oh, and zombie T. rexes. From their first Halloween as babies, Marilee set a high bar for me to uphold." He'd failed miserably last year, dressing them in store-bought ghost getups.

"We'll put our heads together for costume ideas this year." Asher tipped his hat back. "Really good ones that Mom and Marilee would be proud of. I'm told they still have trick-or-treating in downtown Gold Finch on Halloween."

Halloween was two months away.

"I see what you're doing here." Nathan shook his head, opening the horse trailer. "Priming me to stay."

"Don't tell me you expect any less," Asher teased in a tone that brought Nathan back to the good old days. "Especially after Big E convinced you to come."

"I walked right into that." And Nathan was certain it wouldn't be the last time.

"HEY, DAD." TAMARA VAUGHN fell into step with the horse her father had just put through his paces at the exercise track at Richmond Stables in Gold Finch. It was a hot Thursday morning.

"Tammie! As I live and breathe." Dad was in his racing gear, including riding helmet and safety vest. He flung himself off the horse and into Tamara's arms, leaving a groom to walk his horse back to the stables proper. Dad released Tamara and held her at arm's length. They were of the same height—*five foot two*—and the same physique—*a wiry frame*. The perfect size and build for a race jockey. "Haven't seen you since the accident with that Blackwell horse in Paducah."

At his reference to her horse racing accident, Tamara's mind flashed harsh images, her healed ankle twinged and her pulse accelerated.

It's all in my head.

She repeated the mantra and deepened her breathing, trying not to freak out. If she wanted to race again, her fears needed to disappear. Or at least, be controllable. It was concerning that riding anxiety plagued her when her boots were on the ground.

"Great to see you're walking without a limp, Tammie." But Dad must have noted her angst because he added, "How's your head? Feeling confident?"

"I'm good. We Vaughns are tough." Tamara returned her father's regard, registering the empathy in his smile. As a former race jockey, Dad had experienced his share of injuries. He'd understand the emotional ripples a serious racing accident left in a person. "You looked good out there, Dad." He'd ridden the horse at a steady gallop around the racetrack, poised above the saddle with excellent form.

"I may be an exercise jockey but I haven't slacked off in my training on the off chance I get another shot at riding in a race." Dad patted his flat stomach. "And unlike you, I don't have a weakness for chocolate cake."

"Double-chocolate fudge cake is worth the extra time on the treadmill." Always.

"*Vaughn!*" an edgy female voice called from the elevated viewing platform beside the racetrack. "We're already behind and it's almost too hot to continue. Move it!"

"Yes, ma'am." Dad hooked his arm through Tamara's and headed toward the hub of activity at the stables, presumably where the next horse he was scheduled to exercise waited. "That's Caroline Richmond, head trainer and my boss." Dad kept his voice low as they walked faster. "What brings you by, Tammie?"

She glanced over her shoulder at the head trainer. The slender woman was casually dressed in blue jeans and a T-shirt. "I'm looking for racing rides." There were few sanctioned races left in September. "What do you think my chances are of picking up a ride with Richmond Stables?"

"Slim to none." Dad drew her closer, lowering his voice. "There's a flood of jockeys available in this neck of the woods, most let go by Blackwell Stables. I'm sure you heard about the doping scandal they're dealing with. Folks are leaving their employ like rats from a sinking ship. I heard they barely have enough bodies to care for their horses."

Tamara nodded. Everyone in the horse racing world knew about the trouble Blackwell Stables were in. But Tamara was in a spot of trouble herself. "I need work, Dad. No one will hire me after what happened to Frostfire Wind." Nathan Blackwell's horse.

Memories of the race tried to return. Tamara pressed her lips together, forcing herself to focus on the stable activity ahead. A groom with a curry comb. A brown horse playfully nibbling at another groom's hair. The steady clip-clop of a bay horse being led out for exercise.

Stupid anxiety. It's all in my head.

Deep breath in. Deep breath out. "What do you think I should do, Dad?"

"I can put in a good word for you with Caroline. You can even show up at Rosehaven Downs here in Gold Finch on Saturday. But..." Dad grimaced, fiddling with his helmet's chin strap before quietly blurting, "You might lay low until the season starts up again next year. By then, recall of your last ride will have faded."

"I can't wait this out."

"Sorry, Tammie. But I've got to get going." Dad gestured to a groom holding a saddled bay just outside the horse barn. "That's my next ride—Luck in the Mud."

"Clever name." Many racehorse monikers were. But Tamara wasn't ready for their conversation to end. She hung onto her father's arm. "I need a job, Dad." And a place to stay. She'd lost her small apartment at the training facility where she'd worked in Paducah when they let her go. And it wasn't as if she could stay with Dad. He had a room here at Richmond Stables.

"Like I said, I'll put in a good word for you with Caroline. She's the kind of trainer who likes a jockey desperate to win." Dad moved away from Tamara and grabbed hold of the bay's reins with one hand and the saddle with the other. "Give me a leg up, will you, Tammie."

She took hold of his left ankle and boosted him into the saddle. Then she gave the bay a pat on the neck. "Thanks, Dad."

"Show up at Rosehaven Downs on Saturday,"

Dad reminded her. "Your luck's due to change." And then he rode off.

Leaving Tamara to walk back to her SUV, where she had a slice of double-chocolate fudge cake waiting in her ice chest. But why eat it when she had no cause to celebrate?

Luck was ghosting her.

CHAPTER TWO

"HE'S GOT FINE LINES." Asher admired Pest as Nathan led him toward the hay barn pasture. "He's two, right? How's he done on the race circuit?"

"I'm not racing Tempest Wind." Just saying the words out loud made Nathan feel vulnerable, as if he hadn't made the right decision. "Marilee died helping him come into this world and… I protect him the way I protect my sons." T.J., Zeke and Pest were the only living links he had to his dead wife.

Asher looked as if he might have an opinion about Pest not racing but he kept silent.

They reached the hay barn pasture, which was empty of livestock. The grassy field held evidence of idyllic childhood days spent here—a tree house in a cottonwood tree, a rope swing hung from an elm branch in the back corner.

"I have a pasture like this at my horse farm," Nathan admitted, opening the gate. "It's the kids' playground, the same way this one was ours."

Asher led Blaze through the gate. "I'll volunteer to help retrofit the tree house. It could use some new floorboards."

"Is that conditional upon us staying long term?" Nathan teased.

"Yes. Can't blame a man for trying." Asher grinned.

They unclipped the horses' lead ropes. Once free, Blaze galloped off. Pest gave his head a good shake. And then the colt sped after—*and swiftly past*—Blaze. Nathan closed the gate and tipped his straw cowboy hat back, looking around, struck by the feeling that little had changed since he'd left.

Except Dad is dead.

Being here brought the reality slamming home. A wave of grief rolled through him, as familiar as an old friend. A friend he'd prefer to avoid. Nathan turned his face toward the sun, closed his eyes and willed grief away.

"Wow." Asher's voice brought Nathan back to the present. He hung his arms over the top fence rail. "Pest loves to run."

The gray continued to gallop full tilt along the pasture perimeter.

Rather than talking about his colt, Nathan went into avoidance mode, gaze roving across the stables proper, looking for a change of topic. He soon found it. "Big E said you were hurting for staff as well as clients. How bad is it?"

"Devastating." Asher frowned, looking older than his thirty-five years. "Since Pride was drugged by our farm manager, we've lost several clients that had contracted with us for race training. And our employees… They've either left or have been poached. We're down to a skeleton crew."

"It wasn't so long ago that you didn't want to be associated with Blackwell Stables. Or Gold Finch." The same as Nathan and their three other living brothers. When Dylan, the heir apparent, had died, no one offered to return home and take his place. No one wanted to deal with Dad. "Why fight to keep it going?"

"You can credit my change of heart to Big E. He pointed out it's our legacy, and that we can shape it in a way Dad couldn't." Asher blew out a breath as if that had been tough to admit. Then he turned toward Nathan's horses now grazing in the pasture. "After Dad died back in June… I would have been content to let the farm be sold. I only came back because Big E is the executor of the estate and insisted he needed someone trustworthy to vet the business accounts because Dad and Uncle Joe were… Let's just say management was lax in all aspects of the business. And then after I got here… Well… Slowly, the good memories began to outweigh the bad." Asher turned back toward Nathan. "Not to mention, someone doped a Blackwell horse. And Pride… He hasn't been the same since. I can't let whoever did that go unpunished."

"You sound like Big E." Out for justice. Out to set things right.

"He and I are on the same page." Asher led Nathan toward the horse barns. "Now that you're here,

Big E and I can spend more time creating a picture of Elliot. Someone must have seen him with one of our competitors. Someone might know who he hung out with or owed money to. The sheriff hasn't put significant resources on our case."

"In other words, you're going to be nosey and hope folks in town spill all the gossip."

"Well, when you put it that way, it sounds very rinky-dink." Nathan's quick smile fell. "We need you, Nathan. Dad never showed me how to run this place the way he taught Dylan to. Big E used to run a cattle ranch in Montana. Neither of us have experience managing a horse farm like you do. You can keep the place operational while we make our inquiries."

"To be clear, I'm no horse trainer." Nathan had always been more interested in bloodlines and the what-ifs of breeding than race training. "I sell… At least, back when Marilee was alive, we *used to sell* yearlings." In his grief, he'd let things go. Their brood mares. The yearlings. The business itself had been too painful a reminder of his loss, which was why he'd turned to racing Frostfire Wind. "My horse breeding business didn't involve training thoroughbreds. I only raced one of my colts this year and I paid a trainer to get him ready." A trainer who thought Tamara was the best jockey for Frosty.

Oh, how wrong he'd been.

"I know your experience isn't an exact match," Asher allowed. "But now that Uncle Joe has retired, we need you to manage daily activities. I need to pack up my apartment in New York and get it sublet." Asher's tone changed. He sounded all business. "Maybe you can help me put out feelers for buyers of our three-year-olds that didn't pan out."

"Don't forget investors in the two-year-olds."

Asher nodded. "I hope you can use your industry contacts to find a new crop of employees. Like Kelley said, we have few staff. Our last race trainer took off this morning." Asher drew a labored breath. Clearly, he was carrying the stress of keeping the place afloat, an observation that poked holes in Nathan's resolve *not* to stay. "At least, the trainer left his training schedules. But we've only got three employees left. Edie, who you know, Owen, a green stable hand, and Frannie, a green exercise jockey. If you could find one good jockey to keep training our horses, we can get through this rough patch without losing our few remaining clients."

One good jockey?

A woman's face came to mind. Hair as dark as night. Eyes just as black. But those expressive eyes… The last time Nathan had seen them, they'd widened with shock. And then hurt. And finally, near-teary acceptance.

I'm sorry, Tamara.

Nathan wasn't proud of that memory. But he wasn't forgiving her yet, either. He clenched his jaw. "I'm not sure my contacts are worth much anymore." He'd been more of a wounded hermit the past two years than he cared to admit.

"I need more than your contacts, Nathan." Asher placed a hand on Nathan's shoulder. "I need your counsel and fellowship. Since the doping suspension, there have been anonymous offers submitted to buy the farm. And each time an offer is made, the price drops."

"As if someone knows the stable is backed against a wall," Nathan murmured, feeling a prickle of anger between his shoulder blades.

"Yes." Asher's hand fell away. He glanced around the farm. "I know how you must feel being back here. When I first returned, it felt like all I could hear was Dad's negative voice ringing in my ears."

You bring nothing to the operation, Nathan.

Nathan rubbed his forehead, trying to erase his father's words from his memory.

"For me, it was like the bad had to be aired out for me to let it go." Asher captured Nathan's gaze. "You may not come to terms with the past. But you'll remember the good times. And I promise. This place is worth saving. If not for us, for the next generation of Blackwells."

"The next generation..." Despite the heat, Nathan felt the cold hand of shame grip him. He tried to look away but he couldn't. Instead, he found himself admitting, "You shouldn't put your stock in me. After Marilee died, I gave up on my dreams. Everything she and I built is gone. In my grief,

I wasn't up to managing much. I sold too many shares in Frostfire Wind to keep us going. When he died, my share of the insurance money was negligible."

"I don't care about any of that," Asher said in a quiet voice. "You're here now. And you can count on me to help you get back on your feet or find a new dream to aspire to. You should do this, Nathan. If not for yourself, for Marilee and your boys."

Nathan swallowed thickly. It was much the same conversation he'd had with Big E a few days ago. "Okay. I'll try."

I owe my boys that much.

Big E appeared at the corner of the nearest barn. He peeked but leaned back the way he'd come, then plastered himself to the outer wall as if hiding.

Zeke and T.J. ran through the copse of evergreens, spotted the elderly cowboy, then ran over to him, shouting gleefully, "*We found you!*"

Big E made a show of being caught. He was good with the boys.

When was the last time I played hide-and-seek with the twins?

Guilt stiffened Nathan's shoulders. He couldn't remember. Since Marilee died, his days had been filled with the routine of caring for kids and animals while his nights had been plagued by heartache. The only bright spot had been race day. But that was gone now, too. His life had become like the basket of socks he'd brought with them. Nothing was in good shape. And nothing matched.

"Socks are important," Marilee had said to Nathan not long after their marriage. She held up one of his holey socks while they were folding laundry. "They may be hidden in your boots. They may be unmatched or decorated with hearts or superheroes. But socks are a small comfort. You need that foundation to have a good day. And a good life."

Nathan touched his wedding band, smiling wryly. The socks he was wearing had holes in the toes.

"Can you call around for workers?" Asher asked Nathan, bringing him back to their conversation as he waved at Big E and the twins. "To tide us over, we need an experienced jockey."

Again, a woman's face came to mind, only this time it was her smile Nathan saw. Her laughter that rang in his head. The feeling that he wasn't alone enveloped him. Tamara had been the only jockey to race Frostfire Wind as a three-year-old. She'd taken pleasure in making Nathan smile before each race, seeming to recognize his prerace jitters. And for some reason, that made his last words to her that much more painful: *It's best we part ways, Tamara.*

"I know a jockey who might be available," Nathan admitted, having pressured Frosty's trainer to let her go after the accident. He half hoped Tamara was too busy working elsewhere. Because

Nathan doubted Tamara ever wanted to hear from him again.

And the feeling…

The feeling was mutual.

THE THUNDER OF HOOVES. The splatter of dirt on goggles. The roar of the crowd.

All of it had faded.

It was late Saturday afternoon. Tamara walked away from Rosehaven Downs in Gold Finch toward her SUV, her riding equipment duffel on her shoulder. This morning, she'd shown up early looking for a trainer in need of a jockey. She'd been lucky to pick up two rides from Caroline Richmond, placing mid-pack in the first atop a happy-go-lucky mare and barely avoiding last place on a two-year-old colt that didn't start well and slowed down when dirt was kicked in his face.

Wasn't that the metaphor for my life this summer? Dirt kicked in my face?

She'd been tense in both rides, the first races she'd run since her accident two months ago. And if Tamara was honest with herself, she had to admit that she hadn't been brave enough to ride full steam ahead today. In fact, during the race, her breathing had been ragged while her back and shoulders had threatened to cramp. And she kept wondering, *Am I pushing too hard? Is the horse okay? Will this ride end in another death?*

Successful race jockeys couldn't afford to be afraid.

I'm a hot mess.

And yet, Tamara didn't consider the day a total loss. Yes, she had a mental hurdle to overcome and fears to defeat. But she'd been able to ride and now had money in her pocket to pay the rent on the cheap motel where she was staying. Plus, she'd mingled with several trainers, networking in the hopes of finding steadier race employment.

"Tamara." That voice. So deep. So familiar.

It brought her to a halt.

It can't be.

Gold Finch was miles away from Paducah. Miles away from remorse and heartache.

Slowly, Tamara turned to face her former employer and past crush—Nathan Blackwell. Her heart pounded madly in her chest, belying the "past" label in the crush department. Nathan Blackwell looked good enough to wrap her arms around, better than her bittersweet dreams.

She took a moment to drink in her fill of that man. The sturdy, tall frame that required Tamara to look *up-up-up* to meet his gaze. Those soulful blue eyes shaded by his race day brown felt cowboy hat. The way he had his tan cowboy boots planted on the pavement as if he was ready for bad news and prepared to weather it.

Nathan Blackwell had experienced his share of bad luck—his wife dead after being struck by a panicked mare giving birth, his very talented three-year-old colt dead after winning a race with Tamara as his jockey.

It's best we part ways, Tamara.

The hard tone of Nathan's last words to her echoed in Tamara's head, filling her chest with sadness and twinging her neck with guilt over the loss of Frostfire Wind.

I loved that horse.

She'd loved Nathan and his twins, too. She'd lost them in ten furlongs and less than 120 seconds. And nearly lost her life, as well. And now? It was tough enough to be a female jockey in a man's world but to have run a horse to death in a business loaded with superstitious owners and trainers? *Kiss. Of. Death.*

"I didn't expect to see you today, Nathan," Tamara said in a carefully neutral voice since throwing herself into his arms seemed less than professional. "You're a long way from Paducah. Why are you here?"

To ask me how I'm doing? To rehire me as your race jockey? To tell me you love me and can't live without me?

Tamara contained an eye roll. She had an overactive imagination where Nathan was concerned. All she had to do was take in Nathan's closed-off expression to know none of her hypotheticals were coming true.

Silence stretched between them.

Reality check. Nothing good ever comes of awkward silences.

Tamara gave him a small wave as she turned away, hefting her riding equipment duffel higher on her shoulder. "Nice to see you, Nathan. Say hi to the boys for me."

Unexpectedly, the painful memory of her last race for Nathan thundered back, blurring her vision and firing her muscles with adrenaline as if she was reliving that fateful spill.

The pounding of hooves. Her light use of the whip. The roar of the crowd as they crossed the finish line ahead of other horses. The collapse of Frostfire Wind beneath her. The tumble and chaos as other horses veered past. And then the sharp pain, physical and emotional—her right ankle twisted, her heart cracked as she realized she'd let the colt run past his limits.

"Tamara, wait."

She blinked back tears, swallowing hard before turning to face Nathan. "Yes?"

"My family needs a good exercise jockey," Nathan said, all doom and gloom, as if he didn't want to ask her but was boxed into a corner. "The position is at the Blackwell Stables here in Gold Finch."

Tamara had first heard of the Blackwell Stables long ago. But the doping scandal and suspension were new news this summer. Everyone associated with racing was talking about Blackwell Stables for all the wrong reasons, the same as she imagined they were talking about her.

Tamara shook her head. “You don’t need a good jockey. You need a good legal team.”

Nathan grimaced, blue eyes haunted. “There are few people who want to hitch their reputation to Blackwell Stables nowadays.”

Tamara was tempted to say, *That’s not my problem.* Nathan had, after all, severed contact with Tamara and had her fired when she desperately needed his vote of confidence. Without it, no one in the Paducah area had been willing to give her a chance as a race jockey, not even the trainer she’d worked for.

He blackballed me. I should walk away.

But there were his soulful blue eyes. She’d always been a sucker for them.

When was the last time Nathan smiled?

Tamara licked her lips, trying not to worry about him. She had her own problems. “Let’s be honest, Nathan. You don’t want to hire me.” When he didn’t immediately reply, she turned away once more, prepared to shut this chapter of the book of Tamara and Nathan and what might have been. It had been a fairy tale, anyway. Nathan still grieved his wife two years after her death. He might never move on.

But I have to.

“Tamara, wait.” Nathan trotted up next to her. He touched her arm, sending a jolt of attraction racing through her veins. “Please, Tamara. We need insight about the horses we have left and help to identify the ones that have what it takes to win. A good exercise jockey can tell us that. Do me this one favor and then…a month or so from now we can go our separate ways."

Tamara stared past Nathan toward the high wall of the track's grandstand, thinking. Financially, she was close to being forced to sleep in her SUV. She didn't need to add association with the Blackwells to her already tarnished reputation. And exercise jockey… That was a step down from race jockey, practically an admission of retirement. She wasn't giving up on her racing career that easily.

Tamara met his gaze squarely. "Thanks but no thanks."

"The job is salaried and comes with room and board," Nathan coughed out, sweetening the deal.

All Tamara's professional concerns about being further tainted by the Blackwell name and being out of the racing game took a back seat to survival. "Room *and* board?"

He nodded, face a handsome, unyielding mask.

Oh, he hates this. But he's desperate, perhaps as desperate as I am.

But Tamara's desperation wasn't only about a roof over her head and enough money to eat. She needed regular time on a horse if she was going to conquer her fears and ride like a winner again. And if Tamara wasn't worrying about a roof over her head and where her next meal was coming from, she might regain the bravado she needed to return to the winner's circle once more.

Tamara smiled, just a bit, then extended her hand to shake on the deal, trying for a little humor. "Why didn't you lead with room and board?"

Nathan's hand encompassed hers—larger, stronger, warmer.

But his expression didn't soften. "Maybe because I was hoping you'd say no."

SHE SAID YES.

Nathan parked his truck in the rear dirt lot at Blackwell Stables, emotion clogging his throat.

Tamara won't be riding for me on race day. She'll be working for me every day.

Rolling his window down, Nathan tried to clear his throat of all insecurities, all doubt, all feelings where Tamara was concerned. He had to focus on the job at hand—keeping Blackwell Stables running and poised for a resurgence. That was the only way he and the boys would have the resources to start over.

He cleared his throat again.

"You got allergies?" A tall, skinny woman with short white hair approached his truck door. She carried a straw basket filled with vegetables, most likely picked from the small garden nearby, the one Nathan's mother had started when Nathan was a kid. "You should eat onions and garlic to ease your allergy symptoms."

"If I did that, I'd scare more than vampires away." He'd deter potential new employees from agreeing to work here.

Would that have worked with Tamara?

Edie laughed. She wore a pink-checked button-down and blue jeans. Her beige cowboy boots looked older than she was. In fact, she'd been working here longer than Nathan could remember. "I suppose onions and garlic might scare away potential girlfriends for you, too."

The gold of his wedding ring caught Nathan's eye.

Girlfriends? I'm not looking for romance.

He opened his mouth to say just that but Edie wasn't done. "Looks like you're in need of something to smile about."

Unbidden, the defeated stride Tamara had taken as he'd caught up to her as she left the racetrack came to mind.

She doesn't have much to smile about, either.

Nathan reminded himself Tamara's happiness wasn't his concern. "These are tough times, Edie." He cleared his throat once more, gathering his keys and getting out of his truck. "How are things with the fillies?" The elderly woman had been in charge of the filly barn until the mass exodus of employees. Now, she was in charge of all racing two- and three-year-olds, both colts and fillies.

"My girls are fine and dandy." Edie smiled proudly. She'd always considered every filly in her care to be one of *her girls*. "Could use a return to proper training. Those young boys of yours offered to ride them on the track." She pointed toward the hay barn pasture where Zeke and T.J. rode Pest bareback together. "I'm of half a mind to let them try."

"They'd love that but I'm a hard no on letting them do it." Nathan headed toward the colt barn, where they kept the male racing horses and where he was staying with the twins.

"Did you hire a jockey?" Edie fell into step beside Nathan, handing him a large, ripe tomato. "I hope he's not from around here. Wouldn't want to let a rat back into the barn, if you know what I mean."

"*She* isn't a local." Too late, Nathan wondered who Tamara had been racing for today. The majority of the field of horses that raced at Rosehaven Downs was usually made up of competitors based in the region. And the next two largest operations after Blackwell Stables—Richmond Stables and Connelly Thoroughbreds—were on Big E's and Asher's radar as suspects behind Pride's doping.

"If this jockey of yours is up to no good, I'll find out," Edie promised as someone repeatedly rang a bell in the filly barn. "Now, you should gather those rascals of yours. That's the dinner bell. Kelley is calling us to eat."

Nathan's stomach growled at the mention of food. He turned back toward the hay barn pasture while

Edie continued on to the filly barn. “Boys, time to wash up for dinner. Pest! Come here, buddy.”

At his call, Pest walked eagerly toward him. The colt’s long legs soon ate up the distance between them. T.J. sat behind Zeke on his back. No saddle, no bridle, no halter. That was par for the course when it came to Pest and the twins, same as it had been with Frosty.

“Dad?” T.J. slid off the gray colt’s back, then held his hands up as if to catch Zeke. “Can we build a better tree house?”

“That one doesn’t have enough windows.” Zeke’s wrist was out of his sling. “And the floorboards don’t sound so good.” He made a sound more like a creaky door opening in a haunted house than a tree house floorboard.

It was on the tip of Nathan’s tongue to say that Asher had offered to repair the tree house, but just then, Zeke swung his leg over Pest’s haunches and dropped off the colt. He stumbled into T.J. and sent them both onto their backsides.

Two gasps. Two sets of tangled limbs. Two pairs of teary eyes.

Without thinking, Nathan hopped over the fence. “It’s all right. I’m coming.”

But Pest was closer. The colt extended his long gray neck to nuzzle the twins, as if making sure they were okay. By the time Nathan reached them, the boys were getting to their feet and laughing about their tumble.

Pest bumped Nathan's shoulder, a gesture Nathan had come to think of as the colt's way of saying, *I got this.*

"Good boy." Nathan scratched the gray's forehead.

Pest is family. No way am I going to risk losing him in a race.

"You fell on me, Zeke." T.J. brushed dirt off his brother's backside.

"I didn't know you were trying to catch me." Zeke grinned at Nathan. "T.J.'s not a very good dismounting block."

"I was trying to be a good *brother*," T.J. gently chastised.

"Come on." Nathan laid a hand on each of their shoulders and swept them toward the gate. "Dinner's ready."

"Will there be vegetables?" Zeke dragged his feet. "I like Kelley's cookies better than her vegetables."

"Dinner comes with vegetables." Nathan closed the gate behind them. "Whether I make it or Kelley does."

"Will there be dessert?" T.J. climbed onto the closed gate, up and up, until his face was even with Nathan's.

"I don't know what's for dessert." Nathan lifted T.J. back down, then took his boys' hands and led the way toward the filly barn. "But I doubt it's double-chocolate fudge cake."

"Tamara used to bring us double-chocolate fudge cake on race days," T.J. said in a wistful tone.

"We don't like Tamara anymore," Zeke reminded his twin.

"*You* don't like her," T.J. said defensively. "*I* still like her."

"Just for her cake," Zeke countered.

"Not just that. She's nice." T.J. gave up on the argument and ran ahead.

Zeke glanced up at Nathan. "You don't like Tamara, do you, Dad?"

Nathan wasn't sure how to answer that given he'd hired her again. Like Zeke said, his feelings toward Tamara and the accident weren't resolved. He settled for a rather lame "We should give everyone a second chance."

Instead of answering, Zeke ran after his brother.

CHAPTER THREE

"THIS IS YOUR ROOM." Sunday morning, Nathan opened the door for Tamara to a small, air-conditioned studio apartment on the second floor of the filly horse barn. It was the size of a modest motel room. "It's small."

"And so am I." Tamara moved past him, wheeling a large suitcase, carrying a duffel bag and shouldering a backpack, all of which she'd refused help with. She deposited her things near the twin bed and looked around, peering into the equally small bathroom. "It's very compact."

"Every extra inch goes to the horses." Nathan tried to smile but didn't do a good job of it. The easy-going relationship they'd had before that fateful race two months ago was missing, like so many other things in his life he hadn't truly appreciated until they were gone.

"This is perfect," Tamara said.

Nathan watched Tamara move about the room, touching the small desk, looking out the small window. In his opinion, often jockeys were too slim. Most looked half starved. Not Tamara. She was wiry but had lean muscle. She'd earned his respect with her riding skills and also by presenting herself in a businesslike manner with an upbeat attitude. Her black hair was always in a tidy braid. Her clothes were always clean and free of wrinkles. Even now, her khaki shorts and brown T-shirt were neatly pressed. But today, there were none of her trademark smiles. Her petite features were set in serious mode, as if she was pondering something of great importance.

Tamara turned, catching him staring. A hint of rose bloomed in her cheeks.

She's pretty.

Nathan's mouth went dry.

I will not *be attracted to Tamara.*

And yet, he continued to stare.

Tamara fidgeted under his inspection. "Can I get the nickel tour of the farm?"

"Sure." Nathan backed out of the room wondering why he hadn't seen Tamara's beauty before, wondering why he was seeing it now, wondering how he could unsee it. Finding no answers, Nathan led the way downstairs, where ceiling fans in the breezeway tried to reduce the heat for the horses. "My office is in this building, too. There's a break room next to my office where we eat, a small exercise room with a mechanical horse on the other side of the breezeway and a tack room for fillies below the stairs."

"Few fillies though there are," Tamara said matter-of-factly. When he glanced at her, Tamara shrugged. "I saw a lot of cleared-out stalls as we came through the breezeway. Is that the fallout from the doping scandal?"

"Yes. This is my office." Nathan opened the door to air-conditioned comfort.

As offices went, it wasn't fancy. Basic desk, squeaky desk chair, two old dining room chairs for visitors and a concrete floor. There were shelves crowded with trophies and awards. Framed photos of past winners hung on the walls opposite and around two whiteboards with training schedules. Each row was a horse and each column a training routine that had to be completed before a horse was entered into a race.

Nathan pointed to the largest whiteboard. "I updated the dates and activities for training three-year-olds."

"Kind of late in the year to be training three-year-olds hard. You just need to keep up their strength and endurance," Tamara noted, examining the board. "They won't race soon because you've been suspended from all three-year-old races pending the challenge you filed. By the time you get a review, they'll be four-year-olds. If cash flow is an issue, you should evaluate which three-year-olds could be sold and invest your time in the two-year-olds, finding the best trainers and investors."

That's what Asher has in mind.

"You know your stuff." A part of Nathan respected her for that knowledge. But hers was another voice when Big E, Asher and Nathan were already managing by committee. He was leery of her second-guessing his decisions. "I guess it's good to have a broad view of the industry you're in."

"I've been around racing long enough for some business smarts to rub off on me, I suppose." Tamara moved to stand in front of the two-year-olds' training board, giving him a good view of her delicate profile. "I don't see Pest up here. Isn't he of the same breeding stock as Frostfire Wind?"

"Yes." Nathan had hoped no one would notice the omission. "He's more like a pet though."

"So you've said." Tamara faced him, dark slender brows arched. "But if he's anything like Frosty—"

"He's not a topic of discussion." Nathan crossed his arms over his chest and leaned against the wall.

Tamara's expression turned guarded. "You don't want me to ride Pest." Not a question.

Obviously, I don't.

"There are plenty of other horses for you to ride," Nathan said firmly, trying to be businesslike, trying to ignore the myriad of emotions Tamara created inside him—pain over the reminder of the loss of Frosty, discomfort over his reactive firing of her, guilt over his unwanted attraction.

Surprisingly, it was the latter that upset him most.

Nathan touched his wedding band but it felt cool and offered him no comfort.

"Are you saying you're letting your emotions

make business decisions?" Tamara's question didn't make him feel any better, darn it.

"No," he said emphatically. Lying.

She knew it, too. This time Tamara's dark, slender brows rose in silent implication.

Nathan refused to back down. "Pest has nothing to do with the Blackwell Stables."

She made a show of staring at the two-year-olds' training board before addressing him once more. "You said it yourself, Nathan. I'm here for more than exercising racehorses. I'm here to give you insight about the horses you have left at this facility and help identify the ones that have what it takes to win so you won't waste entry fees. Entering Pest in a race is a good investment."

"He's not an investment. He's part of the family." A part of Marilee.

"He can be a family pet when he retires to stud in two years." Abruptly, Tamara faced the wall with the two-year-olds' training schedule and wrote Pest's name on a blank row. She entered dates in various columns, building a timeline with targets for the colt.

"You can't do that." But Nathan didn't move to stop her.

"I'm doing what you hired me to do." Tamara faced him once more, her expression softening. "I know your wife died in Pest's birthing stall. I know that creates a special attachment. But letting a pair of five-year-old boys keep Pest as a pleasure horse doesn't honor your wife's memory, Nathan. Making him a Triple Crown winner will."

And then, Tamara walked out the door.

She can't say that to me. Even if she's right.

Nathan stood rooted in front of the window air-conditioning unit. It blasted on his spine. He should have felt cold. But he was sweating. The sickly kind of sweat that was spawned of devastating heartbreak. The feeling rolled through his body. Drenching his back.

Because he saw *her*.

Not Tamara. *Marilee*.

In his mind's eye, he saw his wife in the large birthing stall. Lying there. Gasping for breath like a fish flung to the shore, unable to fill her lungs after being struck in the windpipe by the mare that was trying to deliver Pest.

Nathan's legs gave out. He collapsed, catching the corner of an old wooden dining room chair next to the wall. It saved him from tumbling to the floor.

I can't risk losing Pest, too.

The office door swung open. "Hey, Nathan." Big E filled the doorway, his astute gaze quickly noticing something was amiss. In two strides, he was standing at Nathan's side. "What happened? Are you okay?"

Nathan nodded. "Heat got to me." He removed his cowboy hat and wiped his damp forehead with his hand. Then he shook the back of his wet, gray cotton button-down as if that would cool him down.

The way Big E is staring at me...

Well, it was obvious that Nathan hadn't sold the concept of him being fine or that his near tumble had been caused by the heat.

But Big E was a compassionate old cowboy. He got Nathan a bottle of water from the small refrigerator and waited until he'd drunk his fill before he started any further conversation. "I came by to meet the jockey you hired."

"You just missed her." And now that Nathan had his wits about him, he was of half a mind to send her packing.

Who does Tamara think she is talking to me like that? She didn't know Marilee. Tamara doesn't know what Marilee wanted.

Only, Tamara's words had him remembering Marilee cradling a newborn foal and saying, "This is the one. A Triple Crown winner. I can see it in his eyes."

He smiled softly. That's what she said about every one of their foals.

She died before she said that about Pest.

Nathan felt dizzy. He didn't want Tamara to be right. Most of all, he didn't want her to sway Big E and Asher to her side. Nathan swallowed thickly and then silently rehearsed the words he needed to say: *I'm sorry, Big E. Tamara's not going to work out.*

But Big E beat him to the punch. "We're lucky to find anyone with significant race wins on their résumé. Asher and I made inquiries when employees started abandoning ship but no one would listen to our job offers after they heard the name Blackwell. Her being here is a selling point."

And that's when Nathan knew the sad truth.

I'm stuck with her.

TAMARA HAD STALKED OUT of Nathan's office, shaking, because it felt as if he was firing her all over again.

He doesn't trust me to race Pest.

But he and his family were in a tight spot. They couldn't afford sentimentality just as she couldn't afford any weakness in her riding.

I'm just here to get my nerve back. I can't let my feelings get hurt.

That was easier said than done. Tamara walked past another horse barn, trying to cool down, trying to convince herself that Nathan's resentment toward her didn't matter. A job was a job. She walked slowly beyond the shaded, hot-walker turnstiles, breathing deeply. Each step brought her closer to a sense of balance, to calm. It was a trick her father had taught her.

You can't let emotions cloud your judgment, Tammie. Win or lose, you have to shake it off. It's business.

Of course, it would have been easier to shake things off if a part of her didn't long to be important to Nathan.

What a pipe dream.

Tamara kept walking.

Several minutes later, Tamara found herself at a pasture just past the hay barn. Two familiar horses were grazing in it—Pest, and Nathan's stable horse Blaze. And two familiar boys were in a cottonwood tree near the horses.

"What are you doing here?" That was Zeke Blackwell, one of Nathan's twins, the more solid of the two boys. He scowled at Tamara from ten feet off the ground. His right wrist was bandaged, which was par for the course. Zeke was always injuring himself in some way because he had no fear. "Go away, Tamara!"

"Tamara!" Despite his twin brother's dismissal, T.J. shimmied down the tree, calling out a warm welcome. "Tamara!" He landed on his feet and then sprinted toward her. "Tamara! You came!" T.J. practically dived in between the bottom two rails of fencing, losing his straw cowboy hat. And then he was hugging her, sandy brown hair ruffling in the warm morning breeze.

After Nathan had revealed he didn't trust Tamara to ride Pest, she needed that little boy's hug, along with his affection.

T.J. gazed up at her adoringly. "Did Dad hire you to race a Blackwell horse?"

"He wouldn't!" Zeke climbed down the tree at a slower pace, favoring that injured wrist. "She's a horse killer."

The roar of the crowd... The feeling of Frosty dropping out from under me...

Despite the heat, Tamara's breath froze in her lungs.

"Zeke! Don't say that." T.J. spun around, hot to defend Tamara. "Frosty ran his heart out. You know how he hated to lose. It wasn't Tamara's fault."

If only I believed that.

Tamara drew a deep breath, then another.

Shake it off, girl.

"It was Tamara's fault and I say she should go." Zeke stomped over to the fence, his injured wrist hanging awkwardly in a sling.

"Everyone's entitled to their opinion, Zeke," Tamara said, tiptoeing into the fray. "But if I leave, you won't get a slice of double-chocolate fudge cake."

The brothers exchanged glances. They had that twin-speak thing down pat, able to silently communicate.

Tamara settled her cowboy hat more firmly on her head and took a step in the other direction, toward the parking lot and her SUV with the rest of her things, including food.

"Wait!" Zeke called out, sounding less territorial. "Is this the double-chocolate fudge cake you used to bring us when you were racing Frosty?"

Back still turned to them, Tamara smiled.

If only winning over Nathan was this easy.

Tamara stuffed that smile out of existence, turning to face the boys with a straight face. "Yes, sir. Double-chocolate fudge cake." She'd picked it up from a bakery this morning, having called all over the county yesterday trying to find a bakery who made that flavor.

The boys exchanged glances once more. After a moment, they both nodded.

"Kelley makes really good desserts," T.J. said, coming over to take Tamara's hand.

"Agreed." Zeke slid between the fence rails and came to flank Tamara's other side, keeping a careful distance between them. No hand holding for him. "But Kelley doesn't make double-chocolate fudge cake."

"Who is Kelley?" Tamara asked, leading them back to the place where she'd parked her gray SUV while they explained that their Uncle Asher was going to marry Kelley and that she made the meals around here.

They reached Tamara's SUV, protected thanks to the shade of a cottonwood tree near Nathan's truck. Tamara popped the trunk, revealing an ice chest filled with her special hydrating water and some of her healthiest, most expensive, high-protein food, plus one small double-chocolate fudge cake.

"You guys are lucky that I travel with a picnic basket full of utensils." Given she had to eat every few hours to maintain muscle, she never went anywhere without it. Tamara dragged the wicker basket toward her, then got out a knife, plates and several forks.

"Did Dad say anything to you about Pest?" Zeke asked while Tamara cut the cake. He was still trying to act as if he disliked her but he pressed his little body to her side. No doubt, his eagerness for cake outweighed his grudge against her. "You can't train Pest. That's my job."

"Congratulations on your promotion from stable hand to race trainer, Zeke." Tamara redirected, slicing cake and putting a piece on each plate for the boys. "How's Pest doing on his training?"

"Mostly, we're working on handling and distractions." Zeke slipped his arm out of his sling, took a plate and dug in, perhaps not aware that those skills he mentioned were what yearlings focused on, not two-year-olds.

"Dad won't let us ride Pest anywhere but in the pasture." T.J. was just as eager to eat cake as his twin, taking a big bite.

"That makes race training challenging." Tamara cut herself a very small sliver of cake. "Maybe you'll get to ride him around the track someday."

"Don't encourage them." Nathan came up behind her, an old cowboy at his side. He introduced the man as his uncle—Big E Blackwell.

The elderly cowboy gave Tamara's hand a firm shake, then eyed the cake she was serving out of her SUV. "Don't mind if I have a piece, do you?"

"Not at all." Tamara cut Big E a slice, then glanced at Nathan. "You want a piece, too?"

Avoiding her gaze, Nathan looked like he was going to refuse.

"It's not like you're a jockey watching your weight." Tamara cut a large slice for Nathan. "Besides, if you can't find something joyful after eating double-chocolate fudge cake, there's something seriously wrong with you." She smiled at the twins encouragingly. "Zeke? T.J.? Am I right?"

T.J. nodded enthusiastically.

"She's right, Dad." Zeke smiled, his teeth covered in chocolate.

T.J. noticed and giggled, pointing at his twin's mouth. "Your teeth are chocolatey."

Big E chuckled while Zeke worked his finger in his mouth like a toothbrush.

Nathan's expression loosened. His lips inched upward ever so slightly before that hint of a smile disappeared.

But a win by a nose is still a win.

Tamara smiled to herself.

"Welcome to Blackwell Stables, Tamara." Big E had a booming voice that conveyed confidence and leadership. "We need more smiles like yours around here."

Tamara handed Nathan that big slice of cake and a fork. He wasted no time digging in.

Big E took a seat on her rear bumper, more interested in Tamara than her cake. "How did you become a jockey? It's an odd career choice for a woman."

"My father is a jockey. He raised me at the track." Tamara smiled at the twins as if they shared a past. The truth was that in a way they had. They'd lost their mothers. However, unlike the twins, her father was more absent.

You don't need me, Tammie. You're tough.

Her father's words echoed in her head, little consolation for how easily he'd forgotten her when horses were around or races were being run. Still, she loved him and nothing would ever break their bond.

"You have fond memories of your childhood, I hope," Big E said softly, touching Tamara's arm. "Good family memories?"

No.

Nathan's blue eyes studied her, as if he knew the truth about Tamara's past just by her hesitation in her reply.

"I have memories," Tamara said slowly, holding on to her smile, if only just. "My mother was a professional barrel racer, so we lived where we could have horses and a makeshift arena. We had a small place outside of Louisville, near Churchill Downs. You'd think two professional riders would be a match made in heaven." Tamara could feel her smile drain away, fearing not even double-chocolate fudge cake could bring it back. "Turns out, they had a lot to teach me about horses and riding but they didn't have a lot in common. Mom left us when I was eight. By ten, I was mucking out stalls at the track. Hot-walking horses by twelve. At sixteen, I had a job exercising horses for a trainer."

"And then it was on to the races," Big E said kindly. There was something about him that inspired trust. "Good for you."

"You make it sound easy. It took a bit longer than that to prove myself." She gestured toward a large, clear plastic box behind her ice chest. It was filled with trophies, plaques and ribbons. "I've done all right. But the big races have eluded me."

Until I rode Frostfire Wind.

Her gaze found Nathan's. If his talented colt had survived, she might have had a chance at Triple Crown rides on other three-year-old contenders next year.

For now, it was back to square one.

CHAPTER FOUR

"We need to complete your tour of the facilities," Nathan told Tamara when they'd finished the cake and she'd gathered dirty utensils and plates in a plastic bag, planning to wash them later. "There are a few people I want you to meet, including those you'll be working closely with."

"All right." Tamara wasn't averse to spending more time with Nathan. Now that they'd both cooled off, they needed to find common ground on which to base their new working relationship.

The late-morning breeze felt hot as they left the shade. The twins scampered ahead. Big E received a phone call and lagged behind. That left Tamara and Nathan alone.

"Zeke and T.J. are enjoying their freedom while they can," Nathan said out of the blue. "They start school tomorrow. Kindergarten."

The twins entered the nearest horse barn, the one with the fillies and Tamara's upstairs apartment.

"Big day for all of you," Tamara said, allowing a teasing note to creep into her words. "You're practically an empty nester."

Nathan grunted, leading her into the filly barn breezeway, which was a noticeable respite from the heat. "The twins aren't looking forward to school. And I don't envy their teacher trying to keep them behaving for five hours."

"Me, either." Tamara grinned when Nathan's mouth dropped open at her comment. "Don't act surprised. I know those boys. They're gems but they don't sit still." She'd shared many a celebratory dinner with the horse trainer, Nathan and the twins after a race. She knew what the boys were like. "Maybe their teacher will bring double-chocolate fudge cake."

Nathan's smile came and went again in demoralizing fashion.

He's determined not to like me.

A tall, elderly woman with short white hair under a blue baseball cap came out of a nearby stall. She stopped and stared at Tamara. "Who's this?"

The twins hid behind a wheelbarrow a few feet away.

Nathan introduced Tamara to the stable hand that Big E and Asher had promoted to barn manager. "Tamara is a former race jockey who's starting tomorrow, Edie."

"*Current race jockey*," Tamara murmured.

Edie took Tamara's measure and found her wanting, if that frown was any indication. "You'll be the one picking up Frannie's training then."

Tamara frowned, glancing around. "I didn't realize there was a horse I'm specifically working with. Is Frannie a two-year-old?"

Edie's bark of laughter had several horses poking their heads out of stalls.

"Frannie has been exercising the horses for us," Nathan explained.

"She's as green as spring grass," Edie announced before addressing Nathan. "We're back on a training schedule then?"

Nathan nodded. "Five a.m. tomorrow. Right after Kelley serves breakfast."

"Don't be late," Edie told Tamara before striding off, walking past Zeke and T.J.'s hiding place without acknowledging them.

"Why were you hiding from Edie?" Tamara asked Zeke when Edie disappeared into the tack room.

"She caught us sitting on top of Fern this morning." Zeke held out a hand toward the brown filly in the stall Edie had just vacated.

The horse sniffed Zeke's hand before turning her attention to Tamara. A brass plate on her halter labeled her as Fern.

"Edie said we didn't have permission to sit on Fern," T.J. added, moving in front of Tamara to greet the filly, his tone drenched in hurt. "She said we might hurt her."

"She's right," Nathan said absently, stroking the filly's neck. "But more importantly, *you* might have been hurt. You don't know these horses the way you know Pest."

"Well, Edie doesn't have to be so grumpy about it." T.J. crossed his arms over his chest, the spitting image of Nathan in his office earlier when he and Tamara had argued about training Pest.

"Edie's always grumpy in the horse barns," Zeke seconded, fixing a disapproving stare on Tamara. "It's not like we planned to take Fern out and race her to death."

Tamara gasped at the shade thrown her way by the boy.

"Zeke!" Nathan chastised while T.J. frowned at his twin. "Apologize. Now."

Zeke was having none of it. He ran off.

T.J. gave Tamara an apologetic shrug. "I should go after him and keep him out of trouble." And then he, too, was gone.

"Sorry." Nathan continued to stroke Fern's neck.

"It's all right." Tamara cupped Fern's soft muzzle, taking small comfort from that touch. "Zeke's grieving Frosty, the same as you are." She shook her head. "It's a challenge. There are so many feelings to try to untangle. And..." She bit her lip, putting a halt to her rambling. "Maybe you should finish showing me around. I'm sure you have lots to do."

Nathan looked as if he might say something else. Instead, he led the way out of the filly barn.

They continued the tour, ending at the elevated

observation deck at the racetrack. It was an impressive training facility. Not only was there a dirt track, but within that oval was a turf track.

"You know what I've learned today?" Tamara leaned on the railing of the viewing deck and watched a pair of doves swoop over spectator seating. "Blackwells don't mess around. These facilities were laid out well and are state-of-the-art."

"Thanks." Beside her, Nathan shifted his weight on the creaky platform before shifting his gaze to hers. "I didn't know your dad raised you alone."

"I don't normally talk about my childhood but…" She stopped herself from blabbing her heart out. Just because she wanted a more personal relationship with Nathan didn't mean she should bare her soul, especially when he still harbored ill will about the accident.

"But…" he prompted, surprising her.

Tamara couldn't get a read on the reason behind his interest. "I don't normally talk about my past because not all my childhood memories are good ones." She gripped the railing tighter, looking out over the track, wishing she was riding. Most times, horses were easier for her to understand than people. "I wasn't so much a latchkey kid as a barn kid. I was on my own a lot at whatever training stable Dad worked for. He gave me plenty of freedom but I felt…unwanted." She chose to keep silent then. She hadn't meant to overshare.

But Nathan didn't seem put out by it. "Overlooked," he said, a faraway look in his eye. "Left to survive on your own."

You don't need me, Tammie. You're tough.

"Yes," Tamara said slowly. "How come…you understand?"

It was Nathan's turn to look uncomfortable. He resettled his brown cowboy hat on all that thick brown hair. "That's the way I felt growing up here, the youngest of six boys. My mom was the glue that held the family together. After she died…my dad was more interested in the business thriving than his kids, except for the oldest. Dylan, Asher's twin." Nathan's blue gaze found hers. "But Dylan died before he could take over. And nothing was the same after that. Still isn't."

Without another word, Nathan headed back down the stairs. And she followed, like a good employee. But her mind wandered…

Nathan had to fend for himself, just like me.

Nathan felt unwanted, just like me.

Nathan still feels like an outsider, just like me.

Once they reached the track gate, he began talking about tomorrow's schedule as if they hadn't just opened the door to each other's secrets.

But now that he'd let her in, Tamara wasn't sure she could let that door close again.

AS WITH ALL employee meals, dinner was served in the break room located next to Nathan's office. It had two large tables, lots of folding chairs, a refrigerator, microwave, sink and dishwasher. Kelley cooked at the main house and brought food over, but the utensils, cups and plates stayed here.

Big E and T.J. sat on either side of Tamara. Zeke stuck with Nathan across from Tamara. They were joined by Edie and Owen, the two stable hands. Asher and Kelley sat nearby, smiling adoringly at each other, reminding Nathan that he was alone.

Nathan was quiet during the meal, distracted from all the work Asher had dumped on his plate. At least, that's what he tried to tell himself. But his thoughts kept circling back to Tamara. After the few things Tamara had revealed on a personal level and things he suspected she hadn't said, Nathan couldn't stop trying to decode the puzzle that was his attraction to her.

How can she fascinate me when she rode Frosty to his death? How can she appeal to me when she pushes back on my training decisions?

Nathan mashed his mushroom risotto with his fork.

"You're as bad as your boys," Edie teased, gesturing toward Nathan's plate with a liverspotted hand.

"I'm distracted." By the worst thought of all: *How can I be interested in anyone after what I had with Marilee?* It felt as if he was cheating on her. He touched his wedding ring but that brought him no peace. It hadn't since he'd arrived in Gold Finch.

"Dad?" Zeke fidgeted in his seat. "Can we get a dog?"

"No dogs," Edie said, emphatically.

Nathan stared at her in shock. "We used to have dogs here." A laid-back Labrador, a bouncy springer spaniel, his mother's toy poodle.

"We're a cat stable now." Edie gathered her utensils and put them on her empty plate. "Dogs are flighty. Joe used to bring his little pooch around and that yapper put all the horses on edge."

Her announcement was met with silence. She stood, then carried her plate to the sink.

"If I had a dog, the horses would love him," Zeke said just as decisively as Edie had spoken earlier about cats.

Edie harrumphed, rinsing her dishes and putting them in the dishwasher.

"He would be loved," Zeke grumped, stirring his small cup of pudding with his left hand. His right was still in its sling. Nathan hadn't noticed that his son's dinner was largely untouched.

He'll be hungry at bedtime.

And Nathan didn't have anything nutritious in their room's small refrigerator.

Kelley brought T.J. a small plastic container. She gave what looked like the same type of container to Zeke.

"What's this?" Zeke was still in grumpy mode. "More vegetables?"

"A peanut-butter-and-jelly sandwich." Kelley

opened the container for Zeke to show him, then ruffled his light brown hair. "When I was a kid, I didn't like adult food, either."

Saved!

Nathan thanked her.

Zeke beamed up at Kelley worshipfully. "If Uncle Asher doesn't marry you, I will."

"I'll hold you to that." Kelley removed Zeke's barely touched plate of pork chop and risotto.

"Sorry, kid," Asher said. "But you won't get your chance. Kelley's mine."

"We'll see." Zeke bit into his sandwich, smiling.

"Haven't you ever had a cat, Zeke?" Edie brought a cup of chocolate pudding back to the table.

"Mom was allergic," Zeke said between bites. "Do cats come when you call?"

"Sometimes," Edie allowed.

"Do they keep away scary people?" Zeke continued his interrogation, expression deadly serious. "Like burglars and evil ninjas?"

Edie shook her head, smiling a little. "No."

Zeke dropped his sandwich on the table. "Then what good are cats?"

Just then, a gray tabby sashayed proudly into the break room carrying a mouse in its mouth.

Edie chuckled. "What good are they? They keep the mouse population down. Good girl, Luna."

The cat dropped the mouse near Edie.

"Cool." Zeke stuck his head under the table for

a better look. "That cat's a killer. I bet she could stop a ninja."

"Maybe if she bit their ankles." Edie scooped the mouse up with her paper napkin, eliciting a chorus of "Ews" from the room. "Oh, grow up," she told them, marching out the door and into the filly barn's breezeway.

Luna trotted along after her.

Edie screamed.

Everyone ran out of the break room to see what was the matter. Even the fillies had their heads poked out of their stalls.

"What happened?" Nathan asked, having gotten there first. But he had a good idea. Edie's paper napkin was on the ground. The mouse and cat were nowhere to be seen. "Was the mouse still alive?"

Wide-eyed, Edie nodded, emphasized by a full-body shiver.

"Oh, grow up," Zeke said, before taking another bite of his sandwich.

Amid the ensuing laughter, Nathan's gaze caught on Tamara's and her pretty, smiling face. He returned that smile.

And just for a moment, he felt things were looking up.

CHAPTER FIVE

"TIME TO RISE and shine," Edie called, knocking on Tamara's door the next morning long before sunrise.

Tamara was already up, showered and dressed. She opened the door to her room above the filly stable and poked her head out. "I'm moving."

"Impressive." Edie paused at the top of the stairs, that gray tabby at her feet. "But there's still a long day ahead and I run a tight stable schedule."

"I'm a hard worker." Tamara gestured toward the cat. "Is that Luna, the mouse catcher?"

"It is." Edie bent down to pet her.

The cat purred loud enough that Tamara could hear her several feet away.

"If she likes you, she'll bring you a mouse, too." Edie straightened, tugging a ball cap firmly on her short white hair. "I'll make sure there's coffee downstairs. Kelley will be by with hot breakfast any minute."

"I'll be there as soon as I put my boots on." And grabbed her safety vest and riding helmet.

Edie was already hurrying downstairs, followed by the cat.

Not long afterward, Tamara joined Edie in the break room, hanging her riding gear on the hooks by one of the two entrance doors. "That coffee smells good."

"Give it a minute to finish percolating." Edie had two mugs out on the counter. "This coffee machine is like me. It gets the job done but not as quickly as it used to."

Tamara came to stand next to her. "How long have you been working here?"

"I was hired before Asher and Dylan were born." Edie's gaze took on a faraway look. "Walter was a joy to work for back then. More like Big E. Organized, friendly, generous."

"What happened? I get the idea that Walter changed." From what little Nathan had said to her yesterday.

"Walter's wife died." Edie stopped staring into space and picked up one of the coffee mugs. "Heart attack. No warning. It was as if a part of Walter died that day, too."

Tamara imagined that's how Nathan felt after his wife died.

The coffee pot finished brewing. Edie and Tamara each poured themselves a cup. But neither moved to sit down.

"Walter always had it in his head that his oldest son would take on the running of the ranch,"

Edie continued, cradling her mug of coffee as if in need of an emotional anchor. "That would be Dylan, even though he and Asher were twins." She paused to blow on her steaming mug of coffee. "But after the missus died… Well, Walter began pushing everyone away, even Dylan. He became a grouchy old man long before his time. It was hard to stick around."

"Why did you?" Tamara wondered aloud.

Edie shrugged. "I'm an only child. I never married. The Blackwells… The staff… The horses I care for… My family is here." She sipped her coffee. "That sounds strange, doesn't it?"

"Not at all. I get it. I'm an only child, too. Found family is important."

She and Edie exchanged knowing smiles.

A door to the outside opened and Kelley entered with a tray of food. The tall blonde was an exceptional cook, although she claimed never to have made double-chocolate fudge cake.

"That smells lovely, whatever it is." Tamara poured herself another cup of coffee.

"Breakfast tacos." Kelley removed the aluminum foil, revealing egg-filled flour tortillas folded the way a taco would be. "I put eggs in a frying pan, break the yokes, sprinkle them with cheese, then put tortillas on top." She served one on a plate for Tamara and another for Edie. "It all melts together. I fold them while they're still hot, then add guacamole, sour cream and a little homemade *pico de gallo*."

"Clever." Tamara brought her plate and coffee over to a table.

Edie and Kelley followed.

"I didn't drown them in cheese or sour cream." Kelley seemed intent upon garnering Tamara's approval. "I tried to keep things as low fat and high protein as possible."

"I appreciate that." Tamara took a bite. It was good and she said so. "The meal last night was great, too." Pork chops with mushroom risotto. "Why aren't you working in some fancy restaurant?"

Kelley fiddled with a diamond engagement ring on her finger. "I did work in a high-end restaurant in New York."

"And then in a diner here in town," Edie said in between shoveling her breakfast down the hatch.

"I still cook at the Galloping Fork Diner. Now, I'm part owner. I've enjoyed adding a bunch of new things to the menu." Kelley finished off her egg taco and looked like she might have another. "Anyway, supporting Asher however I can is my priority in the near future. With the doping investigation happening and all, it's been challenging around here."

Curiosity got the better of Tamara. She had to ask, "Did I hear you say last night at dinner that you went to school with Nathan?"

"Yes." Kelley's bright smile reemerged. "He hasn't changed much. He's still quiet and dependable."

"As the youngest Blackwell, Nathan was a wanderer," Edie added, getting up for a second egg taco. "He roamed all over this place, both when his brothers were still here and after they left. Must know the place like the back of his hand. Broke Nathan's heart when his dad told him he wasn't wanted here anymore."

What?

That very nearly broke Tamara's heart, as well.

A slight woman entered, hanging a riding vest and helmet next to Tamara's on hooks near the breezeway door. She had short blond hair and wore riding attire. She approached Tamara tentatively. "Hi, I'm Frannie. The other exercise jockey?"

"Oh, yeah. The one I'm taking under my wing." Tamara sat back in her chair, trying to hide her surprise even as she shook the woman's hand. She was young but older than Tamara expected. In her twenties when most jockeys started in their teens. "I expected to meet you last night at dinner."

Frannie rolled her eyes. "Blame my sister, Kelley. She had me working in the kitchen of the Galloping Fork Diner yesterday."

"Honestly? Frannie is better at riding horses than she is in the kitchen," Kelley teased gently.

"I'll take that as a compliment." Frannie grinned.

Tamara had a good feeling about Frannie. But…

"Hang on. You two are sisters?" Tamara looked from very tall, willowy Kelley to very short, willowy Frannie.

"Hard to believe, isn't it?" Frannie chuckled, although with a tinge of sarcasm. "Same blond hair and blue eyes but Kelley got all the drive and height in the family. She won't toot her own horn, but she's a classically trained chef. Quite the success story."

"Your story is yet to be written," Kelley kindly pointed out. "Plus, you need drive and passion to be a jockey, Frannie, which you have. Imagine wanting to be a jockey but being my height. So disappointing."

"I suppose you're right about that," Frannie agreed, sounding more genuine.

"Morning." Owen entered the break room looking ready to clean stalls and cool down horses in his muck boots, stained jeans and black T-shirt. He gave Frannie a smitten grin, complete with a blush that brightened his ginger coloring. "How was your weekend, Frannie?"

"Good, since I got paid. But I can still smell the hamburger grease on me." Frannie pulled up the neck of her T-shirt and sniffed it, giving her sister a mischievous grin rather than acknowledge poor Owen's interest. "I hope your weekend was less aromatic, Owen."

Frannie and Owen moved toward the tray of breakfast tacos, exchanging comments about their days off.

Tamara caught Kelley's eye and made a what-gives gesture.

"Nobody knows if that bud is going to bloom," Kelley said cryptically.

"I'm betting no," Edie said flatly.

Poor Owen.

"Great meal, as usual, Kelley." Edie carried her dishes back to the sink for a rinse. "Tamara and Frannie, you've got fifteen minutes before rides begin." She tucked her dishes into the dishwasher, then went out the door, walking with purpose.

"You should hurry," Frannie said, coming to sit across from Tamara with two tacos. "Edie's a bit impatient with those of us who move at a normal pace."

"I'll be fine. It's not wise to bolt your food and hop on a galloping horse." But Tamara drained her coffee just the same and got up to rinse her dishes and load them in the dishwasher. "The food was great. Thanks. I look forward to lunch, Kelley."

"See you then." The chef raised her coffee mug in salute.

Tamara grabbed her riding helmet and vest off the hooks by the door and left.

"This is Dandelion Commotion," Edie told Tamara when she found the stable hand outside a filly's stall. She'd saddled the black filly and held on to her reins, looking at Tamara suspiciously. "*I* call her Dandy. She's feeling frisky today. I won't put you up on her if you can't handle a spirited horse."

"We'll be fine." Keeping a firm hold on her fears, Tamara stood next to Dandy, waiting for Edie to relinquish the reins.

Edie didn't hand them over. "Normally, I'd boost you up and walk you out to the track. But these aren't normal times. Instead of six horses under my care, I've got thirty. That means protocol is shot to the wind. You will not ride Dandy out to the track." Edie clearly wore the pants in this part of the operation. Or thought she did. "You'll walk beside her."

"Because she's frisky," Tamara surmised in her best tone of agreement.

Edie nodded, severe expression loosening. "At least, they hired someone who understands. Not like Frannie."

"I'm learning, Edie." Frannie came out of the break room, not fazed by Edie's brusque comments in the least.

That's telling.

Tamara gave Frannie an approving smile.

"You'll learn soon enough, Frannie girl." Edie finally handed Tamara the filly's reins. "Tamara, when you're done with Dandy, Owen should be at the track to take her for a cool down. Your next ride is Scarlet Debut. But don't get ahead of yourself. Focus on Dandy and don't damage the horseflesh."

"Got it. Dandy is in good hands." Tamara led the prancing filly into the gray, early-morning chill, heading toward the track, talking all the way. "You're a looker, aren't you? Long legs, barrel chest, intelligent eyes. No short races for you."

The filly's hind end swung wide, so that she was walking sideways.

"But you're full of mischief." Tamara bumped Dandy's front shoulder with her own. "Behave. We'll get all that sass out on the track, I promise."

The filly was due to breeze today, a short, fast, conditioning workout. First, they'd warm up, then they'd run a quarter mile with little urging on Tamara's part.

We aren't going at breakneck speed. No need to stress.

Tamara felt herself stressing, anyway. She spent the rest of the walk breathing deeply and thinking lighthearted thoughts. Fuzzy kittens. Waddling penguins. Baby horses.

Nathan stood at the entrance to the track, calming just by his appearance. He wore a brown button-down beneath a blue vest jacket. He tipped his straw cowboy hat when he saw her. "Right on time. Let's get you up."

"I didn't expect to see you this early." Tamara slowed nearly to a stop, letting Dandy dance out sideways.

Nathan closed the distance between them. "As acting manager, it's my responsibility to make sure you're working to plan. Plus, I've got to order supplies before I take the boys to school later. Let me give you a leg up." He came to stand next to Tamara as she gathered the reins and grabbed hold of the saddle. With a smooth movement, he held Tamara's left ankle and lifted.

Taking his cue, Tamara hopped into the air and used Nathan's hold of her ankle as leverage to fling herself into the saddle.

One hand on Dandy's neck, Nathan walked beside them toward the track entrance. "Let Dandy set the pace. Just don't let her gallop like she's neck and neck down the straightaway."

"The very definition of breezing." At the gate, Tamara kept the filly in place by holding the leather reins taut and shifting her weight back. "Any other advice?"

"Keep to the schedule," Nathan reminded her, although it sounded more like a lament than a slight directed at her. "We've got to be ready to race once we get the all-clear."

No way are they getting the all-clear before the end of the season.

"Gotcha," Tamara said, anyway. She allowed Dandy to prance onto the dirt track.

The sun was just starting its leisurely rise in the east. Dandy wanted no part in leisurely. It was clear the filly hadn't been given a proper shakedown in some time. She tried to take the bit in her mouth and run for the roses. But Tamara was on to her tricks and kept her in hand.

"You're a proper racehorse, aren't you, girl?"

Tamara eased the filly into a trot, posting up and down in the saddle.

Dandy tossed her head, sending her black mane rippling across her neck. Then she lurched forward, trying to break into a gallop, as impatient to run as Zeke was to eat when double-chocolate fudge cake was in reach.

After a few minutes of trotting, Tamara allowed Dandy to ease into a slow gallop on the far side of the track, letting the filly find her rhythm. They rounded a turn and Tamara gave Dandy free rein on the straightaway, curious to see what she'd do.

No surprise. The filly was a goer. She probably dreamed of winning races because her stride was long and quick. She didn't want to breeze along. She ran as if she was neck and neck with a contender and determined not to come in second.

Too fast. Too, too fast.

Adrenaline prickled in Tamara's veins, making her hands shake as she reined in the black filly. Or tried to.

"Work with me, girl." *Please.* Tamara managed to bring her to a slow gallop and from there a controlled trot. In no time, they completed another lap just as Frannie was bringing out a leggy brown filly.

They exchanged waves.

Surprisingly, Nathan, not Owen, waited for Tamara at the gate. He took hold of Dandy's reins beneath her chin and walked them back toward the hot-walker station. "What was that? It looked like you two were fighting out there during your breeze."

"Dandy didn't get your training memo." Still feeling shaky, Tamara squeezed her fingers around the reins. "I wanted her to breeze and she wanted to sprint the entire time. I think it's a function of her not being on a regular training schedule."

"So..." Nathan briefly glanced at Tamara over his shoulder, a hint of a smile on his handsome face. "It's not just me you scuffle with. It's horses."

"We had a difference of opinion." Tamara kept her tone light, not wanting him to see her out of sorts. "I always try to do what's right, even if it's not in line with popular opinion."

Nathan scoffed. "Have you always been this stubborn and I just didn't notice?"

"I'm as stubborn as the horses I ride," Tamara said in a get-along tone. "You didn't see it before because we were on the same team."

"Maybe. Maybe you didn't see my stubborn side, either." Nathan gave her a searching glance, one that reminded Tamara of the way he'd looked at her yesterday when they stood on the viewing platform and talked about the past.

The past. Our fathers. Being overlooked.

Tamara wanted to have that connection with him again, wanted it to last longer this time. "My dad always told me stubbornness is a strength."

"Mine just wanted me to fall in line." Nathan

slowed to a stop, staring up at Tamara as if trying to figure her out. “Of course, when I did what he asked, he said I wasn’t doing enough to make this place profitable.”

“Is that when he kicked you out?” When Nathan glanced at her, Tamara added, “Edie mentioned something about it.”

Nathan nodded. “It’s no secret. I was kind of expecting it to happen. I was the last of his kids still living here. Dad felt I was a drain on his resources.”

“I’m sorry.” Tamara had the strongest urge to touch him, to offer comfort.

But they’d reached their destination. Owen was at the hot-walker station. He took the reins from Nathan and held Dandy still while Tamara popped off.

Tamara would have lost her balance if Nathan hadn’t steadied her. She found her footing and smiled up at him. “Sometimes it’s a long way down.”

“Be careful,” Nathan said softly, staring into her eyes…

As if he wanted to kiss me.

That seemed an overreach.

Taking a much-needed step back, Tamara let out a panicky laugh, forced and high-pitched. “Thanks for the escort.”

“Anytime.” Nathan turned and walked away, leaving Tamara feeling as if something had gone unsaid. She waited for him to say it…whatever *it* was.

Wishful thinking on my part.

"Thanks for the assist, Nathan." Owen was already some twenty feet away with Dandy.

His words broke the spell Nathan had Tamara bound in. She started moving, heading toward the filly barn and her next ride.

"I'll meet you at the racetrack gate, Tamara," Owen called after her.

"Great." Everything was great. And if Tamara kept telling herself that, she might just be able to hold her tongue the next time Nathan left her an opening to get to know him better. Because, like Owen's feelings for Frannie, Tamara's feelings for Nathan were one-sided.

"EXCUSE ME." LATER that morning, Nathan dodged a parent towing a child in the crowded elementary school hallway. He held Zeke's and T.J.'s hands as he searched for room 3A, ears filled with the loud conversations of other parents and students milling about.

I can't remember my first day of school. But I'm certain it wasn't this...stressfully chaotic.

"Why do we have to go to school?" Zeke asked, flapping the arm that was in a sling, possibly to indicate to others he needed a wide berth.

"Yeah, Dad. You need us back at the stables," T.J. added, wide-eyed and walking slowly, seemingly taking in every mural and poster.

"Stop complaining." Nathan thought he spotted 3A ahead. He hurried forward. "School is fun. You'll meet new friends. You'll have snacks and recess and lunch."

"We'll have to sit all day." Zeke hated sitting still.

"And sing." T.J. hated singing in public.

A woman in a blue dress and sneakers stepped out of a room just ahead. She carried a clipboard and looked official. "Are you looking for Miss Jenkins kindergarten class? Room 3A?"

"We are." Nathan hurried forward, driven by relief, not to mention a bittersweet feeling of grief. Marilee should have been here on their first day of school. "This is Zeke and T.J. Blackwell."

"I'm Talia Thompson, room mother." She checked her clipboard. "So…we have Zeke and *Tucker* Blackwell."

"Tucker James." Nathan's head bobbed. He was just as nervous as his kids. "He likes to be called T.J."

"Noted." Talia jotted something down, then smiled at Nathan. It was a welcome-to-the-party smile. Innocuous. Innocent. Interested.

In me?

Nathan put his guard up. And yet…there was something about being smiled at in such a manner that had him picturing Tamara with that welcoming smile aimed his way. Now *that* was a smile he could return in kind.

"Ridiculous," Nathan muttered. Letting his attraction for Tamara progress would only complicate his already complicated life further. And letting thoughts of Tamara distract him was holding up the show. He urged his kids forward. They were dressed in their Sunday best. "Have a good day, boys."

The twins dug in their boot heels.

"I'm trying to fill my classroom volunteer spots for the next few months," Talia explained, still sending out interested vibes that now had context: recruiting school aides. "Where is Mrs. Blackwell?"

"There is no Mrs. Blackwell," Nathan said carefully, mournfully.

"Our mom is dead," Zeke said, not one to beat around the bush.

"And our dad is sad," T.J. said, always quick with an overshare.

Talia's smile broadened. "I'm so sorry to hear that. Volunteering can be a way to create community, as well as special memories for your boys."

"I'm actually really busy at work the next few weeks," Nathan hedged.

"I have an opening at Back to School Night." Without waiting for him to reply, Talia jotted his name down. "We always need help that evening at the refreshment stand." She shooed the twins inside, having more success than Nathan did. "Go find your seats, boys. The bell's about to ring. I'll be in touch about volunteering, Mr. Blackwell."

That woman doesn't take no for an answer.

Nathan headed back down the hallway. He hadn't thought about dating or romance since Marilee died. He hadn't felt any jolt of attraction for anyone.

That's not true.

When he'd caught up to Tamara the other day at Rosehaven Downs, there'd been this unusual feeling inside him. It wasn't the burst of enthusiastic attraction he'd felt for Marilee. It was more a warmth blossoming slowly inside his chest when Tamara had first looked at him. He'd actually stared too long at his jockey a few times since then, just trying to figure out what was happening to him when he looked at her.

I can't be attracted to Tamara.

For a variety of reasons, including being her boss, her riding Frostfire Wind when he died and Tamara making a living in one of the most dangerous jobs on the planet.

That last objection… Nathan liked it. He'd buried too many loved ones. He couldn't go through that again.

No. Tamara Vaughn wasn't romance material and never would be.

"WE'RE BEHIND." AND Edie was taking no prisoners. She shook a finger at the two exercise jockeys standing in front of her. "Pick up the pace, ladies."

"Yes, ma'am." Tamara bit back a smile.

"Yes, ma'am," Frannie echoed, also with a straight face.

Tamara liked Frannie. She was friendly and coachable, eager to learn. And boy, did she have a lot to learn.

They'd both just returned from exercising a pair of three-year-old colts, having handed them off to Owen to cool down afterward.

"This is Corny Carny." Edie handed Frannie the reins to a large chestnut colt. "Corny only likes to run on days that end in *y*."

"So he—" Frannie cut herself off and laughed. "That's a joke."

"Corny is no joke." Edie tsked, putting that prickly, serious expression back on. "Give him an inch of rein, and he'll run himself to death. This boy doesn't know the meaning of the word *quit*."

Like Frostfire Wind.

Tamara's breath caught in her throat as fear galloped through her veins. Fear for the horse that might run himself to death. Fear for Frannie, a novice race rider.

"I'll take Corny," Tamara said, easing the colt's reins from Frannie's fingers. "You take Batwing, Frannie." The black colt with white socks was saddled a few feet away.

"Don't know why Batwing is still on the training schedule." Edie led Frannie to where a saddled Batwing was waiting. "He's the opposite of Corny Carny. He's come in last in every race this year."

"But there's always tomorrow." Frannie was an optimist.

The two women led their mounts out to the racetrack. It was coming up on nine o'clock. The sun was firmly in the sky and there was no breeze, which meant it was going to be hotter than blazes soon. They had to put the majority of the horses scheduled to train today through their paces before noon.

Tamara gave Frannie a leg up into the saddle on Batwing. Then she climbed a nearby wooden fence and mounted Corny Carny. He pawed the ground but she held his reins tightly. "What made you want to be a jockey, Frannie?"

"I love horses. I love riding horses. And I love going fast." Frannie's grin was more mischievous and open than her sister's. "Isn't that why you became a jockey?"

"I grew up around horses and since I'm so small..." Tamara shrugged, leading the way through the gate to the track proper, holding Corny to a walk. "The opportunity presented itself and I took it. Haven't looked back since, even though the jockey standards are physically challenging." She'd trained in the gym for months before taking the exam.

"I'm worried about passing the licensing test," Frannie admitted. "It's like military boot camp and I very nearly failed gym class in high school."

"Because you cut class?" Tamara teased, having a feeling that wasn't the case.

"No." Frannie laughed. "Because I can't hit a

baseball, spike a volleyball over a net or strike the broadside of a barn with a soccer ball. I guess I'm not cut out for team sports."

"Racing is more like dancing solo on a moving stage. Let's trot," Tamara said, letting Corny start to groove. The chestnut had a choppy trot if only because he kept trying to break into a gallop.

Frannie had to give Batwing a good kick with her heels to get him moving. Edie hadn't been overstating the horse's tortoise-like attitude. Tamara made a mental note to suggest the colt be sold or at the very least, be removed from the race training schedule. She liked having a reason to talk to Nathan.

Frannie had good posting form, moving up and down in tune with Batwing's stride. "What do you think of Owen?"

"He's cute and seems like a nice guy." Tamara smiled, barely touching the reins to Corny's neck to keep him close to the rail on the first turn. "I've only just met Owen but I know he has a huge crush on you." He blushed every time he saw Frannie.

Now, it was Frannie who blushed, her cheeks a deep pink next to a lock of short golden hair on her cheek.

"Maybe I should have asked you what you think of Owen," Tamara wondered aloud, mind still half occupied by the frisky colt beneath her.

"Owen's my kind of guy. And super sweet,"

Frannie admitted. "But aren't professional jockeys nomadic? Maybe I shouldn't…you know."

"Go out with him?" Tamara guessed.

Frannie nodded. "Work relationships can be torture if things don't work out between us."

Oh, Tamara knew that firsthand. She and Nathan were a perfect example of a relationship turned sour. Even though it was a friendship gone wrong, it made working together a tightrope walk for them.

"But what if it's love?" Tamara hadn't realized she'd given the thought voice until Frannie jerked her head Tamara's way. "Wouldn't it be worth fighting for if it was? Despite the risks?"

Says the hopeless romantic.

"How do I know if what I feel is love?" Frannie asked in a voice barely above the thrumming rhythm of horse hooves.

"How does anyone know they're in love?" Tamara wasn't exactly an expert in that department. Sure, she'd dated. But racing always came first over long-term romance. "I suppose you have to risk testing your feelings for each other to see how important they are."

They continued to trot, both riders posting up and down.

"My thighs are burning," Frannie admitted as they came around the far turn and let the horses gallop slowly. She transitioned from posting to the standing martini position as if she were racing. "Is it bad to admit that when I was exercising the horses before you were hired, I wasn't posting in the trot?"

"Not if you only want to be an exercise jockey. But if you aspire to be a race jockey, you have to build up your stamina, just like the horses." Tamara gave Corny's neck a pat. The colt's stride was quick and smooth. Not a heart-pounding sprint like Dandy. "You have an opportunity here to get good experience. But it's also where the rubber hits the road in terms of your strength and endurance conditioning. If you're sore, you need more gym time."

"And until then?"

"Invest in a good heating pad."

Frannie sat down in the saddle as they crossed the finish line. "There's a small exercise room here."

"I saw that."

"Can we work out together? I'd appreciate the help."

"Sure. I need to get back to training, anyway." Tamara wasn't in top racing form. Her legs were feeling the long hours in the saddle, although they weren't as spent as Frannie's seemed to be. But first, they had to finish riding the horses. And right now, Tamara had to see if what Edie said about Corny was true. She gave the colt some slack on the reins as they finished the far turn.

Corny lurched forward, digging in the way he might when coming out of the starting gate. And then he flew over the straightaway, tossing his head when Tamara reined him back in.

But she didn't give up the fight.

Because this isn't a race. And no horse is dying on my watch. Not ever again.

CHAPTER SIX

Even if the investigation into identifying the culprit in the doping of Sovereign's Pride was slow going, Big E wasn't giving up.

After lunch on Monday, Big E got out of Asher's truck at the sheriff's office in Gold Finch. He stepped onto the sidewalk and took a moment to hitch up his pants, tuck in his red checked dress shirt and straighten his cowboy hat.

"You never looked better," Asher teased, joining Big E on the sidewalk in his new black jeans and black polo shirt. "The sheriff will take one look at you, Dapper Dan, and tell us everything about their investigation into Elliot James." Their former assistant stable manager, a man who'd died in a suspicious single-vehicle crash after they found the drugs used to dope Sovereign's Pride in his room above the colt barn.

"Never underestimate the power of a well-dressed man." Big E was a believer in living the leader look. Appearances counted in confrontational situations. He strode to the front door. "You can't show up asking for respect if you don't give it."

"Is that a Blackwell thing?" Asher asked, no longer teasing. "My dad used to say something similar."

"Walter was a talker." Big E chuckled, opening the door and holding it for Asher. "And so was our paternal grandfather. I'll credit my Grandpa Blackwell for giving us the gift of gab, along with some clichéd words of wisdom that we drop like pearls."

"My dad was more likely to shoot them like bullets." Asher looked grim as he entered the building.

"I'm sorry for that, son." And Big E was. He knew firsthand how the wrong attitude could alienate family.

Once inside, Big E and Asher checked in at the front desk and waited for the sheriff.

Asher gave Big E a sly smile and made a show of tucking his polo shirt into his jeans. "I suppose putting a spit shine on things couldn't hurt."

Big E chuckled, wondering what his cousin Walter had done to alienate his sons. They'd turned out well despite all the family drama.

The sheriff came through a door in his tan uniform. He was older than Asher, younger than Big E and more territorial than a bull in his pasture. "Gentlemen. I have nothing new to share with you."

Oh, really?

"What about the drug given to Sovereign's Pride?" Asher asked, an edge to his words. Like Big E, he didn't believe the sheriff was taking their case seriously. Unlike Big E, the moment Asher felt he wasn't taken seriously, he bared his fangs. "Have you traced the medication to its source? The vial we found in Elliot's room had a batch number on it."

The sheriff pursed his lips.

"What about following the money and identifying who bribed Elliot?" Big E pressed in a calmer tone than Asher had used. "Last we talked, you mentioned finding a large, unexplained cash deposit in Elliot's bank account. Have you brought in other competitors like Patsy Richmond of Richmond Stables? Or Sullivan Connelly of Connelly Thoroughbreds?" Those two had the resources to pay someone to dope a Blackwell horse and they stood to benefit greatly from Sovereign Pride's disqualification and subsequent suspension.

"I can't comment about an ongoing investigation," the sheriff said, gruffly.

"Meaning you haven't done it yet." Asher made no effort to hide his annoyance, not in his tone or his fierce frown.

The sheriff frowned right back. He'd told them previously that he believed Elliot was a disgruntled employee who doped the horse out of spite, then got what he deserved in that accident. End of story.

Fat chance of that.

From what Big E had learned of Elliot, he wasn't the sharpest tool in the shed. It was hard to imagine the man coming up with the plan, much less executing it undetected.

"I can tell you that both Patsy Richmond and

Sullivan Connelly have assured me they weren't involved in either the doping or the crash." The sheriff seemed to be throwing them a bone. "And from what I can tell, they aren't as financially well off as you seem to believe."

I don't believe that for a minute.

"Has there been a ruling on Elliot's crash?" Big E moved between Asher and the sheriff, recalling that someone had told him Patrick Connelly had a gambling addiction that still kept him in the frame. "Was it an accident or something more sinister?"

"There are inconsistencies that make us suspect Elliot's vehicle was tampered with," the sheriff allowed.

Big E nodded. That was something, at least.

"And who is most likely to gain from Elliot's death?" Asher elbowed Big E aside, a dark look on his face. "Patsy Richmond and Sullivan Connelly. That's who you should be looking into." He all but shouted, "*Do your job!*"

"Gentlemen," the sheriff said in a decidedly icy tone of voice. "Solving crime isn't as easy as the one-hour police procedurals you watch on TV. There are protocols and laws to be followed."

"Correct. And not by simply having informal conversations," Big E added, stepping around Asher to be closer to the sheriff. It was time to take off the gloves and play hardball. He lowered his voice. "If you haven't conducted in-depth interviews with the most likely suspects, it looks as if you fear their influence, or perhaps even their loss of support when you come up for reelection."

The sheriff huffed and puffed, his cheeks reddening. He closed the short distance between Big E and himself, chest out. "I've tried to be sensitive to your situation. But I don't have to do so at the expense of my—"

"*Pride*," Big E cut him off. "Let's be honest and call it what it is. I get it. You don't like the pressure of concerned citizens demanding answers to unsolved crimes."

"*Citizens?*" the sheriff scoffed. "You aren't even residents."

"I am." Asher stood in what Big E liked to think of as his corporate boardroom stance—shoulders back, chest out, head high. "Before this crime was committed, the Blackwell Stables were one of the largest employers in the area. We could be again if you solve this crime in a timely manner. Otherwise…" Asher made a show of shrugging. "Lower employment means fewer taxes collected. Which means fewer tax dollars to fund the sheriff's office."

Scowling, the sheriff held his ground. "I think we're done here."

"For now," Asher said before Big E could. He turned on his boot heel and stalked toward the exit, radiating anger with each step.

Big E didn't budge. He wasn't done with the sheriff. Not by a long shot. "Be careful, Sheriff.

Gold Finch may be small but the implications of this crime stretch beyond your bucolic borders." To everywhere horse racing was legal.

"Is that a threat?" The sheriff's tone was cold, sharp and jagged.

"I don't make threats. I state facts." Big E left, joining Asher outside, fuming. But letting his anger ride roughshod wasn't going to do anyone any good. He had to keep his head and do right by Walter. His nephews' futures were at stake.

Asher made a show of untucking his polo shirt. "The whole mutual-respect thing didn't work so well."

"But that doesn't mean we're at loose ends." Big E just had to make some phone calls. "The sheriff and our opposition should never underestimate the power of the Blackwell name."

Particularly when his name was attached to it.

CHAPTER SEVEN

NATHAN CLOSED HIS laptop in the early afternoon, frustrated because he'd posted job listings that should have resulted in responses by now. But… *nothing.* No queries. No applications.

If that isn't an indication of how much trouble we're in...

Was there going to be anything left of Blackwell Stables to pass on to his kids? Nathan slouched, the small movement giving rise to multiple creaks in his office chair.

The lack of job candidates, combined with the dead end Asher and Big E had encountered at the sheriff's office earlier… Well, it didn't add up to anything positive.

This is why I can't commit to this place. It's hopeless.

Tamara entered his office and then paused, staring at him.

Nathan sat up and stared right back.

She'd shed her black, padded safety vest and riding helmet but still wore her gray T-shirt and slim-fitting, olive-green riding pants tucked into her black riding boots. Wisps of black hair had escaped from her long braid, one lock curled on her cheek as if sweat-soaked in place. Tamara looked like she'd put in a hard day's work.

He liked that Tamara was a hard worker. He liked that she brought beauty and energy with her presence. He even liked that she woke something inside of his broken heart. But what Nathan needed right now was hope for the future. And Tamara didn't give him that.

Tamara had closed the door but she kept her hand on the doorknob. "I was going to talk to you about Pest and the two-year-olds. But then I saw the look on your face and I knew you weren't in the mood for that conversation."

"What look is that?" Self-consciously, Nathan ran a hand through his hair. His cowboy hat was hanging on a hook by the door.

"Let me put it this way." Tamara gave him what felt like a carefully modulated smile. "I have double-chocolate fudge cake in my room. And you look like you need it."

She's offering me cake?

For some reason, that made Nathan feel better. He managed a wan smile. "I could use some good news."

"I wish I had some." After a moment's hesitation, Tamara sat in a ladder-back dining room chair on the other side of his desk. "I mean, it's not bad news. I sent Frannie to catch Pest so we could get his training session in and…he didn't let her come near him."

"Just the way I've trained him," Nathan quipped, although it wasn't true.

"That's your theft-deterrent system? Training a blue-blooded horse to avoid strangers in his pasture?" Tamara chuckled, visibly relaxing.

"Something like that." His smile felt easier now, too.

"Maybe you can take Pest on a ride around the track when it cools off after dinner," Tamara suggested.

That's not happening.

"Don't say a word." Tamara held out her hand, palm facing him in the universal gesture of stop. "I see from the change in your expression that you aren't going to ride Pest."

Nathan sat back in his creaky desk chair. "Am I that easy to read?"

"Sometimes. Look." She pointed toward the three-year-old training board and told him about a sluggish colt named Batwing. "He's a waste of time. Edie and Frannie will verify that."

"Thanks." Nathan got up and erased the colt's name from the training board. But he hadn't taken his eye off the ball. He sat back down across from Tamara. "Don't think I didn't notice your quick change of subject. Pest isn't going to be a racehorse."

"And don't you fail to notice that I know how to

bide my time." Her smile returned, tempting him to join in. "That horse was bred to run. And every time I come in here, I'm going to make sure his name is on the training board."

A smile tried to crack his boss-like façade. "You aren't letting this go, are you?"

"Nope." She looked rather pleased with herself. "Stubborn, remember?"

Again, Nathan had the urge to give her a goofy smile. Again, he held on to his composure.

This isn't the time for romance and she's not the one I should fall for.

The alarm on Nathan's phone went off. He was grateful for the interruption. "It's time to pick up the twins from school."

"Exciting stuff." Tamara got to her feet, looking dainty yet sturdy at the same time. This was a woman made to withstand the obstacles life threw her way. "I'm driving into town for socks. Also, exciting stuff."

Socks?

Nathan recalled Marilee's belief that socks were a good foundation for everything and anything. Maybe this was some kind of sign. A sign that he should pursue, not ignore, the attraction between them? Nathan took a moment to reflect on that thought but…

Nah.

"Before I go," Tamara was saying, black eyes intent upon him. "I just want to thank you for this opportunity. I know what happened…" She heaved a sigh, fingers knotting at her waist. "I know what happened with Frosty was hard on everyone. But I… I don't want us to be tiptoeing around our emotions and…and past hurts. That would be like…" She shifted her feet, looking toward the floor. "That would be like having to wear holey socks on a hot day and being unable to find comfort anywhere."

Socks? Again?

Nathan held his breath. Wondering…

Maybe this is a sign.

"A good pair of socks is underrated," Nathan murmured another of Marilee's beliefs.

Tamara stared at him as if he had heat stroke.

"What I mean is…" *What do I mean?* Nathan tried again. "I need to stop at the feed store, too." One of the few places in town to sell decent socks. "Do you want to ride into town and shop together?" He fell back in his creaky chair. Aghast.

That's not what I meant to say.

"Shop for socks together?" Tamara asked, confusion clouding her brow.

"Yeah. Socks are the foundation of your day." And hopefully, would help bring clarity and a turnaround in Nathan's…life?

TAMARA COULDN'T GET a read on Nathan's mood.

Oh, she knew when he felt she was overstepping in her intention to train Pest to race. But the offer to drive her into town? Because he needed socks, too? Where was that coming from?

Upstairs in her small quarters, Tamara cleaned up and changed into shorts, a red T-shirt and flip-flops. Grabbing her water bottle and a protein bar, she hurried back downstairs where Nathan was waiting for her in the breezeway, looking aloof yet attractive with a straw cowboy hat pulled low over his eyes.

It was quiet in the filly barn, empty except for horses who watched them pass on their way to the parking lot. It was quiet in the stable yard, as well.

Tamara struggled to find something to say. "I used to dream of growing up at a place like this. A place of my own."

Nathan gave her a questioning look. "I thought you said you were dumped at the stables while your father worked."

"I was. But I wanted to belong. Looking back… it's probably why I tried to make myself useful."

"I…uh…" Nathan cleared his throat. "I tried to do that, too. Make myself useful?" He didn't break stride. In fact, his steps seemed to lengthen, requiring a faster pace from Tamara to keep up. "I think that's why I gravitated toward horse breeding and left racing to other family members."

Tamara was amazed he'd shared so much. "You don't sound like you regret your choice. And you have skill in horse breeding." As evidenced by Frosty.

Nathan sent her another look, this one dubious and searching.

"You don't believe me," Tamara scoffed. "You should know me well enough to realize I don't hand out false praise."

Nathan grunted.

They passed the hay barn and approached the pasture housing Pest. Nathan's chestnut quarter horse was grazing at the far end of the field. Pest was closer. He ambled over to the gate to greet Nathan, allowing Tamara to pet him.

"You little stinker." Tamara stroked Pest's graceful neck. "You couldn't let Frannie get this close earlier."

"Nobody rides Pest but the twins." There was that boundary-setting tone Nathan used with her sometimes.

Tamara much preferred the pitch of his deep voice when they discussed socks. "Who saddle broke him?"

"I did." Nathan moved on, heading for the parking lot. "He accepted a saddle and me riding him. But now... Well, you've probably seen the twins ride him without tack."

Tamara lingered at the gate, looking into Pest's soft brown eyes. He had the physique and the intelligence of a winner, like Frostfire Wind had. Oh, how she'd love to ride the colt, if only because with his likeness to Frosty, she might absolve herself of the guilt over his death. "It's a shame you're treated like a piece of playground equipment, Pest. They hop on. They hop off."

"And Pest loves it," Nathan called over his shoulder. "If you're going to lecture me..."

"I'm not." Tamara hurried after him, trying to lighten things between them. "That conversation was private. Between me and Pest. You weren't meant to hear."

Nathan opened the passenger door for Tamara, a gentlemanly gesture she didn't expect. "I'm surprised you didn't ask Pest if he'd let you ride him."

"I would." She climbed into the cab and flashed Nathan a playful smile. "Except you made it clear you don't want me to ride him."

"Why do I think that won't stop you?" he wondered aloud before closing her door.

Maybe because I don't believe it, either.

"TAMMIE!"

"Dad." Tamara hugged her father at the feed store after Nathan dropped her off to pick up the boys. "What brings you to town?"

"I need a new pair of riding pants." Her father grinned. "Busted my seams riding a beast of a colt. If you show up at the track on Saturday, Caroline might let you ride Iron Fire's Wing."

Everything inside Tamara folded inward. Iron Fire's Wing was an unruly horse. Huge *and* fast. And with a temper toward other horses. He bit. He kicked. He fought jockeys for control and was an accident waiting to happen.

Dad peered at her, then drew Tamara away from the entrance and into the clothing racks, deeper and deeper until they were at the back wall. “I know that look, Tammie. I’ve seen it on other jockeys. You’ve got PTSD from the accident.”

Tamara shook her head. “It’s nothing.”

Nothing I can’t beat.

Dad glanced around, then moved closer to whisper, “Remember when that horse ran away with you on your first job as an exercise jockey? What was his name?”

“The Devil’s in the Darkest Details?” Yeah, Tamara remembered. The colt had tossed his head until the bit was in the corner of his mouth, rendering the reins useless. “I was sixteen. Just a baby in jockey terms.”

“You refused to do more than warm up horses for weeks.”

“It was more like a week.” But it had been a long week, one filled with soul-searching to decide if she had the guts to be a jockey. “Fears can be overcome in time.”

Dad tipped his cowboy hat back to stare at her, far more serious than his usual self. “We don’t lie to each other.”

That had been their pact the day Mom walked out on them.

“I won’t leave you, Tammie,” Dad had said, holding eight-year-old Tamara while she cried. "But we have to be honest with each other. No secrets. No lies. Because honesty is how two people stay connected." A lesson Dad seemed to have learned too late to save his marriage.

"I haven't lost my nerve," Tamara told her father now, lying to herself and him. Or trying to. "I get up in the saddle just fine. I trot and I gallop just fine. But I feel like I need to protect the horses I ride from what happened. Maybe that's what you're picking up on. Iron Fire's Wing will be hard to protect."

Dad drew her into a hug. "To be clear, when you hit full speed, are you holding the horse back?"

She nodded, feeling as if she was sixteen again and had let a two-year-old colt get the better of her.

"I'm sorry to tell you, Tammie, but you've lost your nerve," Dad said in a whisper before pulling back to look at her knowingly. "Don't show up looking for race rides on Saturday. You're not ready to seriously compete."

"Dad?" Tamara rejected that idea with her entire being. "Has this happened to you?"

Her father hesitated, then nodded. "It wasn't the same. I took a tumble. I let doubts get in my noggin. But eventually, I got back in the saddle. I had to. I had you to support."

Tamara couldn't remember her father ever struggling with his nerve. "Then you should understand. How will I know I can conquer this if I don't race?"

"You keep exercising those Blackwell horses." Dad regarded her with a gaze laden with compassion. And maybe a bit of pity. "When you stop feeling like a horse's guardian and start feeling like you're partners, that's how you'll know you're back."

Dad had a point. But winter was coming. There'd be little racing until the New Year. And with her current employer in jeopardy of going under…

"I'm sorry, Dad. But I have to work as both an exercise and a race jockey." To build both her confidence and her bank account. She hugged her father, knowing he wouldn't approve but would understand. "Tell Caroline Richmond I'm up to riding Iron Fire's Wing."

"WELL, THAT WAS a waste of time," Zeke said when he climbed into Nathan's truck after school.

"It wasn't that bad." T.J. climbed in after him. "Except for the singing. Coulda done without that."

"How's your teacher?" Nathan asked, waiting for the kids to fasten their seat belts before inching forward in the pickup line. "Do you like Miss Jenkins?"

"She's nice," T.J. said at the same time that Zeke said, "She's mean."

"Zeke, did you get into trouble?" Nathan wasn't sure if he should laugh or be stern.

"He didn't come inside after recess," T.J. tattled.

"I *was* coming," Zeke said hotly, raising his fists

to the ceiling. "But I didn't get a turn on the swings. And I waited all through recess."

"I take it you took your turn on a swing instead of going back to your classroom," Nathan surmised.

"Why do you always have to know everything without me telling, Dad?" Zeke lamented.

Nathan decided to let that gripe slide. He reached the end of the school driveway and pulled out on the main road when it was clear. "So, what are you going to do differently tomorrow, Zeke?"

"I'm going to run to the swings first," Zeke announced as if he'd been thinking about it already. "Even if *Carlton* says I can't swing because of my hurt wrist."

Carlton sounded like a pill. But Nathan held his tongue. Chances were that Carlton would be Zeke's best friend by next week.

"Where are we going, Dad?" T.J. had his nose pressed to the window. "This isn't the way back."

"You're right. We're going to the feed store." Nathan turned into the parking lot. "We need to buy socks."

"I'd rather buy candy," Zeke said, sounding drained.

"I think we can cover both," Nathan said, parking.

They went inside. It smelled like a feed store, like hay, dust, grain, with a dose of nostalgia from the old days. The twins ran to the candy counter where some other kids were.

Nathan spotted Tamara right away. She had several pairs of socks in hand. But she wasn't alone. A tall cowboy stood in front of her, his back to Nathan. Jealousy pierced Nathan, sharp, unexpected and unwelcome, puncturing the calm feeling he'd had when focusing on socks and signs.

Tamara spotted Nathan and gestured for him to join her. There was something about her smile that felt strained, like she was trying to send him an SOS, spurring Nathan to hurry through the racks of clothing to reach her side.

Only then did the cowboy she was with face Nathan. His eyes widened in surprised recognition.

While Nathan's narrowed. He knew the cowboy all too well. Patrick Connelly. The Connellys were no friends of the Blackwells. But Patrick, only a few years older than Nathan, had been the worst of the worst bullies in school. Based on his continued dark looks, Patrick hadn't changed his stripes.

"Patrick," Nathan said coolly.

"Nathan," Patrick responded in kind.

Tamara drew Nathan to her side. As if that wasn't unusual in itself, she kept her grip on his arm. "I was just telling Patrick that I'm working as an exercise jockey at Blackwell Stables."

"And I was asking if Tamara wanted to pick up some weekend races for a *winning* operation by wearing the blue-and-red silks." Patrick smirked, sullying his golden boy good looks. "But then… along comes a Blackwell, butting his nose in where it doesn't belong." Patrick's disdain was plainly written on his long face. "Sighting a Blackwell nowadays is like sighting a rare bird. They're a disappearing and dying breed."

Beside Nathan, Tamara sucked in an audible breath.

Nathan squared his shoulders, determined to protect his family's honor. "I hate to tell you, Patrick, but we Blackwells are making a comeback."

Patrick scowled. "You obviously haven't heard of the saying too little, too late."

Nathan leaned forward. "And you obviously haven't heard about the penalties for doping someone else's horse." He didn't know if the Connellys were behind things but it felt like the right thing to say. At least, it gave Nathan some measure of satisfaction.

In response, Patrick's lip curled in disgust.

"Fellas." Tamara stepped between them. "I've got a busy schedule and I promised to help Nathan..." She gave him a quick glance before starting over. "*Nathan's boys...*pick out socks. That'll be hard to do if you two decide to come to blows."

"I'll leave you to it then, Tamara. You know who to call if you want to ride a winner this Saturday." Patrick walked over to a rack with men's shirts, far enough to be out of Nathan's reach, close enough that he could still hear them if they didn't whisper.

Tamara turned toward the sock display.

"What's going on?" Nathan whispered, touching the spot on his forearm where she'd held him by her side.

"He was asking me all kinds of questions about your stables," Tamara whispered back. "How many horses you have left. How many workers you have on staff. If I was well compensated." She grabbed a pair of socks and held them toward Nathan. "How about these?"

"Besides the fact that they're purple, they're women's socks." Nathan put them back.

"Just making sure you're paying attention." Tamara crossed her arms over her chest, still looking shaken. "It was weird."

"The purple socks?" Nathan teased softly.

"The way he asked." Tamara's hand drifted toward a pink pair of thick wool socks. "The way he…kept inserting himself in my space."

"He's a bully. Always has been." Nathan eased her hand away from the unfortunate pink socks. Her fingers were cold. But touching her hand… The calm feeling he'd had when they'd talked about socks back in his office returned.

Everything will be all right.

Tamara looked up at Nathan. "Patrick wanted to know if I was living with you."

"*Me?*" Nathan asked, struggling to keep his voice down.

Tamara shook her head. "Not you…exactly. The Blackwell Stables. He seemed very keen about that point, more so than my qualifications as a race jockey."

Because he wants to bribe you to sabotage us.

Nathan shot Patrick a dirty look. "We need to get back. You need to tell this to Asher and Big E."

"Yes. But first…socks." She handed him a pair and took several to the sales counter where the boys waited with candy.

CHAPTER EIGHT

"PATRICK CONNELLY'S INTEREST in our operations is concerning," Big E said at one of the dinner tables that night.

"Agreed." Nathan nodded, giving Tamara's shoulder a consoling pat, making her hide a dreamy sigh.

Although Nathan's attention was nice, it wasn't the kind of touch Tamara wanted from him. It felt almost…rote.

Like I'm weak. Or collateral damage.

"It's enlightening," Asher added, taking a second helping of meatballs from a serving dish on their table. "That makes Patrick Connelly more of a suspect in the doping of Pride. Maybe the sheriff was right. Maybe Sullivan Connelly wasn't behind it. But his son was."

Tamara had her head bent over her plate, trying to avoid the Blackwell drama, which was hard considering she was at the center of this play. She glanced enviously over to the other dining table, where the rest of the small number of staff and the twins were eating dinner.

For the past hour, Tamara had been grilled about her conversation with Patrick Connelly. Granted, that conversation in the feed store had given her the ick, making her feel uncomfortable on many levels. But the Blackwells were drawing this out, reminding her of all the gossip, cruel assumptions and out-for-yourself attitudes among those in the racing industry.

Let that float over your head, Tammie.

"Could it be possible," Tamara said slowly when the men finally ran out of steam, "that Patrick was just trying to hit on me and…or…identify another local jockey for their stables? I guess what I'm trying to say is…are you reading too much into this?"

The three Blackwell men stared at her for a moment.

And then they all shook their heads.

"Naw," Nathan said.

"If it walks like a duck…" Asher didn't complete that sentence.

"Patrick's behavior… His *questions* add to a greater body of evidence," Big E told her in that patient way of his. "We don't want to make you feel targeted, Tamara."

"I appreciate that." And Tamara did, truly. After her conversation with her father, she only wanted to focus on regaining her race swagger, not get involved in the Blackwells' doping scandal. "I think I'd like to talk about something else now."

The three men stared at her, clearly not ready to change the subject.

"I agree with Tamara." Kelley came over to sit next to Asher, smoothing the light brown hair off his forehead. "Let's talk about something positive. And I can't think of anything more positive than babies."

The dining room went silent.

"Um… Kelley…do you have something you want to tell me?" Asher asked, looking shell-shocked. "In private?"

"Horse babies, people." Kelley's cheeks reddened. "*Horse* babies. Has anyone checked the brood mares lately? Or the yearlings? Edie was just mentioning them."

"We feed the mares and the yearlings." Always the first to finish eating, Edie cleared her dishes from the table and moved toward the sink. "Don't think we've had the veterinarian come out to check which mares are with foal this year."

Nathan tapped something in his phone. "I'll call the vet tomorrow."

"I didn't know we had horse babies here." Zeke came over to lean on Nathan's shoulder, his injured wrist out of his sling. "Taking care of horse babies is our job."

"Your job?" Big E chuckled.

Zeke nodded, completely serious. "Me and T.J. We make sure foals are used to being handled."

"How adorable." Tamara exchanged an amused

smile with Kelley. She could clearly imagine the twins loving on young horses that were more their size than Pest.

"It's not adorable," Zeke said, offended. "It's work."

"Right. Sorry." Tamara tried to look sincere.

But Zeke wasn't her biggest fan. He drifted back to his table, still frowning.

"Looks like we found a nice destination for an after-dinner walk." Big E gathered his dirty dishes. "Who wants to check on the brood mares?"

"I'll pass," Tamara said, wanting to put some distance between herself and more Patrick Connelly conversation.

"Oh, come with us, Tamara," Kelley pleaded, taking Asher's dinner plate. "I won't let this well-meaning trio grill you any more about the Connellys."

"Did you put on a new pair of socks?" Nathan asked.

Tamara chuckled, feeling the humor in life for the first time since Patrick and the feed store. "I didn't."

"You should. You'll feel better." Nathan didn't seem to want to take no for an answer. "And then we'll head out together."

Together? What does that mean?

She didn't know. Nathan kept sending her mixed messages.

Several minutes later, the dirty dishes had been

loaded into the dishwasher and folks assembled on a path that Nathan said led to pastures on the far side of the racetrack. Most of the group set off at a fast pace. Owen and Frannie moved slower than the rest, quickly falling behind.

Does this mean Frannie is exploring her feelings with Owen?

Based on the jockey's smile, it looked like it. Tamara settled into a comfortable pace, giving Owen and Frannie some privacy while letting the bulk of the group take the lead.

"You're moving a little stiffly," Nathan noted, walking next to her.

"I don't usually ride all day." Tamara gestured behind them. "Look at Frannie. She's feeling it, too."

The rookie jockey was walking like a lifelong cowboy, legs bowed.

"Make sure you keep your muscles loose so you can ride again tomorrow." Nathan glanced at Tamara with a lovely, apologetic smile. "Sorry. I'm preaching to the choir, aren't I?"

"Yep." But Tamara liked that he was concerned for her. She glanced around, noting the empty, seemingly endless pastures. The Blackwell operation was huge. It was a shame they'd lost so much from the doping scandal. "Nathan… I've heard you were an independent child, roaming alone on this vast property." The way she used to roam around the stables where her father worked. "Did you ever get lost?"

"No. When I used to wander off, my mom knew she could always find me out with the yearlings or down by the creek." Nathan looked almost… wistful.

She wanted to hold his hand. To offer comfort. Perhaps to take some herself. "Did you run off when you were feeling overlooked?" Tamara guessed.

"Or overscrutinized." Nathan's voice was deep and full of mystery. He lowered the brim of his cowboy hat as the path turned toward the west and the setting sun. "My father had big dreams. Like you, I suspect."

"And you." When he shook his head, she nudged his shoulder. "You can't start a business *just because*. You have to want to be your own boss more than you want to work for someone else. I'm not excusing your father's behavior but it must have been hard for him to build this place to what it is today. Some folks, like your dad and my mom, aren't cut out to be parents. They're just not built for it." Tamara had no way of knowing which camp she fell into. She liked to think she'd be a good parent but she hadn't had as much as a fur baby to care for since she left home. "At least, when Marilee died, you made your boys your priority. She'd be proud of you for that. And someday, Zeke and T.J. will thank you for it."

Nathan's smile was as small as they came. "I never thought of it that way."

Laughter behind them had Tamara glancing back at Owen and Frannie. Even at a distance of thirty feet or so away, Tamara could tell they were both blushing. She fully expected her protégée to talk about her crush tomorrow morning during their rides.

At least someone's having luck in love.

"What will you do when you can no longer be a jockey?" Nathan asked out of the blue.

"Don't say that out loud," Tamara blurted. "It's bad luck." Especially when she was having doubts about her ability to return to the track as a ruthless rider.

An image of the unruly Iron Fire's Wing acting up at the starting gate came to mind, making her catch her breath.

It's all in my head.

But she felt fear in the too-rapid beat of her heart and the bands cinching about her chest.

"Don't you have a backup plan?" Nathan asked, not realizing Tamara was having a mini-panic attack.

"Some jockeys ride well into their fifties. At thirty, I'm too young to think of retirement." *Until I'm forced to.* Tamara studied Nathan's strong features, so dear to her. So out of reach. "What about you?"

"Me?" He chuckled, moving closer to her, although whether intentionally or unintentionally, she didn't know. The path was uneven in places and he might have swerved to more solid ground near her. "I've got to succeed *first* before I think about stopping."

"You've achieved a lot already. Frosty's success counts as yours." When Nathan didn't say anything, Tamara added, "Are you going to move your breeding operation here? Or be content to run operations for your family?"

"Content?" Nathan shook his head. "I don't think I know what that is anymore. I… I get by."

Oh, that's sad.

"You're avoiding the question," she said gently. "What's your future going to look like?"

Could it include me?

There went her overactive imagination again.

They rounded the corner of the track. The voices of those ahead drifted back to them. But there was one voice Tamara wanted to hear that she didn't. Nathan's. So, she kept quiet, watching how T.J. and Zeke scampered ahead, then waited for Big E to reach them before hurrying onward once more.

Such cuties.

Her patience paid off.

Nathan finally started talking. "My brother Dylan used to give me piggyback rides when we came this way." Nathan paused at an empty pasture. "Dad would take away the golf cart and ATV keys if anyone drove *inappropriately*…" He gave

Tamara a sly grin. "Which usually meant one of my older brothers had crashed into something."

"I can just imagine Zeke and T.J. taking a joy ride in one of the many quads or golf carts you have." With much the same results.

"Yeah. Me, too." Nathan's gaze turned wistful before he looked away, out over the empty fields. "As the youngest, I'd always lag behind. And when I did, Dylan would pick me up."

Behind them, Frannie and Owen laughed again. Nathan glanced back, slowing.

"I always wanted a big brother or sister to watch out for me." Tamara took his arm and tugged him along, wanting to give Frannie more time alone with Owen. "I wished for a sibling who'd say, *Hey, it's time to get moving again.*" Not stop, the way her dad did.

"Or *Hey, pay attention,*" Nathan said. "*The world's passing you by.*"

Tamara stared up at Nathan, taking note of his rare smile. "Is the world passing you by?"

"Maybe." He shrugged. "A part of my heart is tied to Paducah but a part of me can't put things there to right."

"Because of your wife," she surmised softly, heart going out to him. "It traps you."

Nathan nodded, turning his wedding ring, a discouraging reminder to Tamara that his heart would never be hers.

T.J. ran back to them. "Why are you guys being so pokey?"

"Because we're old," Nathan told him in a teasing voice, smooshing the boy's straw cowboy hat down on his head.

"You're ancient," T.J. agreed, grinning as he lifted his hat back in place. "But come on. Uncle Asher says the yearling colts are just ahead." He turned and ran back to join the rest.

Tamara and Nathan continued on at their own pace, not too fast and not too slow, as if neither wanted this time together to end.

Tamara sighed, hardly able to keep her romantic notions at bay.

Soon, the yearling pasture came into view. Ten colts of various sizes and colors had their heads up, studying the humans coming to the fence.

Asher had brought two buckets of oats. He gave one a good shake, which was as effective a call as any. The colts pranced over. Asher helped the twins sit on top of a fence railing, then handed a bucket to each of them.

"They need a good grooming," Nathan observed, coming to a stop at the fence corner while the rest of the group was at the gate.

"Daily work on a lead rope or lunge line," Tamara added, coming to stand next to him. "To get them ready for saddle training."

"I like how you think," Nathan said softly, gazing

so deep into her eyes that if they'd been alone, Tamara might have thought he had kissing on his mind.

"Dad, we started riding Pest when he was this size." T.J. leaned over to offer his bucket of oats to a mottled gray colt.

Zeke held his bucket for a bay colt to eat from. But only for a moment. "Hold this, Kelley." He handed Asher's bucket to her and then, without warning, he leaped onto the bay's back.

"No!" Tamara stretched out her hands as if to grab hold of Zeke, even though she was a good ten feet away.

"Zeke!" Nathan shouted, surging forward.

The bay colt raised its head, looked at Zeke, then spun in a tight circle, easily flinging the boy to the ground. Zeke screamed, startling the colts. They galloped away.

"Zeke!" Nathan shouted again, leaping over the gate to come to his son's rescue.

"Dad," Zeke said tearily, getting to his feet and cradling his wrapped wrist. "*Ow-woo.*"

Nathan gathered Zeke in his arms. "I've got you."

"This way." Asher opened the gate to make their exit easier.

"*Ow-woo,*" Zeke wailed.

T.J. kept shaking his oat bucket, hoping to entice the yearlings back. But he wasn't completely heartless. "Zeke, are you okay?"

He wasn't. Nathan had to carry him all the way back to the stables and then drive him to urgent care.

LATER THAT NIGHT, Nathan carried an exhausted, slumbering Zeke up to his small apartment in the colt barn.

The door to his unit swung open. Tamara had stayed with T.J. while he was gone, something Nathan was extremely grateful for. She stood in the doorway, smiling and looking like she was welcoming him home. For once, Nathan didn't fight the ways she made him feel. "I heard your footsteps on the stairs. How did it go?"

"He's got a hairline fracture in his wrist and a real cast this time." Nathan carried his son into the small bedroom and laid Zeke on the bed next to a sleeping T.J., who didn't stir. "Mark my words, he'll ask to stay home from school tomorrow."

"I can't blame him." Tamara gently drew Zeke's black cowboy boots off and set them on the floor while Nathan arranged Zeke's injured arm across his chest and tucked his alligator stuffed animal next to him. "It must have hurt. And you've been gone hours. Was he a trouper?"

"He was." Nathan pulled up the covers and tucked Zeke in. "He was excited that they printed a resin cast for him. Look at this red lattice wrap. It's a breathable, waterproof cast. Zeke said it was *cool beans*." He chuckled.

Tamara moved out to the main living area, which had a sofa bed Nathan had been sleeping on. Nathan followed, watching her tug on her cowboy boots and wishing she'd stay a bit longer. Not that he needed her to stay.

But if she leaves, the world is passing me by.

Obeying instinct, Nathan came to stand at the door, resting a hand on the doorknob. "Early day tomorrow."

"Yep." Tamara stood, her smile weary. "It's almost tomorrow now."

And they both needed rest before another long day.

But Nathan didn't move. At least, not out of her way. He brushed a lock of black hair behind her ear, resisting the idea to run his hand around her head and test the weight of her long black braid. "Thanks for watching T.J."

"He was no trouble," Tamara said breathlessly, barely seeming to move. Her black eyes stared at him with longing. "We had cake and played games."

Nathan let his palm rest on Tamara's cheek, not knowing what to say, not wanting her to leave.

Life is passing me by.

But the only way he knew to counter that was to grab on to something that made him feel more alive.

He grabbed hold of Tamara.

And kissed her.

I've entered an alternative reality.

Because Nathan was kissing her.

And yeah, it was a tentative kiss, as if he expected her to push him away. But she'd dreamed of Nathan's kiss long enough that she didn't care if he took it slow, if his lips gently covered hers or if he didn't crush her against him, as if wanting her to know she was very much on his mind.

He likes me.

Because she'd spent the past year mooning over him, *like* was enough for now.

All too soon, the kiss was over and they were staring into each other's eyes as if waiting for the other to talk first.

No way am I talking first!

More than anything, Tamara wanted to know why he'd kissed her.

Nathan cleared his throat, opened the door and moved out of her way. It was clear he didn't want to say anything. And that he wanted her to leave.

No way, buster.

"Not so fast." Tamara closed the door, still standing inside. "You can't just kiss me and show me out."

Nathan closed his eyes and heaved a sigh. "That's the first time I've kissed someone other than Marilee." He opened his eyes and stared into hers. "It was a big deal for me to kiss you and I'd really rather not go over a play-by-play recap."

"You regret it," Tamara guessed, reaching for the doorknob, wanting to disappear.

But Nathan got there first, holding the knob still.

"I didn't say I regretted anything. There's just a mindset…a headspace I need to be in to kiss you without feeling as if…"

"You're cheating on your wife," she finished for him, catching sight of his wedding ring and finally understanding. Although, given the pained expression on his face, she added, "Or that you're betraying Frostfire Wind."

"Yes," he said simply, as if both applied.

Tamara felt ill. Either one seemed like a tremendous obstacle to overcome. But both?

My odds here aren't pretty.

She removed his hand from the doorknob and opened the door. "Let's make a pact. You won't kiss me again until you figure all that out."

And then she marched down the stairs and through the breezeway toward the exit closest to the filly horse barn. A few horses poked their heads over stall doors. Corny Carny nickered softly as she passed.

Tamara turned back around and greeted him with a pat on the neck. "I'll see you later, boy."

And in the mood she was in, she might just let him run full tilt.

CHAPTER NINE

You won't kiss me again until you figure all that out.

Tamara's command rang in Nathan's head all night, making him toss and turn.

I'm married. I shouldn't want to kiss her again.

Her command banged around his hollow chest in the darkness before dawn, making him cranky.

Even if I'm widowed, I shouldn't kiss her again.

Her command weighed heavy on his shoulders as he got the twins ready for school, thinning his patience.

Okay, I do want to kiss her again. Properly this time. But I'm not going to.

Because he still loved Marilee. They'd built a life together, had kids together, created a business together. She'd brought sunshine and laughter to his life, all without double-chocolate fudge cake.

What am I supposed to do with that love now that she's gone?

By the time he was driving into town with the twins sitting in the back seat, Nathan's head hurt, pounding with guilt and regret.

"Dad, I shouldn't have to go to school today."

Zeke raised his right hand, holding the crisscrossing red resin cast in full view of Nathan's rearview mirror. "I'm injured."

"You're always injured," T.J. told his twin, rubbing his hand over his hair as Nathan pulled into the drop-off line at school.

"Hey!" Zeke countered hotly. "It's not my fault that you don't do a good job keeping me out of trouble."

"*Zeke*," T.J. scolded his brother. "*I* didn't know you were going to hop off that fence."

"I told you I was going to do it."

"Did not."

"Did too."

"Boys!" Nathan eased the truck slowly forward in line, eager for an end to this argument.

"I just don't want to be hurt anymore, Dad," Zeke lamented, sounding tearful. "Never, ever again."

Foot firmly on the brake, Nathan turned to face Zeke, who was sitting behind the passenger seat. "Buddy, that's not going to happen. You're going to get banged up again. And do you know why?"

"No." Zeke's lower lip thrust out.

"Tell us," T.J. urged.

"Because you're a smart, brave boy," Nathan said in a calmer tone of voice, trying to find the words Marilee might have said. Words no one had ever told him when he was a kid. "When you're curious about something, you just do it, Zeke. You don't think about the danger or the consequences."

"Is that bad?" Zeke whispered.

T.J. nodded sagely.

"No," Nathan said with conviction. "Being smart, brave and curious are good things. But it also means you're going to fall down more than your brother."

"Because he's a scaredy-cat?" Zeke asked, a sly smile growing on his face.

"Am not!" T.J. protested.

"Are too!"

"Stop." Nathan waited for the boys to quiet before continuing. "T.J. doesn't fall as much as you, Zeke. Not because he's a scaredy-cat." Someone honked behind him. Nathan turned back around and inched the truck a car length forward. "T.J. doesn't have as many injuries because he learns from your brave actions." Not mistakes.

"My brave actions," Zeke repeated slowly. And then, "I'm brave!" he shouted.

"Yes." Nathan pulled up to the drop-off zone. "Just don't do anything else brave until your wrist heals."

The boys climbed out, both more subdued than usual. Nathan hoped it was because he'd given them a lot to think about.

"Love you," he called after them through the open passenger window.

But his little cowboys were already racing off toward their classroom and probably didn't hear him.

Talia, their room mother, waved at Nathan from

the school entrance, then turned and followed the boys inside. She'd texted him with the date and time of Back to School Night, expecting him to volunteer.

Nathan exited the school lot, his brain turning to the next items on his to-do list—checking his online inbox to see if he had any job applicants, checking with each employee to see how he could help them stay on schedule, checking in with Tamara to see…

Her smiling face.

Nathan ran a hand around the back of his neck, giving his tense muscles a squeeze. He hadn't thought through the implications of kissing Tamara. Apparently, Zeke got his impulsive nature from Nathan.

He came up to a red light and turned the wedding ring on his finger, thinking about what being a widower was supposed to mean. He'd heard a lot of personal advice from well-meaning people since Marilee's death.

It was an unfortunate accident. No one's to blame.

In time, the shock of her passing will fade.

Take your time with grief but don't forget to smell the flowers once in a while.

Nothing anyone had said to him eased the pain Marilee's death had left him with. He'd read somewhere that grief can cling like a stubborn fungus if you don't clean it out. He'd spent two years holding that hurt inside, not trying to clean anything, and certainly not trying to resolve his feelings.

Something Asher said to him came to mind: *In time, the good outweighs the bad.*

He'd like to find that mental space, not just when it came to his childhood memories but when it came to the more recent losses he'd suffered. But wanting and succeeding were two different things.

A hay truck rumbled through the intersection, coming from the direction of the feed store.

Socks.

Nathan smiled. He was, in fact, wearing new socks today, as were the twins. He wiggled his toes in his cowboy boots. His feet felt…pampered. Funny how just a little thing had the power to impact his attitude.

Socks made him think of Tamara once more. She was buttoned up. Wound tight. The way Asher had been upon Nathan's return.

Until Asher and I hugged it out like we meant it.

Last night, he'd taken Tamara into his arms tentatively, careful of both his feelings and hers. He wondered how it would feel to hold Tamara close. To kiss her. To explore a different kind of relationship.

I shouldn't wonder.

But if he didn't, life might just pass him by.

Nathan grasped the steering wheel hard enough that his wedding ring dug into his flesh. The discomfort had him wishing he'd remove it.

No. I'm not ready.

The light changed and Nathan gunned it, speeding away from the intersection and thoughts he wasn't prepared for.

"DROP DOWN TO a walk," Tamara told Frannie while they were galloping at a controlled pace midmorning, kicking up dust as they went. She waited for the younger jockey to follow her lead before asking, "Have you ever taken formal racing lessons?"

"No, but I've watched a lot of instructional videos online." Frannie wiped a hand down the thigh of her black riding pants. "I'm self-taught. Am I that bad?"

They were on the far side of the track from the horse barns. The sun gleamed off the dirt path ahead, promising another hot day. There was no one at the track but them. Edie was inside the horse barn, presumably saddling their mounts for the next round of rides. Owen was cooling down the horses they'd ridden last. Big E and Asher were always scarce in the working area of the property, talking to anyone they thought could shed light on the dead horse doper and, they figured, the person who'd paid him. And Nathan… Nathan wasn't back from taking the boys to school. Although Nathan hadn't been around much this morning.

Good riddance, said a prideful voice in her head, one countered by a mental brokenhearted sob.

He shouldn't have kissed me if he wasn't emotionally ready.

Tamara sighed. She shouldn't have dropped that no-kissing ultimatum on him. She couldn't imagine how it felt to lose the love of your life and start over with someone new.

The grudge about Frosty's death…she understood that all too well.

"Tamara?" Frannie asked. "Are you trying to say I'm hopeless as a jockey?"

"No. You're not a bad rider," Tamara rushed to say, ruing how easily distracted she was this morning. "But you could be better. During a gallop, you want to be in a strong martini glass position." Tamara rose out of the saddle, assuming the racing position as she leaned over her horse's neck. "Your knees should be in line with your belly button. Your back flat. Your head nearly mid-neck on your horse." She lowered herself back into the saddle. "That puts your center of gravity forward. Yours is too far back, which can throw off a horse's stride."

"I can ride like that. But not when my legs are cramping," Frannie admitted, grimacing, not even trying the martini riding pose. "It's my thighs. I don't think I'm going to be able to walk normally again tonight."

"No excuses allowed." Tamara gave her horse a pat on the neck, thinking of the advice her father had given her when she'd first started as a jockey.

"As a female in a male-dominated sport, you have to train harder and have thicker skin than the competition."

I need to take my own advice.

"Okay." Frannie's cheeks reddened from more than the heat.

"I mean…" Tamara searched for a way to soften her advice. "You can vent to me but no one else. Jockeys get hired for their reputations *and* their wins. You don't want to be unprofessional. You don't want to make excuses."

Frannie sniffed suspiciously and nodded. "Thank you for the advice."

"I didn't mean to come down hard. I have a lot on my mind." Wasn't that an understatement! "You've got a good chance to make a go of this and I'll help you train. Gladly." If only to pay forward the mentoring she'd had. "But more immediately, we need to get you hydrated after this ride. And we need to stretch properly in between each ride the rest of the day."

"Just like a real athlete." Frannie's smile reappeared, watery but present.

"A jockey is a real athlete, Frannie. That means you've got to take good care of your body, just like we do the horses." Tamara gave the horse she was riding a pat on the neck. "It's okay to put these horses through their paces without a proper racing position today when we aren't running full speed."

"Thank heavens for that."

Ditto.

Although she suspected they had different reasons behind the sentiment.

Tamara knew this was only a reprieve. Saturday was fast approaching and she'd need a strong dose of courage if she was going to ride Iron Fire's Wing without mishap.

"You haven't asked me about Owen," Frannie said, blushing.

"I wanted to give you space. You seemed to have a good time last night on our walk."

"I did. He's a really great guy. But..."

Recalling their conversation yesterday, Tamara said, "But you don't know if it's love."

She nodded. "I've had crushes before but never anything serious."

"I think..." Tamara tried to assemble a well-thought-out answer. "A crush is surface-level appeal. Love is based on knowing someone and caring deeply for them, despite any imperfections or disagreements." She chuckled. "I mean, no one is Prince Charming."

And that, in a nutshell, was the moment Tamara knew what she felt for Nathan was more than a crush, more than polite affection termed as love. She was *in love* with him.

I'm in deep trouble now.

Because if her love was true, she needed to be patient as Nathan sorted out his feelings.

When they came back around the track, Owen

was waiting for them at the gate. "Right on time," he told them, taking hold of their horses' reins and walking along between them. "How was your ride?"

"Great." Frannie sounded too chipper. "How was your hot-walking?"

"Great," Owen echoed her response, glancing over his shoulder with a broad smile on his face.

They were both blushing.

"Are you two dating?" Tamara blurted.

"*No*," Frannie said, much too quickly.

"It's okay if you are," Tamara added.

"We watched a movie together in the break room after our walk last night." Owen turned around, and led them down the path to the hot-walker station. He was grinning, his blush turning his ginger coloring beet red. But unlike Frannie, he didn't seem to mind. "We're taking it slow."

Tamara reached over and nudged Frannie's shoulder. "Don't overthink it."

The way Nathan did with me.

"No tomfoolery!" Edie called from the colt stables. The head groom wore jeans and a tank top with roses on it. But her mood was anything but rosy. "That means you, Owen. Turn around. Never put yourself in a position of danger. Those horses could run you over when you walk like that." The older woman disappeared back inside.

"Thanks for the tip, Edie," Owen called after her, spinning on his heel so that he faced forward.

There were several moments of silence. Tamara couldn't see Owen's face but Frannie still looked mortified.

"Kelley said we're having leftovers for dinner tonight," Tamara began in her best negotiating voice. "Kelley's cooking is fantastic but leftovers are leftovers. Might be a good time to have dinner out, even if it's only as friends."

"That sounds like a good idea," Frannie allowed. Although she added, "*Friends*."

Owen's sigh was a clear disagreement. He stopped, back stiff, and then faced them without blush or grin. "This is where you gals leave me."

Frannie frowned, perhaps realizing she'd hurt Owen's feelings and perhaps regretting it.

And that brought Tamara's thought full circle—back around to Nathan. If she wanted love to grow between them, she had to let Nathan set the pace.

NATHAN STOOD IN the shade of the bleachers next to the track's viewing platform, watching Tamara thunder past on East End Slugger, a heavy-haunched horse that had been first out of the gate in every race he'd run according to the stable records. But the colt was a short-distance sprinter, no matter his endurance training. He lacked the drive to keep up a fast pace all the way around. Why had Dad and Uncle Joe kept Slugger around? For breeding?

Nathan didn't know. His gaze followed Tamara.

She had good form but something about the way she handled Slugger tickled his brain.

I'm missing something.

Big E joined him, tipping his black cowboy hat back and seeming to watch Tamara's progress on Slugger on the far side of the track. "I've seen a lot of experienced riders in my day. Calf ropers, jumpers, barrel racers and so on. And a lot of inexperienced riders visit my dude ranch in Montana." He turned his gaze on Nathan. "There's a tenseness to Tamara's form. She's not riding as one with that colt. I see it in newbies sometimes. And folks who've had a bad experience on horseback."

The elderly cowboy's words clicked in Nathan's head.

This. This is what I'm missing about Tamara's riding technique.

He hadn't watched Tamara ride a lot here. He had too many other loose ends to handle—workers to find, feed bills to review, a growing list of maintenance projects, vet and farrier visits to schedule. But he'd seen Tamara ride Corny Carny the other morning while she'd tried to rein him in. Granted, she'd been breezing, which wasn't supposed to be a full-on gallop.

But still...

"You see it, too," Big E said in that deep, rumbly voice of his.

Nathan nodded. "The hesitation. The caution."

The fear of speed leading to a heart giving out.

The hard feelings he had associated with Tamara and Frosty's last race softened.

"It's understandable after what she went through on your horse." Big E tsked. "Hope she can work it out before we get cleared to race again."

Nathan made a noncommittal noise. If he had mixed feelings about Tamara riding for Blackwell Stables before, they were leaning toward letting her go now.

Except I kissed her.

He didn't want to see her go. In fact, he wanted to help her heal.

Big E continued to stare at Nathan. "I came to check on you."

"Me?"

"Yep. As tense as Tamara seems in the saddle, you seem more tightly coiled than a startled rattler." Big E leaned against a bleacher support post. "I'm here if you need to talk about your father or grief over losing a loved one."

"Grief?" Nathan's body stiffened. "I don't need a lecture on grief."

"It's a complicated journey, as you know," Big E continued as if Nathan hadn't spoken. "Not only do you have to deal with the hole a loved one's passing leaves in your life but you have to tackle any regrets you have. Or any suspicion you have that they'd still be alive if you had done something differently."

Like hire a different jockey to ride Frosty?

Nathan glanced back out toward Tamara, imagining the guilt she carried about the horse's death was heavy. He should have accepted her apology earlier.

If I was a better man, I might have.

"I'm guessing you carry both types of grief, Nathan," Big E went on, much as Nathan wanted him to stop doling out advice. "That's why you still wear your wedding ring, isn't it?"

"No. I—"

"You still feel like you're married." The old man paused for breath and seemed to be considering his next words. "I've had plenty of friends struggle with the same thing. But sometimes, just taking the ring off helps you move on your journey."

"My grief journey is coming along just fine, thank you very much." Although Nathan didn't feel fine. There was too much second-guessing about Tamara and his feelings toward her muddling his head. But he couldn't confess that to Big E. "Actually, I have an idea I'd like to run by you. I was thinking we should have a showcase sometime soon."

Actually, that had been a brief thought and he'd had it days ago.

Big E's brow furrowed. "I'm not familiar with a showcase."

"It's when a stable puts on its own races to show off how well their horses are coming along." Nathan glanced back at the nearly empty stables behind him. "You invite current and potential clients to the showcase. Dad used to host them once a year. It always brought new clients in as well as offers to buy or invest in a horse featured that day."

"I think you might be on to something." Big E smiled broadly. "Don't you need more jockeys for that?"

"Yeah." Nathan scratched the back of his neck. "And other workers, too. That's the problem. We've only got two jockeys and two stable hands. I haven't been able to find any more."

Tamara and Slugger trotted past on their cool-down lap. She posted with perfect form, rising up and down in tune to the colt's steps.

"She looks more relaxed at that speed," Big E noted.

Nathan nodded.

"You know..." Big E turned back to Nathan. "You could ask Tamara if she knows of any other jockeys who'd want to ride in this showcase. Didn't she say her dad is a jockey?"

"Yes." Nathan returned his attention to Tamara, wondering how she'd feel about working with her father. She'd said she loved him but she'd also spoken of him in guarded terms.

"Do you want me to talk to her?" Big E asked.

"About jockey referrals?" Nathan shook his head. "No. I'll do it."

Big E tsked again. "I meant about her having lost her confidence."

"No. I'll do that, too." It would be tricky considering their last conversation after that kiss. But she was his employee. He was responsible for the safety of his horses and his jockey.

But am I willing to take responsibility for her heart?

"THERE'S MR. I-NEED-A-SLICE-OF-CAKE." Tamara approached Nathan in the shady breezeway of the filly horse barn after lunch. She sipped from one of those fancy water bottles, then gestured toward her face and that too-bright smile, the one he suspected was an indicator of her unease with him after he'd initiated that kiss. "Unlike me, you've got that *unhappy* expression on your face."

A smile tugged at Nathan's lips, despite all the things he needed to work out when it came to Tamara, including his grief over losing Marilee and Frosty. Just talking to Big E had made him more aware of the emotional rut he was in.

Well, I knew I was in a rut but no one challenged me to get out. Thank you, Big E.

And maybe…just maybe, Tamara's mental block and his grief needed to be challenged if they had a chance at something real.

If love can be found twice in one lifetime.

Tamara stopped in front of Nathan, tilting her head as she regarded him. She'd shed her black riding vest and helmet. Her black hair was in a tousled braid. Her gray riding pants and black boots were streaked with dirt. “Wow. Things must really be bad. You’ve been shocked into silence.”

Get it together, man.

“Sorry. My mind is trying to solve several operational issues.” And concerns for his top jockey. Nathan studied the gentle lines of Tamara’s face. “I don’t suppose you know of anyone looking for work or a new place to work. Jockeys, stable hands, hot-walkers?”

“Not really.” She wrinkled her nose. “I’m too new in town. My dad is an exercise jockey at Richmond Stables. He’s all I know locally.”

“Interesting.” He filed that fact away for future consideration. “Sadly, Dandy’s owner is moving her to Richmond Stables.” Apparently, Blackwell Stables hadn’t yet hit rock bottom and was still bleeding clients. “I told the owner that Dandy was being ridden by an experienced race jockey here but since Dandy can’t race while connected to our stable, it made no difference.”

“I’m sorry.” Tamara glanced around, her expression as soft as her hair. He knew that from experience now. “The loss of Dandy will make it feel more like a ghost town in here.”

“I saw you ride Slugger earlier.” Nathan dived right into the hard stuff. “Looks like he gave you trouble when you had him at speed.”

Tamara’s dark gaze landed on Nathan, cool and boundary setting. “He…he didn’t give me trouble. Not really.”

Don't fight me on this, please.

Nathan tried to look understanding. "You had him on a tight rein and he fought you on it."

"Because we're only breezing and he wanted to race for the hills." Her tone was as guarded as her gaze. "He's three. There's no sense risking injury at the end of the season by riding him hard."

Nathan nodded slowly, mind spinning at high speed. He'd assumed she'd confess her fears. But perhaps he'd been too vague. "I was just wondering if you had another reason for holding him back."

"No," Tamara scoffed. Her cell phone rang. She took it from a pocket and glanced at the screen. "It's Patrick Connelly."

Without thinking, Nathan replied, "Don't answer."

Tamara frowned. "You forget my position."

"I haven't." That came out as hard as a cold winter horseshoe. He tried again, softer this time. "You're a jockey employed by Blackwell Stables."

"And jockeys are disposable, as you well know." She stared at the phone screen, not Nathan. "I may not like Patrick, but I can't afford to ignore him. He could blackball me the way…"

You did.

She didn't have to say the words. He'd been grieving over losing Frosty when he'd fired her and challenged his trainer to do the same. It wasn't his finest moment.

"I'm sorry about that. Truly. But you don't need

to take jobs with Patrick Connelly," Nathan said, more forcefully than he'd intended.

Tamara gave Nathan a quizzical look. "In a profession where I can be fired without notice, I need to stay on the good side of everyone in the business. You, of all people, know this." She moved off to answer the call.

Leaving Nathan annoyed, jealous, worried and regretful. The emotions tangled, turning his stomach.

"She's right, Nathan." Edie stepped out of Dandy's stall, wiping a tear from her eye. She was particularly fond of that filly they were losing. And so was Luna. The gray cat was curled up on Dandy's black back. "Jockeys don't have job security."

"Exercise jockeys do," Nathan said mulishly.

"She's a race jockey at heart." Sniffing lustily, Edie scribbled on a clipboard containing the day's schedule. It hung from a nearby support post. She gathered her grooming tools, then headed for the tack room. "Race jockeys come and go, as free as the wind they race."

I could lose Tamara. In so many ways.

Unbidden, he recalled watching Tamara tumble beneath Frostfire Wind, reliving the fear for both horse and jockey. In the aftermath of losing Frosty, Nathan had forgotten he'd been terrified of losing Tamara, too.

I'm such a jerk. How could she want to kiss me?

Nathan pretended to study Edie's clipboard, battling his tension back while he waited for Tamara to return. And when she did, he couldn't wait to ask, "What did Patrick want?"

"He asked me to ride a horse for him Saturday at Rosehaven Downs." Tamara smoothed the wayward strands of dark hair away from her face and behind her ears. "He's got a promising two-year-old."

"*We've* got promising two-year-olds." As soon as he said the words, Nathan wished he could take them back, suspecting that Tamara would bring Pest into the conversation. He may be midway through his grief journey but he wasn't yet on forgiveness's doorstep. He couldn't bring himself to allow her to ride Pest.

Dandy poked her head over her stall door, extending her nose toward Tamara.

"You aren't entering any of your *promising* two-year-olds in any races because of the temporary ban on your stable," Tamara pointed out, stroking Dandy's graceful neck. "And with the end of the primary season around the corner, I need to ride in as many races as I can."

"Like a squirrel gathering nuts," Nathan muttered, concern for her safety tying him up inside.

"Nobody faults squirrels for preparing for lean times." Tamara peered at Nathan, moving closer. Temptingly close because she was within reach. Within kissing distance. "Is there a problem with me picking up a race for another stable?"

"Yes." Nathan hadn't meant to say that. He swallowed, removing his cowboy hat and running a hand through his hair. Apologies and forgiveness had to come before more kisses…didn't they?

"Yes?" Tamara came closer still, until the toes of her riding boots almost touched the toes of his cowboy boots. "Why?" she whispered.

"Lots of reasons." Nathan tried to think of one. But his mind had gone blank, glitching because he was trapped between the thought of kissing her again and the need to properly let go of the past. He ended up saying, "As you know, the Connellys might be up to no good."

Tamara chewed on her bottom lip, taking a few steps back. "Well, until you have proof, I'm going to take the ride and the money." She took a drink of water and then licked her lips.

Those lips.

Nathan licked his, thinking about their kiss last night. Wanting a deeper, longer kiss.

Focus!

He'd wanted her to open up about her riding difficulties.

"Are you sure you should be racing?" he asked, point-blank.

"Why wouldn't I?" Again, her dark eyes took on a guarded look.

Nathan hesitated. But it had to be said. "Because—"

The alarm went off on his cell phone, interrupting him. It was time to pick up the twins from school. Priorities needed realigning. He was a father first, before being the stable manager and certainly before being anything personal to Tamara.

"I've got to go. We'll talk about this later." Nathan hurried back toward his office to collect his wallet and truck keys. But he thought he heard Tamara say "*Or not.*"

"I DON'T USUALLY butt into someone else's business," Edie said, stepping out of the filly tack room as soon as Nathan shut the office door. Luna sauntered after her, tail twitching. "However, that man is trying to protect you. And you—"

"Don't need to be protected." Tamara stood tall, despite being a dusty, sweaty mess, not to mention a woman shaken to her core by Nathan's assertion that she shouldn't ride in races.

He and Dad are on the same side.

Doubt wove through Tamara's thoughts, trying to take hold.

Be gone, fears! Be gone!

Tamara took in Edie's disapproving expression. "You don't think I should be racing, either." Had she noticed a fault in Tamara's careful rides the way Nathan had?

"You're a good jockey." Edie leaned down to pet Luna, then picked up a straw basket, the one she used to collect vegetables in the garden. "But I don't want you to race for the competition. Whether it's the Connellys or the Richmonds. They're trouble."

"Trouble?" Tamara fell into step with Edie, heading out of the filly barn. "They can't pay me to sabotage a Blackwell horse. What other trouble can there be?"

"The kind of trouble that never takes the blame when something is their fault," Edie huffed. "Now, I'm not one to gossip but I've known folk who've worked for both their stables. If a horse loses or pulls up lame, it's always the fault of the jockey, stable hand or trainer. You know how it is. These horses are athletes. And soft injuries or the mental state of a horse on race day can't be predicted. Bad things happen and no one's specific actions are to blame." She gave Tamara a knowing look.

As if she knows I blame myself for Frosty's death.

Tamara chose to ignore that message. "I can handle prickly owners."

"Can you?" At the barn door, Edie paused to stare at Tamara with a challenging gaze. "The Connellys and the Richmonds have the power to destroy your reputation, such as it is today." And with that chilling statement, out the door she went, Luna trotting behind her.

Leaving Tamara second-guessing her decision to take a ride on a Connelly horse. But knowing she wouldn't go back on her word.

CHAPTER TEN

EVERY YEAR, GOLD FINCH closed up shop at noon on a Friday in September and had a Fall Festival. The event was part farmers market, part county fair, and every bit as unique as the horse racing town itself.

Nathan picked up the twins from school and found a parking spot just off Main Street, which had been blocked off for the event. "Let the fun begin, boys."

"Honk, Dad," T.J. commanded from the back seat. "There's Tamara."

Nathan glanced around, seeking the woman who occupied too many of his thoughts.

Tamara walked along the sidewalk, nearing their truck. She wore sunglasses, khaki shorts, a red T-shirt, and sneakers. Her long black hair fell freely across her back, swinging with each confident stride.

If only she raced with that kind of confidence.

"Dad!" T.J. cried when Nathan hadn't hit the horn.

Zeke leaned over the center console from the

back seat, having unbuckled himself. He tooted the truck's horn—*beep, beep-beep-beep!*

Tamara and several others on the sidewalk startled, staring their way.

"Sorry." Nathan gave a sheepish wave, easing Zeke back where he belonged. "For the record, Zeke, honking is rude."

"Tamara stopped though, didn't she?" Zeke lost his footing and collapsed into his seat. "And T.J. stopped yelling."

"I wasn't yelling at you," T.J. said, affronted.

Zeke made a derisive noise.

Their mild bickering didn't bother Nathan.

Meanwhile, Tamara had stayed put while other folks moved on toward Main Street. She smiled but it wasn't a happy-to-see-you smile. It was more like an oh-shoot-I'm-trapped smile. Not that Nathan could blame Tamara for feeling caught. Things between them hadn't been great lately. In fact, he felt as if Tamara had been avoiding him.

Now that bothers me.

Zeke was already moving, hopping out of the back seat and joining Tamara on the sidewalk. He removed his straw hat and fanned his face, seeming to talk non-stop, although Nathan couldn't hear a word his young son said.

"Dad?" T.J. undid his safety belt, moving to stand behind the truck's center console where Zeke had been moments before. "Can Tamara hang around with us today?"

"That's up to her." Nathan didn't think she'd agree to it. He got out of the truck and helped T.J. to the ground. Heat seemed to rise from the asphalt, enveloping them.

T.J. scurried to Tamara's side. "Dad says you can go to the Fall Festival stuff with us!"

"Did he?" Tamara gave Nathan an arch look.

"Hey there, in fact, I said it was up to you," Nathan clarified, joining them on the sidewalk.

A family with teenagers passed by, tipping their cowboy hats to everyone. Nathan and his boys raised their hats in return.

"That's her," the woman said in hushed tones to the man who held her hand. "The female jockey I told you about."

The family glanced back at Tamara, who graciously waved, although she turned to whisper toward Nathan, "Since when am I a celebrity?"

"Since..." *The day we met.* Nathan swallowed back the words, afraid they'd be taken in a romantic context. Instead, he said, "Since you came to Gold Finch. Female jockeys are as rare and special as four-leaf clovers."

Her smile blossomed.

Before Nathan could wonder how Tamara had contextualized his words, Zeke took Nathan's hand and tugged. "I smell burgers."

"And popcorn." T.J. took Tamara's hand and tugged.

Tamara laughed. “I’m hungry, too.” She allowed herself to be led forward.

As if she’s used to dealing with small boys.

My boys.

Unbidden, Nathan smiled.

He and Zeke hurried to catch up.

Main Street was crowded with people. There were booths set up on both sides of the street. The offerings were eclectic. Fresh produce. Arts and crafts. Saddlery and tack. Further down, several food trucks had parked, filling the air with a pleasant mix of barbecue, fried food and popcorn. Beyond the food trucks, more stalls lined the street offering activities.

Someone must have done something amusing because the crowd roared its approval near the clothing boutique.

The boys ran over to a woman carving a pumpkin at a produce stall.

“What a great community event. I wish it wasn’t so hot.” Tamara gathered her shiny black hair and twisted it over one shoulder. “Was it like this when you grew up here, Nathan?”

“It was.” He hadn’t thought about any local celebrations in years. But this…

This was like a homecoming. In his mind’s eye, he could see his older brothers running ahead through the crowd. He could remember that pang of being left out and left behind. Except… It hadn’t stung back then, not when he, Mom and Dad had taken in the celebration at a much slower pace.

"These community events were an opportunity for me, as the youngest, to have my parents all to myself." He hadn't meant to admit that. Nathan lowered the brim of his brown felt going-to-town cowboy hat.

"Dad and I didn't go to things like this," Tamara admitted. If she noticed his discomfort, she didn't let on. "They're mostly held on weekends, which is when he'd race."

"Gold Finch is a horse racing town. That's why this event is held during the week." Nathan gathered the boys. "Let's walk to the end before we decide to do anything."

Rather than protest, the boys skipped ahead, heedless of the heat.

Tamara and Nathan walked in silence, each taking in the lay of the land.

"Do you notice all the stares we're getting?" Tamara asked.

"I've been too busy looking at peanut brittle, brownies, and the like to notice." It wasn't only the twins who were hungry. But now, as Nathan glanced around, there did seem to be a lot of people turned their way. "I guess you're more of a celebrity than you thought."

"No. It's you," Tamara teased. "Blackwells are like celebrities around here."

He chuckled. "I disagree. Pretty jockeys are rare."

Roses bloomed in Tamara's cheeks. "Flattery will get you everywhere."

Will it?

Nathan's smile broadened, although he wasn't exactly sure where this attraction to Tamara would end up.

"Dad! Dad!" The twins called to him from a booth where kids and adults alike were decorating and then eating cupcakes. "Can we do it?"

"I shouldn't let them." Even though Nathan was tempted. "They haven't had lunch."

"Ha!" Now it was Tamara who tugged him forward, her small hand on his. "Your kids are like bottomless pits. They can eat a cupcake and then demolish a cheeseburger and fries."

"And still have room for a second dessert later." Laughing, Nathan agreed.

Soon, the twins found a place to stand at the decorating table. Nathan paid for two plain cupcakes while the boys snatched sprinkles, colored sugar, and tubes of frosting. In no time, they were engrossed in the task.

Two elderly women came to stand next to Nathan. They wore matching pink visors over their silver hair and had thin, matching pink sweaters tied over their shoulders. They looked vaguely familiar to Nathan, although he couldn't place them.

"Isn't it lovely to see kids being kids, Beatrice?" one of the women asked, nodding toward Nathan's twins.

"Instead of having their noses in a gadget?" the other replied in a knowing tone. "Yes, Lynette."

The pair smiled expectantly at Nathan.

Tamara nudged him with her elbow.

"Oh, yes," Nathan agreed, nudging Tamara back.

"And they're enjoying the freedom of creativity." Tamara moved closer to the twins. "How's it going, boys?"

"Great!" T.J. didn't look up from his work. "I'm making a mountain with snow on top." He'd created a swirl of black frosting dusted with white sugar and rimmed with mini-marshmallows.

"That makes me want to go skiing," Tamara said in a praiseworthy voice.

"I'm making a space alien cupcake." Zeke glanced up at Tamara, revealing a streak of blue on his cheek as well as blue on his fingers. He'd covered his cupcake with blue frosting that overflowed onto the sides. "He's a blob. Kinda like a slug. He absorbs everything in his path."

"Does this alien slug have a name?" Leaning in for a closer look, Tamara held her twisted hair in place.

"No." Zeke wiped at his cheek, creating another slash of blue.

"What about Bob?" Tamara asked. "Bob the Blob."

Both boys giggled.

"Dad?" T.J. motioned at Nathan, grinning broadly. "Can we name our next colt Bob the Blob?"

Tamara caught Nathan's eye, her smile full of mischief. "I've heard of worse names."

It was on the tip of Nathan's tongue to say, "*We'll see,*" but he didn't speak fast enough.

"Truer words." Beatrice chuckled, tugging on the arms of her sweater. "All the best names are taken."

Lynette nodded, fanning her face with the local newspaper. "Bob the Blob is memorable."

"And my Bob tastes good." Zeke swiped his fingers through all that blue frosting and then shoved them in his mouth, swallowing all that goop before adding, "Like a winner."

T.J. stared at his twin and giggled. "You're eating Bob!"

Tamara swooped in, grabbing some napkins from the table and wiping Zeke's face and hands.

The woman behind the table handed Tamara a wet wipe. "Your boys are adorable."

Nathan held his breath, waiting for Tamara to correct the woman. They weren't *her* boys.

"They are, aren't they?" Tamara said instead.

A flicker of warmth…of *rightness* wrapped around Nathan's heart.

"She's a keeper," Beatrice murmured, as if aware that this was a monumental moment for Nathan.

"A heart of gold," Lynette seconded, having stopped fanning to clutch the newspaper over her heart. "That's as rare as a triple crown winner."

"As rare as true love," Beatrice added softly,

smiling at Nathan as if he needed help sorting his feelings where Tamara was concerned.

Nathan felt warmth give way to a cold reality.

I found true love once before.

And when Marilee died, his heart had been ripped from him. He'd known he'd never find true love again. Considering such a thing…

Nathan took a step back.

He wasn't ready to believe it was possible.

THE COOL, UNCOMPROMISING Nathan was back. His face was a guarded mask. His steps stiff.

Sometime during that cupcake decorating session, Nathan's good humor had dissipated, like that weak, occasional breeze Tamara felt.

She walked beside Nathan while the boys scampered to the next booth where they could win a goldfish by tossing a ping-pong ball into one of several bowls filled with water and fish.

"Dad?" The twins turned as one. "Can we?"

Before Nathan broke out of his funk, Tamara reached into her pocket for some cash. "Here you go. My treat." She handed them enough for several tries.

Zeke and T.J. stood in line, craning their necks to watch others toss ping-pong balls.

Beside her, Nathan made a noise that sounded like annoyance.

Tamara tsked. "Every kid needs a goldfish once in their lives."

"You didn't ask me," Nathan groused.

"I'll ask you this then." Tamara twisted her hair tighter over one shoulder. It was hot. But the temperature felt fiery with that unhappy look in Nathan's blue eyes. "What have I done to upset you?"

"Nothing." Nathan tugged down his cowboy hat brim. "I'm just thinking."

Tamara frowned. "About naming a colt Bob the Blob?" That was all she could think of that might have upset him.

"No." Such a sharp little word.

She refused to let it cut her down, choosing instead to cajole. "Personally, I like Bobby the Blobby better. I'd rather be a fun blobby than a blob. But hey, that decision isn't up to me. You Blackwells go for high falutin' names like Frostfire Wind. If you keep with the wind theme… Well, Bob the Windy Blob doesn't quite cut it."

Nathan stared at her from beneath his hat brim, lips twitching.

"And Windy Bobby the Blobby…" She forced out a chuckle. "That sounds like Bobby has flatulence." Tamara was quick to add, "Not that I haven't ridden a gassy horse into the winner's circle, but the name doesn't carry the gravitas of most Blackwell thoroughbred names, does it?"

It looked like Nathan was biting the inside of his cheek in a poor attempt to suppress a smile.

Mission accomplished.

"Come on, boss." Tamara looped her arm through

Nathan's and swung him around until he was facing the goldfish booth. "Your kids are about to win a fish." She hoped it would be two. "If you're lucky, Zeke will call the fish Bob the Blob and get you off the hook in the colt naming department."

Nathan chuckle-coughed, able to cover his reaction but not before giving himself away.

Tamara laughed, turning her attention to the boys.

Zeke tossed all five ping-pong balls at once, sending them scattering without any luck. He turned toward Nathan with a pouty face. "Dad?"

T.J. tossed his five ping-pong balls one at a time. All his balls bounced off the rims of glass fishbowls. "Darn it." He turned and gave Nathan a pouty face. "Dad?"

"This is the moment of truth," Tamara whispered to Nathan. "If you don't want to hear a race announcer say, '*It's Bob the Blob by a nose,*' I suggest you fund another round of goldfish attempts."

Her humor finally cracked Nathan's bad mood. He reached for his wallet. "One more time, boys. But only if you name your goldfish Bob the Blob."

"Yay!" the twins cried, rushing toward him for a quick hug and to take his money.

Zeke stared at the five dollar bill he'd been given, a frown on his face. "But Dad… What if we both win?"

T.J. had gotten into line again. He stared at Nathan. "Yeah. What if we both win?"

Nathan seemed to hesitate. But then he said, "Then the second fish will be called Bobby junior, son of Bob the Blob."

Tamara grinned.

"Bob and Bobby junior," Zeke said slowly, testing the idea.

T.J. repeated the names just as slowly. And then he brightened. "I like it!" he announced.

"Me, too!" Zeke trotted over to join T.J. in line.

"Situation saved." Tamara patted Nathan on the back. "Good job, Daddy-O."

Nathan tipped the brim of his hat upward, studying her intently. "Let's not kid ourselves. That was all you."

Tamara shook her head. "I cued you up and you took the shot. That's what good dads do."

Nathan sighed. "You're good."

"At what?" Tamara wondered aloud.

"Very good." Nathan doubled down.

"We need a brave volunteer for the dunk tank!" a white-haired man called from across the way before Tamara could get a straight answer out of Nathan. The man stood at a table fifteen feet or so from one of those dunk tanks where an accurate ball thrown could send someone into the water. "How about a Blackwell?"

"Do you know him?" Tamara asked.

"I think that's Mr. Shepherd, my old gym teacher." Nathan waved his hand as if to decline and told the man, "Not today, thanks."

The twins were moaning behind them, dragging their feet as they left the goldfish booth, faces flushed from losing and the heat.

"We didn't win," T.J. said.

"Not so much as a Bob," Zeke echoed.

"What about Mrs. Blackwell?" Mr. Shepherd wasn't one to give up easily.

"Who is he talking about, Dad?" T.J. took Nathan's hand.

"Yeah. Who is Mrs. Blackwell?" Zeke glanced about.

Nathan stared at Tamara. "He thinks Tamara is your...your mom."

It didn't escape Tamara that Nathan hadn't said his wife. His choice of phrasing felt like a challenge.

"She's not our mom," T.J. said.

"Nope," Zeke echoed.

"She's just..." Nathan's blue eyes sparked but quickly dimmed "...Tamara. Our jockey."

Annoyance slithered beneath her hot skin. She felt like more than an employee to Nathan. Or perhaps she wanted to be. But this was a reality check.

She considered bidding Nathan and the boys farewell, but she wasn't a quitter. And she didn't back away from a gauntlet tossed to the ground, either.

So Tamara raised her hand. "I'll take a turn in the dunk tank."

The boys stared at her in open-mouth wonder.

"What's a dunk tank?" T.J. asked.

"Is it that thing?" Zeke pointed at the tank.

"That's it," Tamara confirmed. "More fun than a barrel of swimming monkeys."

Nathan sighed.

"Come on over here, ma'am." The elderly man waved Tamara over. "I've got a bowl here for you to put all your valuables in so they don't get wet."

Tamara took a step toward him.

Nathan held her back with a touch to her arm. "Let's think about this for a minute. I've seen how abrupt the drop on these things can be. And…" He glanced around as if searching for something. And then that blue eyed gaze fell on her once more. "You don't have a bathing suit under there, do you?"

"No. But I'm sweating…and so hot that a swim sounds great right about now." Plus, Tamara wasn't savoring the way Nathan was staring at her—like he didn't think she was qualified to be Mrs. Blackwell or the target in a dunking tank.

The two weren't mutually exclusive. And this female jockey was going to enjoy breaking another stereotype.

Tamara marched over to Mr. Shepherd, emptying her pockets of her keys, wallet and cell phone into a small blue bowl. Nathan and the boys followed.

"The Gold Finch High School baseball team thanks you, ma'am." The old man stowed the bowl beneath his table, which had a bucket of baseballs on it. "We're raising money for a new set of bleachers."

"I love a good cause." Tamara stared down at her sneakers. "I can take my shoes and socks off, can't I?"

"Leave them at the bottom of the steps." Mr. Shepherd smiled at Nathan. "We appreciate the support of the Blackwells. Good to have some back in town."

Nathan grunted and continued to look slightly shocked, definitely aghast. "Be careful."

She nodded, suddenly struck by a bout of nerves.

"What are you doing, Tamara?" Zeke asked, a note of interest in his tone, as if he might like to try it, too.

"Is it safe?" T.J. asked, looking worried.

"How long is her turn?" Nathan asked, looking similarly concerned.

I should be asking that.

The fact that Nathan was worried enough to ask for her was heartening.

"Mrs. B goes until she's dunked." Nathan's old teacher grinned, patting a stack of folded beach towels on the table. "I hope for a lot of missed throws." And then he leaned on the table and spoke directly to the twins. "Your brave mama is going to sit above the water in that tank until someone hits that round circle with a baseball. A direct hit drops her in the water."

Nathan gave another sound of displeasure but

didn't otherwise correct the old man for referring to Tamara as his wife or the twins' mother.

What does that mean?

Tamara's throat went dry.

Meanwhile, the twins' mouths fell open. And then they started to giggle and turned to their father with pleading expressions, begging for a turn to throw.

"Let's get this going." Mr. Shepherd led Tamara toward the dunk tank.

Nathan stopped Tamara with a hand on her shoulder. "If you're sure..."

His unease was confusing. But touching, as well. "It's for a good cause. I'll be fine."

"I want to do it next," Zeke piped up.

"Then me." T.J. didn't want to be left out.

"Sorry, boys." Mr. Shepherd stood at the dunk tank. He waved for Tamara to join him. "You've got to be eighteen to get dunked."

While the twins protested and pleaded with Nathan to break the rules, Tamara went to the ladder and removed her shoes and socks.

Mr. Shepherd held her elbow to help keep her upright. "I'm happy to share that your husband never played on my baseball team," he said, softly.

"Are you saying..." Tamara chuckled. "You think Nathan will miss?"

"I've worked this dunk tank for over thirty years." The old man moved back to give her room on the ladder. "It's always better for a couple when they can't dunk their significant other."

"Oh, we're not..." Tamara ascended the plastic steps to sit on the carpet-covered seat. "We're not like that."

Mr. Shepherd laughed. "Don't say I didn't warn you."

Tamara adjusted her position on the seat, dipping her toes in lukewarm water. Plexiglass surrounded her on three sides, amplifying the heat and giving her second thoughts. "Hey, it's hot in here. What if no one hits the target?"

"Don't worry." The old man laughed again, taking money from Nathan and handing him six baseballs. "Never happens."

"OKAY, BOYS. TAKE YOUR best shot." Nathan handed each kid a baseball. He doubted they'd be able to strike the target.

Frankly, Nathan had mixed feelings about this dunk tank business. The last thing either of them needed was Tamara getting hurt. He had enough worries as it was. He didn't like being stuck in a funk because people were assuming Tamara was his wife and her efforts...well-meaning though they might be...had just added fuel to his dark mood. A downer mood that Tamara was actually trying to lift.

My happiness isn't her responsibility.

And yet… He appreciated that she'd tried to get him to lighten up.

"I got this." Zeke threw his ball with all his might, missing the dunk tank completely. His ball bounced off a sheet of plywood behind the tank and rolled back to Mr. Shepherd.

"My turn." T.J. threw an arcing ball that landed inside the dunk tank walls and was caught by Tamara.

She grinned and tossed it back. "Nice try."

Mr. Shepherd caught her ball and dropped it into his baseball bucket. "Two more tosses each. Make each throw count, boys."

"You can do better, fellas," Tamara teased them.

Nathan gave each boy another baseball. "See the target. Throw the ball." It was something he told them the few times they'd played catch. Nathan made a throwing motion.

Zeke's chin jutted out. He mimicked the motion of a major league pitcher and threw the ball hard.

It hit the side of the dunk tank, missing the target lever by inches.

"Argh!" Zeke cried, stomping his boots in frustration.

Tamara laughed, splashing water with her feet. "So close."

A ball flew through the air, striking the plexiglass in front of Tamara's face.

She flinched, shrieked, and fell against the back wall of the tank.

Nathan's heart took a tumble toward his toes. "Are you okay?"

"Fine and dandy as candy." Tamara straightened.

It might have been Nathan's imagination but she looked pale.

Tamara twisted her dark hair over one shoulder and smiled weakly. "Who's next?"

"Me!" the twins cried.

Nathan handed them each a baseball. A crowd was forming behind them. If the twins didn't dunk Tamara, someone surely would. He didn't like that idea. He'd probably stand nearby and wait for her until she hit the water and worry about her safety the whole time.

He scoffed.

It's not like she's the first person to use that tank.

But she was the first woman he cared about that had climbed into that tank.

The boys looked at each other.

"Together?" T.J. asked his brother.

"Together." Zeke nodded, assuming the pitching position. "One…two…*three!*"

They threw at the same time.

And by some bit of luck, both baseballs struck the target.

With a loud *clunk*, the seat fell out from under Tamara and she dropped into the water with a scream and a splash.

The boys squealed triumphantly.

Nathan grabbed a towel on the table and ran to the tank. "Tamara?"

Tamara stood in the tank, pushing all that long, dark hair out of her eyes. "Yes?"

Their gazes met. Held.

Something inside Nathan tried to shift, tried to open, tried to break free.

This woman did this to make me smile.

It seemed fitting that Nathan smiled. In fact, he smiled for all he was worth because Tamara deserved kudos for having some faith that he hadn't completely buried his good humor beneath the cares and burdens weighing on his mind. "That was spectacular, Tamara. The boys are never going to forget it."

"I hope not." Tamara climbed out of the dunk tank and down the ladder, letting him wrap her in that beach towel. "I hope you won't forget it, either."

I won't. Not ever.

He nodded but knew that he was holding something back when it came to Tamara no matter how much he was drawn to his spirited jockey.

CHAPTER ELEVEN

"HAVE YOU SEEN the twins?" Nathan poked his head in the break room while Kelley was setting up for dinner several days later.

"Not today." Kelley glanced up from uncovering a bowl full of fluffy rolls. "Do you need to assemble a search party?"

"No. Not yet." Nathan hurried through the filly barn, checking each stall for his missing boys. Coming up empty, he rushed out the door into the heat and headed toward the colt barn.

Edie and Owen were feeding the horses. They hadn't seen the twins, either.

"They might be with Tamara in her room," Edie suggested. "She's always got cake. Or they might be at the main house with Asher and Big E. You know Kelley always has cookies there."

"They didn't tell you where they were going?" Owen asked.

"No." Nathan supposed that was karma coming back around for all the times he'd disappeared as a kid. Sending a silent message of thanks to his mother in heaven, Nathan hurried back to the filly barn and climbed the stairs to the staff apartments.

Tamara opened the door at his knock. She wore a fuzzy pink bathrobe and a blue towel wrapped around her head. Her toenails had a coat of blue nail polish.

They were cute toes. Small as pebbles.

But he had no time to admire her toes. He'd had no time to admire anything about her since the Fall Festival. And frankly, it was simpler and safer that way. But more to the point… Obviously, the twins weren't here. Nathan explained that they'd gone missing.

"I'll help you look." Tamara snapped the door closed.

He sat on top of the stairs waiting for her, telling himself the twins had just gone out exploring the way they might have done at home. On a much smaller property where they were familiar with all the dangers.

Tamara reappeared with her black hair in a perky ponytail coming out the back of a tan baseball cap. She was dressed for the search in a blue tie-dyed T-shirt, blue jeans and sneakers. "Did they say anything after school? Something that might be a clue as to where they'd have gone?"

"Just the usual." Zeke had gotten into a scuffle over the swings with Carlton, his nemesis. T.J. had complained about singing, although he'd hummed all the way home.

Tamara took the lead going downstairs. "And Pest is in the pasture alone?"

"Yes."

"Horse or ATV?" Tamara asked once she reached the lower landing. At his blank look, she added, "Do you want to search on horseback or use one of the ranch vehicles?"

"ATV." He hadn't checked to see if any of them were missing and he didn't have the patience to saddle a horse. Now it was Nathan who took the lead, heading out the door toward the side of the filly barn where most of the ranch vehicles were parked when not in use. As far as he could tell, none were missing. "I should have known they'd get bored sticking to one pasture." He sat behind the wheel of the nearest vehicle.

"Don't beat yourself up over things you did as a child." Tamara sat in the passenger seat. "We should check the yearlings' pasture and any place that might have frogs or a rope swing. You know, some of those wondrous places you mentioned before." She gave him a bolstering smile.

Very forced, that smile.

"A wondrous place," Nathan murmured. "We have something like that." Behind the far pasture where Pride and the retired horses were kept.

He put the electric ATV into gear and off they went, following the path around the track.

"Stop!" Tamara cried as they rounded the turn. She hopped out of the vehicle before it came to a complete stop. "It's a sock." She held up a child's sock that had been left in the ditch.

"That's one of theirs." An older sock without a mate.

"At least, we know we're going the right way." Tamara settled into her seat.

"I'll never again feel like a failed parent because they wear mismatched socks. Those socks are like breadcrumbs."

"You're a great parent," Tamara assured him.

"Save the praise for after we find them safe and sound." Nathan put the quad back in gear.

"You're a good parent," Tamara insisted. "And I know this because your kids are—"

"Runaways?"

"—well-behaved."

"Rascals?"

"Kindhearted kids who are bright enough to stay out of serious trouble." Tamara was looking at him with an expression that indicated she wasn't quite finished. "Accidents happen but what kid hasn't had a few broken bones?"

"Me. T.J."

"Well." She faced forward once more, crossing her arms over her chest. "You're in the minority."

He frowned, shaking his head. "I didn't realize you were a Pollyanna."

"I'm hardly glass-half-full." But she laughed, loosening up enough to place a hand on his arm.

"Now, when we find them—*and we will*—you need to love all over them. No rants or lectures."

"Oh, no. Lectures come first." If only because they'd given him a scare and should learn from the experience.

"No." Her hand was still on his arm, warm and comforting. "Think back to your childhood. How would you have wanted your parents to react when you wandered off?"

They passed a pasture where Dad used to keep nonracing fillies while he decided their fate as breeders or to be put up for sale. Nathan and his mother used to visit those horses with oat treats and curry combs, keeping them domesticated for whatever role awaited them.

Mom never scolded me for wandering off.

Tamara removed her hand from his arm. "When my parents were still married, we had a hunting dog that would bolt out of the gate whenever someone—mostly me, to be honest—left it open. Buckley would run off for hours. And when he came home, usually around dinnertime, my mom would scold him practically nonstop. He was her dog, originally."

"Your mom needed an outlet for her fears."

"I think so." Tamara braced herself on the dash as he raced over a bumpy part of the path. "But the result of all her rants was moot. Buckley ignored her."

"Whereas you probably welcomed him home with open arms."

"He was a good boy for finding his way back home. I gave him treats for returning." She smiled at Nathan, bringing hope and sunshine to combat his worries. "But then something amazing happened. If I left the gate open, he'd follow me."

"Because he was expecting treats." Nathan smiled.

"Well, I like to think of it as he and I being part of a pack but yeah." She continued smiling. "It all started with a bribe."

Nathan shook his head. "The problem with greeting my boys with honey is that they won't learn anything."

"I bet they will," Tamara insisted. "When they become fathers, they'll think back on what type of parent you were. And they'll do so fondly."

The way I think of my mom and Marilee.

Nathan heaved a sigh. "You want me to play the long game."

Tamara nodded, drawing her long ponytail over one shoulder without taking her eyes off him. "You don't have to be like Buckley and pretend nothing happened. You can tell them how worried you were while you hug them."

He supposed that was something to consider.

Nathan glanced at Tamara, who was sitting up tall, presumably trying to look over the hedge at the racetrack.

I suppose she's something to consider, too.

"Is that Sovereign's Pride?" Tamara had gotten out of the ATV to open the gate to what Nathan referred to as the far pasture.

A very tall, very grand gray horse had his head up high, nostrils flaring and ears swiveling back and forth, sometimes almost flat against his neck.

"That's him. He shares some of the same breeding lines as Pest." Nathan sounded worried. "Watch out. I'll try to drive through the gate quickly. But from what Asher says, Pride has gone from being a well-behaved horse to wary of people and defensive of his space."

"What a good boy," Tamara crooned without looking into Pride's eyes and possibly being seen as a challenge. She opened the gate just enough for Nathan to pull through. "We're the good kind of people, Pride. Ones who mean no harm." Once Nathan was clear of the gate, she closed it and hopped back in her seat.

"Poor guy hasn't been the same since they doped him." Nathan drove to the far side of the pasture, giving Pride a wide berth. "The vet told Asher he's one of a very few that find it hard to shake the effects of the drug."

"It's hard to get past trauma," Tamara said, thinking of her own challenges.

Pride reared and whinnied, but otherwise kept his distance.

"If Zeke and T.J. came this way, how did they get past Pride?" Tamara wondered, suddenly afraid for the roguish twins. She searched the pastures for trampled boys, thankfully finding none.

"They don't always take a straight path. They might have come through the empty pasture next to this one." Nathan looked grim. "But a part of me, the worst-case-scenario thinker, fears finding them down by the creek, too wounded to—"

"Hey, hey. None of that nonsense." Tamara gave his shoulders a quick, bolstering rub. "Those boys live a charmed life."

That's probably how Nathan had thought about Frosty. He'd led a charmed life, too, short as it was.

Tamara drew a deep breath, trying to crowd out the feelings of guilt and grief. She watched Pride watch them. The other horses, all retired racers, paid them no mind. With a sigh, she looked ahead, gaze sweeping the land for any clue to the whereabouts of the twins.

"They're here!" Tamara cried as they reached the end of the pasture and a wide swath of blackberry bushes on the other side of the fence. A faded child-size sock was stuck on the brambles near a gate. She shook Nathan's arm. "They have to be here."

They got out and hurried to a small gate. On the other side of the pasture was a narrow path that led past the blackberry bushes and down a dirt bank to a slow winding creek that was sheltered from the sun by a thick canopy of a tall willow tree.

And there they were.

Zeke and T.J. were on their knees in front of a

pile of rocks with a bunch of sticks balanced across the top. Their cowboy hats had been tossed to the ground. Their boots were wet up to their ankles, as if they'd waded into the creek with them still on. Two more socks had been removed and tossed aside. The water was clear nearest the boys, a darker green at the bend where the water seemed deeper.

Nathan stood at the top of the bank, staring at his children with soft blue eyes.

Tamara came closer, laying a hand on his arm and whispering, "I know this has been scary for you. I know you're probably thinking this wouldn't have happened if Marilee was alive. But whatever guilt trip you're laying on yourself, put a smile on that handsome face of yours." Tamara hesitated, then patted his cheeks with both hands because he still seemed lost. Then she turned and picked her way down the slope. "Hey, boys. What are you doing?"

"Tamara!" T.J. grinned at her over his shoulder. Then his eyes lit up.

And Zeke's did, too. "Dad! Come see our baby frogs!" He was so excited. It would be a shame if Nathan erupted on them.

Tamara was close enough now to see that the rocks weren't in a pile. They were stacked like a box with those sticks as a lid.

"Come see the fort we made them." Zeke smiled at Tamara for what felt like the first time since Frosty died. He moved some sticks and reached inside, then cupped a small frog in his hands so they could see. “We remembered Dad telling us about frogs at a creek once. And look! We found them.”

The frog took that opportunity to leap from Zeke’s hands into the stream, landing with a small splash.

“No!” In his rush to recapture the frog, Zeke’s booted toe knocked the corner of the rock prison. As the stones scattered toward the bank, the frogs jumped free. “Help!”

Zeke and T.J. scampered about trying to catch frogs, splashing in the shallows.

Tamara laughed at their antics. She spared a glance behind her. Nathan hadn’t moved from atop the bank. A hint of a smile graced his handsome face.

Good.

The boys soon tired, slowing to spend more time searching for their prey than lunging into the water.

“There’s one.” Zeke dived into the deeper, darker water, all the way under. He floundered and sputtered. Zeke came up for air but was swept away almost immediately by the current into deeper water, head sucked under the flow.

“*Zeke!*” Tamara rushed forward, panic making every step shaky.

Nathan pushed past her, tossing his straw cowboy hat aside. He waded through the shallows and then dived in after Zeke.

“T.J., get out of the water.” Tamara wrapped her arms around T.J. when he joined her on dry land.

"Zeke," T.J. said weakly. "Is he dead?"

"No. Your dad's going to get him." Despite those reassuring words, Tamara's body flooded with a current of fear rippled with helplessness.

But Nathan was a strong swimmer. He had a better chance of saving his son than she did. He disappeared under water and when he resurfaced, he carried Zeke in his arms. The boy coughed and sputtered as Nathan towed him back to safety.

Nathan carried Zeke to the bank and set him down. They were both dripping wet. Nathan looked thunderous. "Are you all right?"

Zeke shook his head, sweet features crumpling. "I lost my boot." And then he started to cry.

Without a word, Nathan turned and waded back into the water.

"Good thing your cast is waterproof. But this..." T.J. tugged off his brother's remaining black cowboy boot and poured water out of it. Then he smiled at Zeke. "Hey. Next time, we're putting the frogs in our boots, not a rock house."

"There will be no next time!" Nathan cried before diving into the deeper bend in the creek.

With his boots on.

"ARE YOU OKAY, DAD?" T.J. held Nathan's hand on the walk back to the ATV. "You look the way Zeke did when he took a bite of Kelley's clam chowder."

"He'll be fine once we get him dry and in bed." Zeke held Nathan's other hand, seemingly having forgotten that he was soaking wet, too. “If we don’t take care of him, Dad could catch cold and die.”

“I’m not dying,” Nathan claimed, breaking his self-imposed silence.

I’m wet and recovering from being scared out of my wits for my kids’ safety.

“He looks sick to his stomach. If you have to hurl, Dad,” T.J. continued in that bossy tone he used with Zeke, “wait until we get a bucket or find a toilet.”

“That’s the sick-tummy rule,” Zeke said, glancing over his shoulder, presumably explaining things to Tamara. “No hurling on the carpet.”

“I’m not sick,” Nathan insisted, suspecting it was going to be a long drive back to the stables. A noise behind him, one that sounded suspiciously like muffled laughter, had him turning and glaring at Tamara.

She didn’t care. Her dark eyes sparkled. Her smile was deep and broad, just the way he liked.

The way I thought I liked.

He didn’t like it now, not when he hadn’t yet recovered from the afternoon’s scares. Lost boys. Boys who were almost swept away in the creek. That wasn’t something you got over in a minute. Or even five.

Still gawking at Tamara behind him, Nathan stumbled. He caught himself before he fell, and focused on the path ahead. But the thought of Tamara smiling behind him got under his skin. He felt all hot and prickly.

"We should put Dad to bed when we get back," T.J. went on.

"He can sleep with my alligator stuffy," Zeke added. "That always makes me feel better."

"You boys are too nice to your dad," Tamara said in a voice that was far too upbeat for Nathan's peace of mind.

"That's because he's nice to us," Zeke said.

"He *loves* us," T.J. said.

"Yep." Zeke swung Nathan's arm.

Love.

"I love you two." Nathan felt a weight lifting. He could breathe easier. He stopped walking and knelt to give his boys a heartfelt hug.

"And there it is," Tamara said from behind him. "What we've all been waiting for."

Nathan glanced at her. "What?"

Tamara grinned but it wasn't a teasing grin. "The response Marilee and your mother would be proud of. Bravo, Nathan."

It almost felt as if… Tamara was proud of him, too.

Something inside Nathan shifted. It felt as if his heart was making room. For Tamara.

How can that be?

He glanced at the hand that held T.J.'s, catching sight of his wedding ring. It didn't seem to belong there.

How can that be?

Nathan was still wondering about the state of his heart at dinner.

Tamara and the twins sat with the rest of the staff—Edie, Frannie and Owen. And although Tamara had been a cheerful talker on the drive back to the stables with the twins, she and Edie were in a heated discussion about the potential of Slugger.

“He doesn’t have the traditional build of a winner,” Edie argued, referencing the colt’s unusually strong hindquarters. “We should drop him from training.”

“He’s got the will to win *and* with the right endurance training, he could really be something,” Tamara countered.

“We should consider putting him in the showcase.” Asher sat across the table from Nathan. “Great idea to have a showcase, by the way, Nathan.”

“Let’s hope we have enough horses left to field one.” Nathan was feeling very pessimistic in general. He fiddled with his wedding ring.

Big E suggested I take it off.

Nathan stopped fiddling with his ring.

“We’ll be fine. All we need now is a date.” Big E gave a mock salute with his water glass. “Things are looking up. I found someone in town today who told me they saw Elliot drinking several times at the Lucky Lane with Luke and Patrick Connelly from Connelly Thoroughbreds.”

"That makes the Connellys our prime suspect in the doping of Pride." Asher nodded, returning Big E's broad smile with one of his own. "I heard whispers that Patrick has a gambling problem."

Nathan was unable to share their enthusiasm on a day when one of his kids almost drowned and he felt his attraction to Tamara strengthening. "That's still no proof the Connellys did it."

That comment stole the smiles off their faces.

"A showcase?" That caught Tamara's attention. She leaned back in her chair to catch Nathan's eye. "We'd need a few weeks to get the horses in shape. We've just been taking them for breezy runs this week."

"Can I ride in the showcase?" Zeke asked. "I could ride Pest."

"No!" Nathan didn't have to think twice about that.

Tamara's eyebrows went up. She gave him a look he took to mean *Respond like Marilee would.*

Zeke's brow furrowed. "*Dad.*"

"Pest isn't a racehorse," Nathan insisted, drawing all kinds of looks from the assembled, from sympathy to disbelief. "You're too young to be a jockey, Zeke."

"Is he? Do you remember when you rode in a showcase?" Asher asked Nathan.

Nathan's mind went blank. He shook his head. "I never rode in a showcase."

"Oh, yes, you did." Asher chuckled. "Dad added a race with jockeys age thirteen and under. Dylan and I were too old. Mom convinced Caleb and Ridge that you needed the spotlight with Dad because you'd gotten into trouble at school, defending some little girl from bullies."

Nathan didn't remember that, either.

"Did he win?" T.J. asked.

"He did." Asher was smiling joyfully, as if this was a fond memory. "Dad had the biggest smile on his face when Nathan got the winner's circle."

"Why don't I remember this?" Nathan wondered aloud.

"Maybe because you were ten and so nervous that you passed out as they put the drape of roses on your horse."

"Oh… I remember waking up in the winner's circle." His hands had been cramping from clutching the reins. He'd always been afraid to ride a racehorse at speed. Which seemed ironic now as he looked at Tamara, who was flashing him that approving smile.

"You woke up." Asher grinned. "And then, you threw up."

"Did he hurl in a bucket?" Zeke asked with the enthusiasm boys usually gave to the gross and disgusting. "That's a rule, you know."

"Let's just say this." Asher leaned forward, lowering his voice. "He missed."

"Hey, I was only ten." Nathan didn't know whether to laugh or get upset. "And Zeke, you won't be riding in a showcase until you're older than I was."

"We'll see," Zeke said with a ton of attitude.

Laughter filled the break room, broken by a sour meow from Luna. She stood in the doorway with a mouse in her jaws. She dropped it on the floor and trotted over to Edie.

They all stared at the mouse, waiting to see if it was still alive.

Thankfully, it didn't move.

"Good girl, Luna." Edie got up to dispose of the cat's tribute. But that wasn't her only concern. When she returned, she said, "We'll need more staff to put on a showcase—starting-gate crew, riders, hot-walkers, stable hands."

"I'm on the same page, Edie." But there was something off-key that needed Nathan's more immediate attention—his feelings toward Tamara. He caught her eye. "Can we talk after dinner?"

"We should iron out the details of the showcase first," Big E advised.

Asher agreed. "Might take hours."

"We can catch up tomorrow," Tamara promised, gathering her dishes. "Or you can leave me a note telling me what you need done."

She thinks I want to talk to her about work?

Nathan didn't know whether to be relieved or annoyed.

CHAPTER TWELVE

FRIDAY AFTERNOON, TAMARA returned from a trip to town with a fresh supply of nuts and protein bars. Her SUV's air conditioner gave up the fight on the way back, making her glad she'd worn thin blue capris and a white tank top. She parked and gathered her purchases, heading toward the filly barn.

She wasn't thinking about Nathan, who'd been giving her a wide berth. And she wasn't thinking about her ride tomorrow on the headstrong Iron Fire's Wing.

In the hay barn pasture, T.J. and Zeke were sitting on Pest's back and shouting, "Yah! Come on! Let's go!"

Despite their prompting, Pest wasn't moving anywhere.

Tamara stopped by the gate, despite the urgent desire for air-conditioning and the need to discard her socks and sneakers for flip-flops. "Hey, guys. What's up?"

"Nothing," Zeke said with attitude, apparently having reset himself to believing Tamara was a villain.

"We're trying to train Pest to race in the showcase," T.J. told her. "But he won't move."

Big E joined Tamara at the pasture gate. Unlike Tamara, he never looked wilty in the heat. The elderly man stood tall and unfazed in his cowboy attire and black hat. "Kind of hard to control a horse when you haven't at least got a bridle on him."

"We want to do it our way." Zeke was in a mood. His wrist was out of its sling. The red lattice cast the brightest color in the pasture, other than Blaze's chestnut coat.

"I bet Tamara can make him go." T.J. slid off the back of the gray colt. "Come on, Tamara. You try."

"No." Zeke scowled, answering before Tamara could. "I'm Pest's trainer."

"There's a difference between being a trainer and being a jockey." Big E used a conciliatory tone with Zeke but then leaned closer to Tamara and whispered, "Are you up to try mounting him? This is the perfect opportunity to prove to Nathan that he's trainable, at least."

"NATHAN WON'T APPROVE," Tamara whispered back as T.J. approached the gate.

"You and I both know that Nathan has let himself fall into a rut of grief." Big E nodded sagely. "He needs an intervention."

"You think my sitting on Pest is an intervention?" Tamara had a bad feeling about this. Trepidation rolled around her stomach like a circular hot-walker set on high speed. "If Nathan finds out, can I tell him it was your idea to try and ride the colt?"

"It was my idea," T.J. said brightly. "Not Big E's."

"Hey!" Zeke called. "I can't get down."

"We're coming." Big E opened the gate, pausing to whisper to Tamara, "If that colt lets you near him, hop on."

"Hop on an unsaddled, unbridled horse?" Sounded foolish to her.

"He won't go anywhere," Big E countered. "Look at him. He's not moving a muscle. You said Frannie couldn't catch him. Now's the time to see if your relationship with Pest inspires trust in the colt."

"Let's hope he doesn't buck me off." Tamara put her bag of purchases near a fence post and entered the pasture, anyway. There was something tempting about hopping on Pest. What harm could there be in sitting on him? "I'll need a leg up."

They reached Pest easily since the colt hadn't moved with a panicked Zeke on his back.

While Big E held Pest's halter, Tamara eased Zeke to the ground.

"It's now or never," Big E said softly, slowly moving into a lunge near Pest's left shoulder and gesturing to Tamara to use his knee as a mounting block.

Pest turned his head to look at her.

"Why do I feel like I'm going to regret this?"

Tamara grabbed hold of Pest's mane at the base of his neck, stepped on Big E's knee and swung herself onto the colt's back. He was of similar height and breadth as Frosty had been.

Big E let go of the halter and took Zeke's hand. "Let's give them room."

"Room?" Tamara shifted her weight back. "I thought I was just sitting."

"I just want to see what he'll do," Big E said.

Pest backed up a few steps, gray ears on the swivel. Then he shook his head.

"Uh-oh," T.J. said. "That head shake means he's about to run."

"Hang on, Tamara," Zeke told her, pulling Big E backward.

The words were hardly out of his mouth when Pest bolted, tearing off toward the back of the pasture. He was fast, like Frosty. He was sleek, like Frosty. But did he respond to her leg and foot cues like Frosty? Nope.

I'm just a passenger. A...a guardian.

Not a partner on this ride. Fear of another horse accident clogged her throat, making her breath ragged.

Pest galloped at full speed toward the back fence. He didn't slow.

I have to do something. Or this green colt is going to hurt himself by running into a fence. And then Nathan will never forgive me.

Tamara yanked Pest's mane backward, shifted

her center of gravity away from his withers, and then pulled that mane with her left hand to force his head off center.

His pace faltered. But he refused to turn.

Time slowed. Tamara considered bailing. But she couldn't.

There will be no more injuries on my watch.

She heeled Pest with her left foot and yanked harder on his mane with her left hand. "Come on, boy. Turn."

Pest finally slowed, turning left.

"That's it. Now you're cooking, boy." Tamara leaned forward once more, easing her hold in his mane.

With a mighty shake of his head, Pest poured on more speed.

And now, Tamara faced a different problem.

Big E and the twins stood directly in the colt's path.

SHOUTS DREW NATHAN'S ATTENTION.

He'd been walking toward his office from the colts' barn. But at the sound of indistinct, young voices, Nathan turned toward the hay barn pasture. He rounded the corner of the barn and immediately started running. "Hey! Stop!"

"Move, guys! I can't control him." Tamara rode Pest bareback at a racing gallop and was headed directly toward his boys. Without a bridle to control him.

"Stop! Pest! Stop!" Nathan waved his arms. But he wasn't going to reach the pasture in time.

Luckily, Big E was urging the boys back toward the corner near the gate, shielding them with his body.

Nathan kept running, waving and shouting, "Pest! Stop! *Pest!*"

The gray colt's head came up and he shifted course, heading toward Nathan. But instead of slowing as he came to the fence, Pest turned on the speed, ignoring Tamara yanking on his mane.

"He's going to jump!" Tamara cried, leaning over his neck at the last moment.

Pest flew gracefully over the fence as if he was a trained jumper, then came to a skidding halt in front of Nathan and shoved his head into Nathan's chest as if seeking comfort after a traumatic experience.

He's afraid.

Adrenaline crashed through Nathan, prickling his skin, spiking his temper, pointing that anger at Tamara.

What was she thinking?

But he couldn't ream Tamara when Pest was upset. He'd learned that lesson yesterday with the twins.

"Is he okay?" Tamara dropped to the ground and began running her hand down Pest's rear leg. "Tell me he's okay. The last thing I want is for him to be hurt." She moved to the other side and ran her hand down his other hind leg. "Nathan, he's okay, isn't he? He's trembling."

Nathan was stroking Pest's neck and making soothing noises. He glanced at Tamara, who was now moving to the colt's front leg. The hand she laid on Pest shook.

She's afraid, too.

It struck him then—both horse and rider could have been killed. Nathan's anger drained, sucking the strength from his legs until he thought it wise to drape his arm over Pest's neck to keep him upright.

"It's all right," Nathan said, softly, to both horse and jockey.

"I don't know. I just don't know." Tamara passed beneath Pest's neck to check his other front leg. And then she came to stand in front of Nathan. "Is he okay?"

"Yes." Nathan put his arm around her shoulders and drew her closer. "It's okay. You're both okay." Or they would be when they stopped trembling.

"That was awesome!" T.J. ran up to join them. "I didn't know Pest could jump fences."

"I want to jump fences," Zeke cried, tossing his cowboy hat in the air.

"Asher is training some of the retired racehorses to be jumpers." Big E picked up Zeke's hat and stuck it on the boy's head. "Maybe he should be working with Pest. There's a good market for jumpers."

"Pest's not a working horse. Nor is he for sale."

Besides, Nathan knew by the way Pest was still trembling that this wasn't something the colt had any love for. "We need to cool him down."

"We'll do that while you debrief with Tamara." Big E gave Tamara a knowing smile before taking hold of Pest's mane. "Come on, boys. Let's head over to the hot-walker. One of you run ahead for a halter and lead rope."

Both boys ran toward the colt barn. Big E followed at a slower pace.

Nathan realized he had Tamara tucked into his side. He released her and crossed his arms over his chest. "Well?"

"You want an explanation." Tamara still looked limp. Her hands still shook. She glanced in the direction Big E had disappeared with what seemed like an unfocused gaze. "You're sure he's all right. I was so worried for him."

"For him? If you were so worried about Pest, why didn't you jump off him? No. Forget that. Why did you get on him in the first place?"

"Why didn't *I* bail?" Tamara faced him once more, still looking out of it.

She's in shock.

"Come on. Walk with me." Nathan took a few steps and when Tamara didn't follow, he took gentle hold of her hand. "You need a cool down just as much as Pest does."

Tamara didn't protest. That's how scared she was.

Nathan led her to the garden his mother had

started, the one Edie still tended. There were more flowers here than he remembered. Tall wildflowers that Tamara held out her hand to touch as they passed. There were tomatoes and peppers growing in the center bed. He plucked a cherry tomato and handed it to her.

She popped it in her mouth, ate it and then drew a deep breath. "Wow. There's nothing quite like a homegrown tomato, is there?"

He ate one and agreed. "A taste of home. Every spring, my brothers and I used to dig in this patch with our mother." And he had a vague recollection of his father helping, as well. Which was odd.

I don't remember him doing anything with us that wasn't horse related.

In fact, those memories he had of both his parents with all his siblings seemed to have been buried beneath Dad's impossible standards and general disappointment.

"Zeke needed help getting off Pest," Tamara said after eating another tomato. "Big E and I went into the pasture and… It was his idea that I hop on." She shook her head. "He said Pest wouldn't budge. I had my doubts. And…obviously neither Pest nor I were dressed for a proper ride. But everyone wanted me to try."

"It was Zeke's and T.J.'s idea?" Nathan frowned. Zeke wasn't Tamara's biggest fan.

"Yes. No. It was Big E's idea more than theirs. A bad one, it turns out." She drew another deep breath and clenched her fingers as if trying to get them to stop shaking. "I didn't drop off because I thought Pest might hurt himself. I had to be heavy-handed in my cues to get him to turn but he wouldn't slow down. I pulled so hard that I'm surprised I didn't pluck out chunks of his mane. Are you sure he's saddle broke?"

"Yes, I'm sure." Nathan let some of his frustration through in his words. Although it had been nearly a year since the colt had worn a bridle. "That's not the point."

"He's fast." Tamara laughed but it wasn't her usual joyful laughter. It was more…maniacal. "So fast. Like Frosty fast. Now that I'm not thinking about my lack of control—"

"No." Nathan didn't want to hear that. "We're not racing him."

Tamara turned her big, dark eyes his way, still looking shocked. "You need to reinforce his saddle training."

He scoffed. Had she heard a word he said? "No."

"He has to be trained. If not to race, for the safety of your boys." She clenched and unclenched her fingers once more, staring at them. "They're riding on him but he's deciding where they go."

Pest isn't safe to ride.

Nathan finally got the message. In fact, he got more information than Tamara probably thought she was giving him. "You're afraid of Pest."

"No. I mean…" Her pretty eyes widened. "I…

I'd be a fool not to have been afraid. It was like riding a bullet train on a too-short track. But if he was saddled—"

"You have every right to that fear. But I've seen you ride some of the better horses we've got left here, saddled horses, and…" He recalled how it looked as if she held the horses back on the straightaway. "You're afraid. Afraid of going full tilt on a horse."

Tamara bit her lower lip, a silent confession.

"You can't be a race jockey if you're afraid to run for the roses." His frustration built. This was only common sense. "It's not safe for you or the horse you ride if you're afraid. And it's not fair to the owners."

"I know," Tamara whispered, looking pained. "I'm trying to work through it."

Finally. An admission. Nathan placed a supportive hand on her shoulder. "You need to call Patrick and tell him you can't race."

"No." Tamara hung her head. "How can I conquer my fears if I don't ride?"

"You're not ready to try." He took one of her hands. It was clammy. "And if you're not ready, you could have another accident." Horse jockeys had to be cutthroat—edging the competition off the rail, riding a horse through the tiniest of gaps, pushing themselves and their horse to the limit down the homestretch.

The way Tamara pushed Frosty.

Nathan's breath caught.

Tamara was just doing her job. A job I paid her to do.

A wave of cold drenched him in sickly sweat.

I killed Frosty.

He swallowed the lump in his throat.

I'm just as much to blame as anyone.

"I have to race tomorrow." Tamara lifted her face to his, dark eyes as liquid as a silky midnight sky. "And I… I will be. I'm getting in a lot of rides every day. And I'm getting more confident."

That false confidence could be the end of her.

Nathan's breath felt heavy, laden with fear. But there was something about the way Tamara had spoken. Her brave words a contrast to her tenuous tone. "Are you trying to convince me? Or yourself?"

"Both?" Tamara attempted a smile and began to back away. "Don't worry about me. I'll be fine."

Nathan watched Tamara walk away knowing he'd continue to worry about her.

Because she was anything but fine.

And he didn't want Tamara to get hurt. In fact, surprisingly, he wanted to protect her with the same fierceness he protected Pest and his boys.

CHAPTER THIRTEEN

THERE WAS NO reason for Tamara to feel trepidation when she parked her SUV at Rosehaven Downs early on Saturday morning. She'd raced here before.

But that was before Nathan knew about her struggle to push a horse to its limits. Or let them push themselves. Somehow, Nathan knowing and caring for her safety and well-being had shifted her fears back to the forefront, until they roared in her ears like crashing ocean waves on a stormy day. She spent a few minutes doing deep breathing exercises before getting out of her SUV and grabbing her duffel with her riding gear.

It was a clear, sunny day with a light breeze, perfect for racing. It was still hours before the first race. Cars, trucks, and SUVs continued to fill up the employee parking lot while the larger, visitor lot was empty.

"Tammie!" Dad had a large backpack over his shoulder as he approached her. His black hair was cropped short but his smile was miles wide. "Guess what? I'm racing today, too."

"I'm happy for you." Tamara hugged him. "What horse are you on?"

"Caroline Richmond put me on Goldfish Road." Dad hooked his arm through Tamara's. They walked together toward the racetrack's outbuilding. "I'm in the same race as you on Iron Fire's Wing. The last race of the day."

"I won't take it easy on you," Tamara teased. Her father's exuberance was infectious. Some more of Tamara's angst receded.

"Ha! I'd expect no less." Dad was practically skipping toward the jockey rooms. "This is a new beginning for both of us."

Tamara chuckled. "What's that supposed to mean?"

"We're both exercise riders getting a chance to make a mark in the racing world. Me, after a very long hiatus." He tipped his head toward hers, lowering his voice. "And you, after losing your nerve."

"Don't say that." Tamara cast furtive glances around them, but no one was close enough to hear. "My confidence has never been better."

Dad leaned back to look at her, a challenge in his eyes.

Tamara scrunched her nose. "It's true. Just yesterday, I rode a two-year-old at Blackwell Stables at full speed." She waited for that to sink in before adding, "Bareback and without a bridle."

"Hoo-whee!" Dad crowed. "That's my girl. You're my idol."

"And you're mine." Tamara tugged playfully on his arm, feeling more confident than she had in weeks.

It helped to have her own personal cheerleader.

And a new pair of socks.

"HAVE YOU SEEN TAMARA?" Nathan asked Edie from the vegetable garden gate on Saturday morning.

Edie placed a large yellow summer squash in her woven basket. "She left early. Took her riding gear."

"I was afraid of that," Nathan murmured, gaze caught on a budding red rose. The flower reminded him of the winner's circle, a place he didn't expect Tamara to visit today. Worry lodged itself under his skin, sharp and prickly as that thorny rose.

I need to do something.

"I see you." Edie moved toward the strawberry tower, smiling in a troublesome manner. "I've seen the lovestruck expression on your face when you look at Tamara."

"I'm not… I don't…" Nathan floundered. Did he?

"You are and you do." Edie came to the vegetable garden gate. "And now, you're hurt bad that she's riding for someone else instead of being happy that she's seen as being a skilled jockey, satisfied to only ride for you."

"What if she's riding when she shouldn't?" Nathan voiced his concerns. "What if she's putting herself in danger?"

"Whoever caused Elliot to crash isn't going to target Tamara. That would be foolish." Edie patted his shoulder, misunderstanding the context of his words. "Admit it. You're jealous."

Nathan scoffed. "I'm not jealous." Oh, those words felt like a lie. "I'm concerned for Tamara's safety."

Edie laughed. "Do you know what makes a good horse person?"

He shook his head.

"Someone who understands himself and his feelings." She walked away, chuckling as if she didn't believe he was a good horse person.

Or a good romantic prospect for Tamara.

Nathan rubbed the back of his neck. His feelings were confused where Tamara was concerned. But that could be sorted in time. But not today. Today, he needed to find Tamara. If he couldn't stop Tamara from racing, he could at least be there to support her if something went wrong.

Nathan turned on his heel and headed toward the horse barn pasture, calling to his kids as he did. "Hey, boys! Let's go to the races."

THE TRACK WAS FAST. The three horses Tamara rode throughout the day had been strong contenders. Tamara had been focused, riding well, her fears at bay. She'd even come in first on Patrick's promising two-year-old, Red Sunset.

"Tamara." Caroline Richmond turned from Tamara's father and Goldfish Road to Tamara, who stood near Iron Fire's Wing, a large chestnut three-year-old. Caroline looked sophisticated in black slacks, a formfitting black blouse and black heels. "Fire is a nervous starter. Don't worry if he blows off steam before getting in the starting gate. It seems to help him settle down."

"No worries." Tamara moved to the colt's head, greeting him with soft words and a friendly pat on the neck.

Fire struck her chest with his head—*hard*—bumping her several steps back.

"Ow." Tamara rubbed her sternum over her teal-and-silver silks. "Point taken, fella." He wanted her to stay out of his way.

Caroline chuckled, a cool, humorless sound. "None of my horses are sweethearts. We don't coddle our stock at Richmond Stables." Set-down delivered, Caroline continued with her race instructions. "Make sure Fire's in position to move ahead as you come out of the first turn. He doesn't like the rail."

"Got it." Tamara gave the colt a wide berth as she came around to prepare to mount. She tugged her racing gloves on tighter, all while holding her whip, then took hold of the reins and the saddle.

A stable hand started leading Fire and Dad's horse forward.

Caroline leaned down and grabbed Tamara's

ankle, giving her a leg up into the saddle. "Do us proud."

"We will," Dad promised.

Fire tried to bite Goldfish Road, sending the palomino skittering sideways.

"Behave." The stable hand drew Fire's head back to his left shoulder. "Geez, we're only going fifty feet to a track pony, Fire. Why do you always have to be difficult?"

The colt pranced, then tried to kick Goldfish Road with his hind leg. Granted, it was a weak attempt at a kick.

"Hey, you." Tamara drew him to a stop, anyway, causing the stable hand to halt. Then she scolded the colt. "None of that."

Fire turned his head to look at Tamara. It wasn't a repentant look. He huffed with the intensity of a bull about to charge and then faced forward.

"Now you've done it," Dad said, a sparkle to his dark eyes. He also wore Richmond teal-and-silver silks but his cap was silver while Tamara's was teal. "Fire thrives on proving he's boss."

"Great." Unruly horses rarely won. They spent too much energy fighting their jockey. Although Tamara got paid to ride, placing first, second or third earned her a bonus. "Let's get this show on the road."

"THERE'S TAMARA! HI, TAMARA!" T.J. waved from the grandstand at Rosehaven Downs even though they were too high up for her to notice.

Nathan sat in between the twins at the racetrack. He'd held his breath every time she raced. And every time she raced, she did well.

This time, Tamara rode a very large chestnut past them, accompanied by a track pony. The colt kept tossing his head as if unhappy with the bit in his mouth or the rider on his back.

"Wave to Tamara, Zeke," T.J. encouraged.

"Why? She's not riding a Blackwell horse." Zeke tugged at the sling around his neck. "When can I stop wearing my sling?"

"Not for another few weeks."

Groaning, Zeke slumped in his seat.

The horses headed back to the starting gate, where they were loaded in order by odd numbers first. Tamara's horse was in the second gate.

The chestnut reared when the gate handler reached for his reins.

A gasp rolled through the crowd.

Tamara quickly brought the colt under control. Nathan couldn't see her face, but she looked rigid in the saddle. Uncomfortable.

This race is going to test her confidence.

Nathan laid his arms over his sons' shoulders. "Let's think good thoughts."

"After this race we can go home," Zeke said, still slumped in his seat. "That's a good thought."

"Tamara's going to win." T.J. hadn't taken his eyes off the starting gate.

The last few horses were loaded. The rear gates all shut.

A hush fell over the crowd.

The starting bell rang. The front gates were flung open. And the horses leaped out.

Tamara's horse sprang nearly half a length ahead of the colts on either side. He managed to keep that small lead from the rest of the pack even though he tossed his head the way he had during his warm-up lap, as if trying to take control.

Tamara and the horses thundered around the track, heading for the finish line. Her horse tossed his head once more and this time the length of rein snapped from the snaffle rings at his mouth.

The crowd gasped.

The colt surged forward.

Tamara let the useless reins fall across the colt's withers. She grabbed on to the chestnut's mane just like she'd held on to Pest's yesterday.

If I hadn't seen her do that yesterday, I'd be terrified.

Instead of simply scared to death.

Nathan got to his feet.

"Dad, Tamara's in trouble." T.J. stood, too.

"Where? What?" Zeke scrambled to his feet, looking toward the pack of horses rounding the turn.

"Her reins snapped off," T.J. explained.

Nathan's mouth was too dry to speak.

"But she's ahead." Zeke sounded awestruck.

"Come on, Tamara!" T.J. shouted.

"Come on, Tamara!" Zeke echoed.

The horses approached the far turn. Other jockeys began using their whips.

Not Tamara. Nathan didn't know if she was afraid to let go of her horse's mane or if she wasn't using her whip for fear of history repeating itself. Not that it mattered. She was ahead and her lead lengthening.

By the time Tamara crossed the finish line, she was two lengths in front of everyone else.

TAMARA'S RIDE CAUSED a stir.

After crossing the finish line, she was able to slow Fire down and bring him back toward the finish line, where a stable hand clipped a lead rope on him. From then on, Tamara was a passenger, which was a blessing. She was shaken and doubted her legs would hold her after that wild ride.

Smile like you meant for that to happen.

Oh, Tamara smiled. She smiled hard.

Crowds gathered. The Richmond family surrounded her, full of praise for both horse and rider. There were pictures. So many pictures. It allowed Tamara to regain some equilibrium, to breathe and be thankful neither she nor her horse had been hurt. When it was time to get back on the ground, she barely swayed on the dismount.

Her father was waiting for her, linking his arm through hers. "I came in second."

"I saw that." Tamara paused to hug him. "You kept Goldfish Road close after the reins snapped off."

Dad nodded. "Just in case you needed an exit strategy. But then Fire took off." He hugged her tighter. "Scared me half to death."

"Ditto." Tamara's pulse pounded as she relived some of the scarier moments of the ride—the energetic toss of his head that slowed his stride, the snap of the reins, the way Fire pranced and pretended to obey her after the win.

That horse has been thinking about this for a long, long time.

"Tamara?" That was Caroline's cool voice. When Tamara faced her, she said, "Thank you for keeping your head. Both of you. Great rides today."

"And as a thank-you, you'll invest in a better set of reins for Fire," Dad said archly, as if Caroline didn't scare him.

Dad's boss gave him a hard stare. "I'll see you Monday, Mr. Vaughn. Don't get cocky." And then she left them, marching off in her high heels.

"She's as scary as her horse," Tamara said, only loud enough for Dad to hear.

He chuckled. "Come on. Let's change out of these silks and then I'll buy you dinner."

Several minutes later, Tamara exited the female jockey room.

"You placed on three of four horses." Patrick Connelly greeted her with that too-slick smile of his. "Great outing. That last ride is going to make you a legend."

"Thanks." Tamara glanced around but couldn't see her father. "But if it comes down to it, I'd rather win with the reins in my hands."

"So pragmatic." Patrick was all smiles. "I was wondering if you'd be interested in earning some extra cash."

The hair on the back of Tamara's neck stood on end. Instinct told her Patrick was up to no good. But she had to ask, "Doing what?"

"Are you interested?" Patrick didn't answer her question. And he looked… Well, he looked like he wanted to cause mischief and pay her for it.

Tamara hesitated.

"She's not interested in working for you."

Tamara turned to find Nathan and the twins nearby. She hadn't seen them approach. They looked like cowboys, not race folk, in their faded blue jeans, T-shirts and cowboy hats.

"I think the decision to work for me is Tamara's," Patrick said coldly. "It's not a Blackwell decision."

Both men looked at Tamara.

"You'd have to tell me more details, Patrick. For now, I'll just take the rides." Tamara hitched her equipment bag higher on her shoulder, relieved when Patrick was hailed by someone else and left them.

The crowd ebbed and flowed around them, heading for the exits.

"Tamara, you're a rock star!" Zeke made a human X with his body, grinning at her the way he used to.

Tamara's heart melted a little.

"You have to teach us how to ride like that," T.J. added, giving her a hug.

Tamara's heart melted a little more.

"Tamara isn't going to teach you how to ride like that," Nathan said in what for him was a low-key voice. He took tender hold of Tamara's hand. "It's too dangerous."

"Oh," the twins said in unison, looking crestfallen while Tamara's heart soared.

"Are you all right?" Nathan asked Tamara, blue gaze softening.

"I'm fine," she assured him, possibly staring at him with an adoring gaze.

The boys latched on to a metal support post and began spinning around it.

"You could have pushed Baseball Bobby to second place if you'd have used your whip," Nathan said softly, just for her.

"That's a jockey's decision," Tamara replied in a starchy tone, even if she agreed with him. She'd done well without triggering her anxiety about pushing a horse too hard until that last ride. "But Nathan, I just had the craziest, most thrilling *and* most terrifying ride of my life. Not to mention, I came out unscathed. Please don't poke holes in my joy by making me second-guess my other race decisions."

"Point taken," Dad said, coming up from behind Tamara. He stared coolly at Nathan, then frowned at their joined hands. "Who is this fella, Tammie?"

Nathan dropped her hand.

Immediately, Tamara felt bereft. "He's my boss, Dad." She introduced them all.

"You came in second on that last race." Nathan shook her father's hand. "Great ride."

Dad's chest puffed out. "I tried to protect my little girl. But in the end Fire was quite literally on fire. No one could catch him."

Tamara didn't want to examine the idea that the race would have been closer had she been holding a pair of reins attached to Fire's bit.

Nathan tipped his cowboy hat back. "Larry, the Blackwell Stables are looking for jockeys for a showcase we're hosting in a few weeks. We'd sure like to have you on board."

"If it's okay with Tamara, it's okay with me." Dad's gaze caught on someone in the crowd. He gave Tamara a side hug. "I see someone I need to talk to. Tammie, will you take a rain check on dinner tonight?"

"Of course, Dad."

Her father hurried off.

"So?" Nathan asked. "What's the verdict? Can I hire your dad to ride in our showcase?"

"You can." Tamara faced Nathan, taking in every strong angle on his lean face and committing it to memory in case things didn't work out how her heart wanted. "But I'm warning you, he's stubborn and opinionated."

Nathan flashed her a big smile. "Oh, I'm used to that in my jockeys." Then he leaned closer to whisper, "And I'm really starting to like it."

"Me, too," she murmured, trying not to look like a lovestruck fool.

CHAPTER FOURTEEN

"I GOT IN touch with a friend who knows someone at..." Big E stopped himself from saying where. Even among family, it was dangerous to identify his sources. He took his sunglasses off and wiped them clean on his shirt before putting them back in place. "Anyway, she says we can trace the erythropoietin to the veterinarian who ordered it." He always hated rattling off that long word. But that was the drug that had been injected in Sovereign's Pride. Some people he'd run across called it EPO. "That will give the sheriff something concrete to go on."

He and Asher stood at the pasture where Pride was spending time on Monday, mid-morning. At the sight of the humans, the gray three-year-old reared and charged the fence, ears back.

Big E didn't play chicken with large livestock. He backed away from the fence.

"Whoa." Asher held up his arms, making himself larger.

The colt skidded to a halt in front of Asher and released a shrill whinny.

"It's okay, buddy," Asher said in a low voice. "We're not going to hurt you. We know the drug did this to you."

"I think that window is closed." Big E hated to burst Asher's bubble. But the veterinarian the stables contracted with, Dr. Julia Eisler, had been emphatic about this point a while back. "It takes weeks for EPO to flush through a horse's system. It's coming up on three months. Whatever the drug did to Pride, he's clinging to the effects. There's no medical reason for him to behave this way."

With a huff, Pride galloped across the pasture away from them.

"You think Pride's physical reaction to the drug has now become a…a…learned behavior?" Asher tipped back his cowboy hat.

"Bad habits are easy to come by." Big E marveled at the fine form of the stallion. "It's getting rid of them that's a challenge. If you want that horse to race again, you need to call in a specialist."

"A horse whisperer," Asher said half under his breath. "That will be a challenge given the poor reputation of Blackwell Stables. I'll try to get word to my brother Caleb. He used to be really good with problem horses. But he's finishing up a rotation for the army overseas. And, like Nathan, he's not good at staying in touch under normal circumstances. I'm not exactly sure when his tour ends."

"Reach out to him." Big E clapped a hand on Asher's shoulder. "I know not having answers quickly is frustrating. But it also gives us time to put things right here at the farm before Caleb returns. Hopefully."

CHAPTER FIFTEEN

TAMARA WAS SPRAWLED on her bed and resting when she heard the twins run through the filly barn Monday afternoon.

"I'm going to ask her!" That sounded like T.J.'s voice.

"No. Let me." That was definitely Zeke's voice.

Footsteps raced up the stairs.

"Tamara! Where are you?"

Tamara sat up and went to open the door to her room.

T.J. rushed in, flinging himself at Tamara for a hug. "We need your help."

Zeke appeared in the doorway, looking less than happy. His sling wasn't tied around his neck. "I wanted to ask her."

Tamara released T.J. and gave Zeke a tentative hug. "What do you need?"

The twins exchanged silent glances, both adjusting the straw cowboy hats on their heads.

"Do you have cake?" Zeke blurted. "We think this talk needs cake."

"I'm out of cake." Tamara did a quick mental

inventory of her stores. “I have chocolate squares. Want one?”

Zeke came over to her small refrigerator. “You have chocolate in here?” He opened the fridge. “You have strawberries. I like strawberries and chocolate.”

“With whipped cream,” T.J. added.

“I don’t have whipped cream. But you’re welcome to eat strawberries with one square of chocolate.” Maybe chocolate would loosen their tongues and they’d tell her what mischief they had in mind.

“I’d like two squares,” Zeke said, taking out the basket of strawberries.

The boys sat on the floor and ate their treats. It didn’t seem as if they had any urgency to explain their presence in her room or that cryptic request.

“How was school today?” Tamara asked.

“I got to go on the swings first at recess,” Zeke announced, as if this was important. “And I got to be at the front of the line when we walked to the cafeteria, which made Carlton mad at me.”

“We had to sing.” T.J. sounded less happy with his day. “And I got in trouble for writing on the board.”

“Really?” Tamara was surprised by that. Zeke was the one who was always out of line. “Why was that trouble?”

T.J. wrinkled his nose as if the memory was distasteful. “I took Miss Jenkins’s sparkly marker and wrote my name on the board.”

“She couldn’t get the name off,” Zeke tattled.

Tamara tried not to laugh. "Did you write your name in permanent marker?"

T.J. nodded, shoulders slumped. "I had to sit in the corner during story time."

"But do you know what?" Tamara tried to think of something to cheer him up. "Your name is going to be on that board forever. You're going to be a legend."

T.J. seemed heartened by that idea.

The boys finished eating.

"Are you going to tell me why you're here?" Tamara asked.

The boys exchanged a silent look that ended with Zeke's defeated shrug.

"We want Pest to compete in the showcase," T.J. told her.

"But we need someone to train him." Zeke stared at Tamara intently. "We think you're the best person for the job."

That's so sweet.

Tamara took a moment to enjoy being asked before she had to burst their bubble. "I can't train Pest. Not without permission from your father."

"Pest is our horse." T.J. raised his chin, adamant on this fact.

"It's our decision." Zeke mirrored his twin's stubborn chin lift. "And I guess it comes down to you. Because Dad won't let me ride in the showcase."

He won't let me ride Pest, either.

"Boys—"

"We want someone to ride him with saddle and bridle on," T.J. continued. "To show Dad he's got potential."

Zeke nodded. "And if he does well, we'll need a jockey. And you're the best."

And now you've put me between a rock and a hard place.

She couldn't ride Pest without Nathan's permission. But selfishly, she wanted to make these boys proud. Plus, riding Pest to a win without tragedy striking would absolve her of some of the guilt over the other ride. A kind of do-over.

"Help us, Tamara," T.J. said. "You're our best chance at making Pest a racehorse."

"Dad listens to you more than he does us," Zeke deadpanned.

I beg to differ. Not when the conversation is about Pest.

Someone else knocked on her door. It was Big E.

"Nathan is with the veterinarian." The old cowboy tipped his cowboy hat back, surveying the chocolate wrappers and earnest faces of Zeke and T.J. "He asked if I'd watch the boys while he and the vet check out the brood mares on the other side of the property."

"All right, boys." Tamara picked up their snack wrappers. "Time to go with Big E."

"But what about Pest?" Zeke didn't budge.

"Tamara's going to train him to ride in the showcase," T.J. told Big E, a bright smile on his sweet face. "We think he can win."

"Is that a fact?" Big E gave Tamara a searching look.

She held up a hand. "They asked. I told them it was Nathan's call." Tamara knew enough to assemble some cover.

The twins launched into their ownership speech, trying to sway Big E to their side.

"I think we should saddle Pest and give it a try." Big E had no qualms with the idea of going against Nathan's wishes. "In fact, we should give the colt training time on the schedule."

Tamara explained to Big E how Pest didn't work with anyone but Nathan and the twins. "Not even Frannie could catch him."

"Dad always says we have to give new things a try," T.J. argued with a tremendous eye roll. "Like singing in school."

"And learning how to make new friends," Zeke backed his brother up. "We want Pest to try something new."

"What's the harm in trying to ride Pest in the pasture?" Big E asked in a booming voice full of good humor. The man clearly didn't know this was Nathan's hot button. "If he's that unruly, he'll never be ready to race in a few weeks."

"Are you going to tell Nathan about this?" Tamara asked, not mincing words. "I was hired to follow orders."

"Then we'll hire you." T.J. stood up taller.

"We'll offer you a hundred..." Zeke sneezed.

"Dollars?" Tamara filled in the blank, intending to refuse.

"*Smackerels*," Zeke corrected.

"That's a big sum." Big E pretended smackerels were real currency. "Tamara would be a fool to pass up that offer. You should shake on the deal."

"Big E, we're going to regret this." Tamara gave the old man an exasperated look. But in the end, she shook each boy's hand.

"I'll handle Nathan. You handle Pest. We'll start now while Nathan is preoccupied." Big E led the boys downstairs, calling over his shoulder, "Put your riding gear on, Tamara."

This is a big mistake.

Not to say that Tamara wasn't eager to give Pest a try with proper riding gear.

And Big E did say he'd handle the heat.

Although she'd taken it the last time.

Tamara glanced out her tiny window. She liked this place. She loved Nathan. All that added up to *not* riding Pest.

But what if he's the key to overcoming my fears?

It was hope that had Tamara changing clothes.

After putting on her riding pants and boots, Tamara went downstairs, stopping to gather a bridle and saddle from the tack room, plus a lead rope, curry comb and hoof pick. Edie wasn't there to witness her actions. She was either upstairs napping or in the vegetable garden.

Several minutes later, Tamara reached the hay barn pasture, where Big E and the boys had Pest on a lead rope. Tamara rested the saddle and bridle on the top fence rail.

"You boys need to groom him." Tamara gave them the curry comb and hoof pick. "We can't train him if he doesn't want to be handled."

When Tamara entered the pasture, Big E said in a quiet voice, "That colt is one fine piece of horseflesh."

"That doesn't mean he can race." But Tamara hoped he could.

Hope was something they all needed.

NATHAN SAT IN the passenger seat of Dr. Julia Eisler's veterinary rig as she drove out to the brood mare pasture. "Thanks for coming out on short notice."

"I like getting out of the clinic." Julia drove with capable hands along the dirt road that circled the racetrack. "And besides, I haven't been out to check on Blackwell mares since a few weeks after they were bred."

"I was pleasantly surprised to discover you're our veterinarian of record." Nathan knew Julia from school, although she'd been a bit younger than him. "You always loved science."

"I loved healing people and animals." She spared

him a soft smile. "While you were the class protector."

"Was I?" He couldn't remember. And that bothered him. He should remember the things he could be proud of, like winning a showcase race or standing up for a friend.

Julia nodded. "You stood up for quiet, nerdy me more than once. That meant a lot. It gave me the confidence to…" She slowed as they approached the brood mare pasture. "This is going to sound sappy but you gave me the confidence to reach for my dreams."

Nathan scoffed. "I'm sure I wasn't the only one to believe in you."

"There were a few people." It sounded as if Julia added under her breath, "A very few." She brought her truck to a stop at the brood mare pasture and turned off the ignition, facing Nathan. "Never underestimate the power of a kind word or a protective gesture. It's true what they say. A little goes a long way."

Nathan was reminded of Tamara's determination to keep riding and pursuing her dreams. He should shift his strategy with Tamara to be one of support. That felt like something his mother and Marilee would approve of.

They got out and entered the pasture with the brood mares, most of which looked very pregnant. Julia carried her portable sonogram equipment. Nathan carried a clipboard with the names of each mare, which stud they'd been bred to and initial confirmation that they were pregnant.

Nathan went to work catching and leading mares to Julia to check. Most were very friendly, coming to him when they noticed the oat cube treats in his hand.

Rosey, a rotund roan, proved harder to win over. Nathan tossed her oat treats like breadcrumbs until he could get close enough to clip a lead rope to her halter. When he tried to lead her to Julia, the mare yanked her head back and dug in her hooves.

"What's wrong, girl?" Nathan stopped trying to move forward, choosing instead to give the mare some affection. He rubbed behind her ears and along the top of her mane. He whispered sweet nothings. "You don't trust me, do you?" Nathan whispered. "I don't think Tamara trusts me, either."

But just remembering how she'd looked at Rosehaven Downs, when he said he was learning to like her stubborn attitude, made him smile. Her gaze had gone soft and was welcoming. She'd stared at him as if her feelings were blossoming the same way his were—toward love.

That wasn't as scary to think about as it had been a week ago.

The mare curled back her lips and stuck her tongue out, sending a horrid stench toward Nathan.

"Whew. Your breath is rank, Rosey. I think we need a dental treatment over here, Julia."

The veterinarian came over. "Let's do the sonogram first." She conducted her exam, frowning as she faced Nathan. "Twins."

"That's not good." Twin births were high-risk for both the foals and the mare. Every horse lost wasn't just a tragedy; it impacted the bottom line.

"We could've protected Rosey and aborted one if we'd found out about this earlier." Julia ran her hand over the large swelling of Rosey's belly. "As large as she is, she should be larger to support those twins. That tooth problem probably keeps her from eating enough. Bring her over to the gate. I have what we need to fix that tooth. And then I think you should put Rosey in a stall for a few days, just to make sure she's eating enough calories."

It took another hour to lightly sedate Rosey, insert a dental speculum and file down the mare's jagged tooth. And when they were done with the exams, Nathan bid Julia farewell and walked the mare back to the stables.

THE RIDE ON Pest had been successful. The colt responded well to Tamara's commands.

Tamara and the boys were putting the saddle and bridle back in the tack room when they heard Nathan's voice.

"It's all right, girl," Nathan said.

Tamara and the twins looked at each other, guilt written all over their faces.

But then the twins grinned and darted out the tack room door. Tamara followed at a slower pace.

"That mare is preggers." Zeke skipped to meet Nathan in the filly barn, swinging both arms enthusiastically, even the one in the red cast.

"Super preggers," T.J. agreed, skipping after his brother.

Tamara might have skipped after them if she hadn't just ridden Pest around the pasture. Instead, she sucked up her guilt, walked up to Nathan and greeted the chubby roan. "What's she doing in here?"

Nathan explained about Rosey carrying twins and not gaining enough weight due to a snaggle tooth.

"Twins!" Zeke giggled. "Like us."

"Wouldn't it be great if we could each keep one?" T.J. piped up.

Without waiting for an answer, the twins pressed their ears to Rosey's bulging sides, as if they could hear the foals' heartbeats.

"Poor thing." Tamara scratched behind the roan's ears.

"Poor thing? I'm the poor thing." Nathan's smile invited Tamara to share the humor in the situation. "They want to keep two horses bred for racing."

"You mean horses like Pest?" Maybe Nathan was ready to see the light when it came to the two-year-old.

Nathan's smile fell. He looked away. "It always comes back to that, doesn't it?"

Tamara laid a hand on his arm. "Maybe because it should."

Nathan didn't look like he agreed. But he didn't reject the idea outright.

The dinner bell rang in the break room.

Tamara walked with Nathan to dinner, where Big E suspiciously praised Pest and the twins laughed each time like nobody's business.

Tamara kept her head down, afraid Nathan would realize something was up.

After dinner, the twins went inside the colt horse stables to shower in their apartment.

Tamara went to sit outside in the shade where she could see the hay barn pasture and Pest. She was liking the colt more and more. He was filling the hole left by Frosty. And she would have felt great, ready to ride for the roses on any horse, if not for the manner she'd gone about achieving this change inside.

I need to tell Nathan.

He appeared in front of her as if summoned by her thoughts. "I think I owe you an apology."

"You do?"

"Accidents happen in this business." Nathan stared at his clasped hands. "From what happened with Frostfire Wind to mares like Rosey carrying twins. I blamed you," Nathan said, quietly. "And I apologize for that."

Tamara felt cold. She'd waited a long time for him to say those words but now they were soured by her riding Pest behind his back. She rubbed her arms until the chill faded. "It's not cars we're racing. These animals have personalities. You were grieving." She placed her hand over his. "And you grieved alone."

"I was still grieving Marilee." Nathan seemed to stare at her hand on his. "I feel like I've been stuck in limbo for the past two years. All because of grief." He lifted his gaze to hers. "Grief is a mysterious thing."

"It's only mysterious if you don't talk about it." Tamara made to draw her hand back, but Nathan turned his hand over and held hers.

Tamara's pulse pounded erratically.

"I want to talk to you about my grief, Tamara. Because I feel a kinship with you. We were both alone during our childhood. And..." Nathan tipped his cowboy hat back. "I want to be on the same team."

Same team? No. I need to tell him that Big E and I went behind his back and rode Pest.

Guilt speared through Tamara. She didn't dare move for fear he'd realize what his touch meant to her. But she had to tell him about riding Pest today. She had to.

Only the words didn't come. Perhaps because she sensed he was opening up to her. And she craved that from him more than she'd ever craved double-chocolate fudge cake.

Nathan sat forward, leaning his elbows on his knees but keeping hold of her hand. "I was lost when Marilee died. It was just so...unexpected. And..."

He licked his lips. "I was angry. Angry at myself. Angry at the mare that struck her. Just…angry."

"Nothing felt right, I bet," Tamara said, softly. "Not the anger. Not the hole her death left in your heart."

"No." He blew out a breath. "It was the same anger that consumed me after Frostfire Wind died. But I had a person to blame, even if you were cleared by the racing commission. And for that, I'm sorry. I believed in you enough to approve you racing Frosty. You deserved my support."

He was saying all the right things. All the things she'd ever wanted him to say.

Well, maybe not all the things.

She waited to hear what he had to say next.

Nathan turned toward her, blue eyes filled with warmth.

Her heart pounded frantically in her chest.

"Tamara, do you think—"

"Dad!" T.J. came running around the corner. "Zeke is trying to take his cast off. He went looking for scissors."

"Duty calls." Nathan released Tamara's hand and got to his feet. But he hesitated, staring into her eyes. "Thanks for the talk."

"Anytime," Tamara murmured as he walked away.

Every time.

Until she told him the truth and he'd no longer seek her out.

CHAPTER SIXTEEN

"WE NEED TWO more jockeys for the showcase," Nathan told Asher and Big E at breakfast the next morning. The break room was empty except for the men. "We have Tamara, Frannie and Larry, Tamara's dad."

"How many horses do you have ready to race?" Big E asked. He'd been the one to call the meeting. He had a large mug of coffee in front of him that he seemed more interested in cradling than in drinking.

"Maybe twenty," Nathan estimated, sweeping a biscuit through the last of his gravy and thinking about Tamara. He'd apologized for being so hard on her after Frosty died. But he hadn't been able to remove his wedding ring.

"Can we get to twenty-five horses?" Asher pushed his plate away. "If we had five jockeys, that would give us five races for folks to observe. That's a full afternoon."

Nathan nodded. "I suppose we can put one of the five weakest horses in each race." Would Tamara be upset if he assigned her the weakest horses to ride in each race? He thought she would. But at least, she'd be safe.

"We'll need food and something special for each guest." As usual, Big E was decisive. "Something commemorative, like a travel mug."

"I'll authorize the money for catering." Asher sounded uptight. "But we don't need to provide guests with trinkets."

Nathan agreed. "I'm still afraid no one will come. We don't have a marquee race or featured horse to draw them in."

"You don't think folks will want to come to witness our downfall?" Asher looked grim. "Everybody likes to watch a dumpster fire."

"Especially when offered trinkets," Nathan quipped with a heavy dose of sarcasm.

Big E shifted in his seat, resting his forearms on the table and fixing Nathan with a determined stare. "We need a little optimism here. Why don't we run Pest in a race? Given his bloodlines, he could be a draw."

Nathan's gut clenched.

"I like this type of thinking." Asher sat up taller in his chair.

"I think it's enough that we have Tamara in the saddle for each race." Nathan was reaching for straws. But he kept reaching. "After that epic race on Saturday, folks will want to see her ride."

But not the nags in the stable.

Nathan hid a grimace.

There goes that idea.

"But Tamara could get a better job offer any day," Big E pointed out, much to Nathan's chagrin. "It's the horses folks need to see. Fast horses. Well-raced horses. Horses that make the crowd envious of our training."

"My horse, you mean," Nathan grumbled.

"Well..." Big E beamed. "Yeah."

Nathan pushed his chair back. "I need to get to work."

"Hold up." Big E planted a hand on Nathan's shoulder, as if wanting to keep him seated. "We have more to discuss."

"WHAT'S *HE* DOING HERE?" Edie confronted Tamara in the breezeway of the colt barn as Tamara led a saddled Pest toward the racetrack. "Isn't he supposed to be a pet?"

"Look at him, Edie." Tamara was tense. Big E was keeping Nathan occupied so she could exercise Pest but she didn't know how long Big E could keep Nathan busy. "Does he look like a pet to you?"

"No," Edie allowed, no less sourly. "Do you have Nathan's permission?"

"Big E's taking care of it." Tamara didn't have time for questions. She led Pest out of the horse barn, heart pounding in her chest.

There are so many ways this can go wrong.

Although Pest had accepted her control when she'd saddled him yesterday afternoon, who's to say how he'd react to her riding him around a racetrack. He could turn out to be as unruly and untrainable as Fire.

Owen led Frannie and her horse back toward the hot-walker. He stopped, staring at Tamara. "Oh, snap. Pest is on the training schedule?"

"No. He's not. But can you give me a leg up?" Tamara waited for the stable hand to give her a boost into the saddle while Pest very politely held still. "Thanks."

"So..." Owen glanced from Tamara to Pest. "If Nathan asks, Pest was never here?"

"If Nathan asks, don't lie." Tamara knew she was breaking Nathan's trust. But Big E had convinced her this was for the greater good of Blackwell Stables. And riding Pest was good for her. "Just...don't offer up the information."

Owen nodded, returning to Frannie and her mount.

"Okay, Pest." Tamara gave the colt a pat on the neck. "I hope you're as well-behaved as you were yesterday in the pasture." She gave him a bit of rein.

Pest started walking quickly, ears perked forward and head held high.

"You know something big is about to happen, don't you, fella?" Tamara could feel it, too. "You know, I'm commanding top dollar...er...*smackerels*...to train you. That means, you do what I say so that we're both safe."

They passed through the gate and onto the loamy soil of the track.

Pest danced sideways, lowering his head as if checking out what was beneath him.

"You'll like this track, buddy. It's softer than your pasture. Let's trot." Tamara gave him a little more slack on the reins while simultaneously giving his flanks a gentle kick. Pest eased into a smooth trot. Tamara began posting up and down. "You trot just like your brother." Frosty.

Just the thought of Frosty had her stomach tied in knots that hindered her breath.

It's all in my head.

"We can do him proud," Tamara continued babbling, trying to regulate her breathing as they trotted down the straightaway toward the first turn.

Pest's ears swiveled around toward her and then forward again.

"That's right. I'm here with you." She encouraged him into a lead change as they neared the turn. The colt executed her command flawlessly. "That's right. Left lead around this corner." Left leg first to give them a bit of momentum.

Without warning, Pest shook his head and tried to break stride, tried to move into a gallop.

Tamara held him back. "Not yet, fella. It's your first day on the track. Don't want to pull a muscle."

Pest tossed his head but settled back into a trot.

They rounded the turn without incident and headed across the back stretch. Tamara had planned to let Pest gallop down the home stretch but nerves took hold.

What if something happens to him?

She noticed Edie watching them from the entry gate. There'd be more questions than she'd like if she didn't let Pest run.

It's all in my head.

And suddenly, it was in her head. The mad dash to the finish line. The feeling of the world being swept out from under her. The pounding hooves, pelting of dirt, pain so sharp it sliced disbelief to shreds.

She gasped for air.

I can't do it.

They came around the turn. The long straightaway was empty before them.

Pest shook his head once more and leaped forward into a gallop.

Without thinking, Tamara rose to the martini position and let the colt do his thing.

His very fast thing.

He's just like Frosty.

And for that reason, Tamara didn't allow him full rein.

But she wondered what it would feel like to ride him in a race. And for the first time in a long time, she didn't shrink back at the thought.

"SEVENTEEN...EIGHTEEN...NINETEEN...TWENTY." Tamara finished counting Frannie's wall ball squats that afternoon. "Now squat down and hold it for two minutes."

Frannie grunted. She had a large inflatable ball between her and the wall. She lowered herself into a squat, holding her position with the ball at her back, saying in a strained voice, "How did you make this look so easy?"

"It's only easy after you've done it several times a week for a lot of years." Tamara glanced at the clock hanging in the small exercise room. "It could be worse. My dad used to blow me away on all the exercises. And he wasn't humble about it."

Frannie's face was turning bright red.

"Don't forget to breathe," Tamara reminded her.

The door to the exercise room opened and Nathan's twins rushed in.

"Can we ride the mechanical horse?" T.J. asked, although he didn't wait for permission before climbing on the life-size practice horse.

"Um…yes?" Tamara didn't think they'd get hurt on it or break it.

"I'm next." Zeke came to stand next to Tamara. "What's Frannie doing? She looks angry."

"I'm helping her become a licensed jockey."

Predictably, Zeke said, "I want to be a jockey. Can I go next?"

"You don't want to go next. It's torture, kid." Frannie gasped out the words. Then she glanced up at Tamara. "Time?"

"You have a minute and fifteen seconds to go."

Frannie groaned.

"I could do it." Zeke lowered himself in a squat. "I could do it easy."

"Okay, buddy." Tamara gave him an encouraging smile. "You hold that position until Frannie is done."

"Can do." But despite the determined expression on his face, Zeke was already rising out of his squat.

"My horse won't go," T.J. complained, shaking the reins on the mechanical horse.

"It's not electric. You have to make it go using momentum, like you would with a rocking horse." Tamara helped the boy stand in the stirrups and then guided him through the movements until he had it going.

"How. Much. Time?" Frannie ground out.

"Oops." Tamara glanced at the clock. "You're done."

"Woo-hoo!" Frannie slid to the floor, letting the large ball behind her bounce free. "My legs are done."

"That's okay. We're doing planks next." Tamara smiled.

"Ugh." Frannie flopped over sideways. "You're evil."

"Watch me, Tamara." Zeke put the inflatable ball behind him and scootched down a few inches. "I'm doing it."

"Great job, Zeke." Tamara helped Frannie to her

feet. "Come on, Frannie. We're almost done. Only planks are left. And then it'll be time for dinner."

"Promise me there'll be ice cream." Frannie pressed her hands into the small of her back. "I can hold a plank for two minutes if there's ice cream."

T.J. had lost all momentum on the mechanical horse. "It's broken, Tamara." He hopped off, looking disappointed.

Immediately, Zeke stood, letting the exercise ball bounce away. He hurried to get on, struggling a bit because of the injury to his right wrist. "Tamara, help me get started."

"Okay, but then you've got to ride on your own, the same way T.J. did." Tamara provided the leverage to get the horse moving.

"Tamara, am I doing this right?" T.J. was trying to squat with the inflatable ball at his back, but it squirted out one side.

"This is a sign," Frannie said, sprawling on a yoga mat on the floor. "And the sign says our workout is over."

"But we just got here." Zeke didn't have enough strength to keep the horse going. "Tamara, help me. I can't do it."

T.J. wrestled the ball around his backside. "Tamara, I can't do it."

"Tamara, I can't do it," Frannie echoed, chuckling.

"All right. Workout over. Everyone out." Tamara

opened the workout room door but quickly pivoted away and screamed.

"What is it?" Frannie staggered to her feet. "Does this mean we don't get ice cream later?"

"Mouse!" Tamara pointed at a dead mouse in the breezeway.

Edie hustled over from a stall down the way. "I told you Luna would bring you mice if she liked you."

The twins came out and knelt on either side of the rodent.

"I think Luna brought him to us," T.J. said. "We always pet her."

"Yeah." Zeke nodded. "I gave her a piece of my tuna fish sandwich at lunchtime."

"Ew. It's all yours." Tamara backed away, letting Edie scoop the mouse up with a dust pan. "I won't fight you boys on this one."

"It's okay." Frannie gave Tamara a side hug. "But now you really need an ice cream."

"WHAT'S GOTTEN INTO PEST? Why isn't he at the gate?" Nathan asked his boys, having found them outside the hay barn pasture gate. "Park that question for a minute. Where'd you get those toys?"

They were playing in the dirt with yellow metal dump trucks, excavators and tractors. Toys Nathan remembered playing with as a kid.

Those were the days.

He smiled.

"Uncle Asher said he found them in the garage at his house." T.J. filled the dump truck with dirt from the excavator bucket.

Zeke was making engine noises, rolling a tractor up a dirt hill.

Nathan picked up an unused dump truck. "This reminds me of the summer of road construction. My brothers and I built a road system all around this pasture. It took us a week." They'd had so much fun. Working together. Arguing with each other. Laughing until they thought they'd bust a gut.

"Uncle Asher said he was going to fix the floor in the tree house and build us a window." T.J. finished filling his dump truck. "Maybe this can be the September of the tree house."

"The fall of the big fix." Zeke sent his tractor zooming down their dirt hill.

"Thirty days of healing," Nathan murmured.

The boys were having a good time. Nathan's gaze sought out Pest. Surprisingly, he stood beneath a cottonwood. He was usually incredibly social and affectionate.

Zeke pushed the tractor up and over his dirt hill, laughing when it crashed, falling over sideways. "Dad, can we keep Tamara?"

"What?" Nathan felt as if he'd had the wind knocked out of him.

"She's part of the family," T.J. said matter-of-factly. "Just like Edie, Frannie and Owen."

"Our work family," Nathan qualified.

"She's good with Pest." Zeke rolled the tractor easily end over end. "She's a good jockey."

"The best jockey," T.J. qualified.

"That's high praise." Especially from Zeke.

"You like her, too, don't you, Dad?" T.J. stared up at him. "You held her hand at the races."

That caught Zeke's attention. He looked up at Nathan. "Did you?"

"Yes. I like Tamara, too," Nathan confirmed. Out loud.

And inside, something shifted in his heart, falling into place and making him feel…

Like things were looking up.

NATHAN FOUND TAMARA on the viewing platform before dinner where she'd been doing something she hadn't done in months—taking a mental turn around the track.

Nathan leaned on the railing next to her. "Penny for your thoughts."

"I'm just imagining racing around this track." And for the first time in a long time, she didn't feel panic rising inside while doing so. Was this the Pest effect?

"Were you imagining winning?" Nathan smiled softly.

"I hadn't quite gotten that far." Tamara pointed directly across from them. "I was on the back stretch." She allowed herself a small smile. "I'm boxed in at the rail and when I see a small opening ahead, I know I need to urge my horse faster."

"Using your whip?" His question surprised her.

"A good jockey knows how to encourage a horse, with or without a whip." She hadn't completely beat her hang-ups.

"You still don't want to use yours, though." Nathan was no longer smiling.

"Just because I have a mental block doesn't mean I won't overcome it eventually." That was a bold statement. One Tamara hoped she could back up with action. "Did you come to find me because it's dinnertime?"

"No." He hesitated before saying simply, "I came to tell you that I'm falling for you, Tamara."

Yes!

A smile split her cheeks in a millisecond. But then she noticed Nathan was still wearing his wedding ring. Her smile fell. "Why are you telling me this?"

"I thought that after our kiss—" he resettled his straw cowboy hat on his head "—I should tell you how I feel."

Pride bristled along her spine. "You feel the need to protect me."

"Well…yes. Because I care for you."

"I don't want to be another burden you need to carry."

"You're not a burden." Nathan tried to tuck another lock of hair behind her ear.

Tamara took a step back. "And yet, you still aren't ready to move things forward with me. You might never be ready. We need to be honest with each other. No more leaving things unsaid."

"Just because I have a mental block doesn't mean I won't overcome it," Nathan parroted her words back at her, without sarcasm or malice. "I thought you'd want to know the state of things."

"I do. But not enough has changed, has it? You still see yourself as married. I don't want you to feel guilty about having feelings for me." Just like she didn't want to feel guilty about the joy she got from riding Pest, albeit behind his back.

But instead of opening that can of worms, Tamara left Nathan on the viewing platform and went in search of ice cream.

Tonight, dessert came first.

CHAPTER SEVENTEEN

PEST WAS A dream ride.

Tamara knew it. And everyone else did, too. Everyone came out to watch her ride him around the track. Everyone but Nathan and the twins, that is. She always put the colt through his paces when Nathan was driving the kids to school.

This morning, a sunny day, was the first time they were practicing coming out of the starting gate. There was an old starting gate in the covered arena. But first, Tamara led Pest and Blaze around the large contraption, which had all the gates open, letting Pest learn that it wasn't a threat.

"Keep going for another few laps," Edie told her. "Until he starts to plod."

"Pest doesn't plod," Tamara replied.

The colt was always alert and curious. On the other hand, Blaze, Nathan's chestnut quarter horse and Pest's stable mate, was already plodding and bored with the process.

Asher strode over to the gate in his fancy duds. No worn blue jeans or checked button-downs for the oldest Blackwell. He wore slate-gray jeans and a bright blue polo shirt. His shiny new cowboy boots kicked up dirt. "I'll walk in and out of the gate while you do laps."

"Frannie, go get Slugger," Edie directed. "Don't saddle him. Just put a lead rope on his halter."

Frannie didn't budge. "Why?"

Edie frowned, putting a hand on one slim hip. "Because Slugger is used to the gate and I think it'd help to have an example for Pest to see. Now go." She made a shooing motion with her hand.

"Hang on. I think we should saddle Slugger." Big E jumped into the fray. "Might just as well have a rider on him. The closer to reality for Pest, the better."

"Yes. Yes. All right." Edie turned to Owen. "Go with Frannie and help her saddle Slugger."

"I don't need help saddling him," Frannie said, nose bent out of shape.

Edie scoffed. "Height-challenged jockeys always need help saddling tall thoroughbreds. Hurry up."

The pair left the building. But not before Frannie could be heard telling Owen, "I can saddle a horse."

"I don't know many horses that get trained by committee," Tamara said, half under her breath. She still led the two horses around the starting gate.

Asher heard her as she walked past him. He chuckled. "Maybe that's what we need more of around here. Management by committee."

"At some point, someone's going to have to tell Nathan what we're doing." Tamara felt incredibly guilty about going behind his back. But there was just something about Pest that made her feel more like herself. More confident in her riding abilities. "And that someone was supposed to be Big E."

"We'll tell him today," Big E promised.

"We?" Tamara continued getting her steps in around the starting gate with the horses until Frannie and Owen returned with Slugger.

"Move Pest back," Edie directed. "Let him watch Slugger enter the gate."

"First, let's open the doors and ring the starting bell," Asher suggested. "Keep Pest a good thirty feet away so he knows what to expect. Then we can put Slugger in there and let Pest try."

"But only if the horses remain calm." Big E leaned against the arena wall.

"Everybody's got their two cents in," Tamara said to no one in particular as she led Pest and Blaze to a spot thirty feet in front of the starting gate.

Asher banged the doors open and closed, over and over.

Pest took a step back, staring at the gate. But he didn't look rattled. Just curious.

Then Asher rang the starting bell.

Pest nickered and crowded Tamara, watching the starting gate suspiciously.

"Good boy." Tamara stroked his neck. "You're going to be fine."

Asher repeated operating the gates and ringing the bell until even Pest was bored with it.

“Frannie, walk Slugger through the gate a few times,” Edie commanded. “We’ve got to get back to our regular schedule soon.”

Pest watched intently as the other colt interacted with the gate.

“I think it’s your turn,” Big E told Tamara, nodding toward the gate.

Tamara handed the older man Blaze’s lead rope. Then she unclipped Pest’s lead rope and asked Big E for a boost into the saddle. Pest turned his head to look at her. “It’s time, fella.”

She rode him to the starting gate. And then she rode him through the starting gate several times before Asher closed the gate in front of him.

Pest tried to back out but Tamara held him steady until Asher opened the front gate and they walked through. Things were going well.

“This is taking longer than I thought it would.” Edie checked her phone. “We need to move along before Nathan gets back.”

“Too late,” came a voice from the door.

Everyone turned.

Tamara’s heart dropped to her toes.

It was Nathan. And he wasn’t happy.

“SOMEBODY EXPLAIN TO me what’s going on.” Nathan was determined not to shout. But the fact that his family and his employees were all involved in training Pest behind his back had anger burning through his gut. "Now."

Everyone began talking at once. Everyone but Tamara.

She rode Pest over to Nathan and hopped off, looking all business in her riding clothes, safety vest and helmet. But what she'd done wasn't professional. "The twins hired me to train Pest."

That shut everyone else up.

"The twins?" Nathan scoffed. "How are they paying you? With frogs?"

"They promised me one hundred *smackerels*." Tamara made that announcement with a straight face.

Nathan knocked his cowboy hat back and rolled his eyes. "You had no right to—"

"Blame me." Big E still held Blaze's reins. "The twins told me what they wanted to do and I encouraged Tamara to go along with it. We treated him like fine, breakable china and—"

"You lied," Nathan groused, staring at Tamara.

"—and Tamara only rode him in the pasture at first."

"You've run him on the track?" Air burned Nathan's lungs the same way he'd been burned by his family, making it hard to breathe. Toxic to breathe.

"We've all been making sure Pest is safe." Asher walked over to stand near Nathan. "We know how important Pest is to you. But he's a natural."

"A fast natural," Big E added, smiling as if Nathan should be happy about it.

Edie, Owen and Frannie took Slugger out a side door.

"How long has this been going on?" Nathan demanded, almost breathless.

"This is only the second day," Tamara said softly, regret in her dark eyes.

"The second day?" Nathan worked even harder to keep from raising his voice. "You rode him yesterday? Before we talked at the track?"

Before I told you I was falling for you?

Feeling a fool, Nathan grabbed Pest's and Blaze's reins. "How dumb am I? I should pack up and head home."

"Now, Nathan," Big E began.

"No." Tamara finally found her voice. "He's got every right to be angry. We went behind his back to train a horse he wants to protect."

"I wish you wanted to protect our legacy as much as you do this horse." Asher shook his head.

"He has priorities." Again, Tamara stepped in for Nathan. "He's lost so much. You can't expect him to risk what's most dear to him. I've got to move on to other horses." With a nod to Nathan, she walked out.

"I'm sorry, brother." Asher scratched Pest beneath his headstall. "I thought Pest would be a great addition to the showcase."

"I'm sorry, too." Big E laid a hand on Nathan's

shoulder. "I thought showing you how much potential that colt has would lift your spirits."

"And give you something to be excited about," Asher added. "You just exist, going through the motions."

"How do you know?" Nathan's mind spun at dizzying speed. Off-kilter from the combination of hard truth, spiked betrayal and ice-cold anger. "How do you know I'm just going through the motions?"

"Because that was me before I came here, stuck in limbo and missing out on life." Asher stopped petting Pest and moved to hug Nathan. "I want you to be happy. I'm sorry if this wasn't a good surprise. I love you, brother."

"I love you, too," Nathan parroted back. But his tone didn't convince anyone, including himself.

"TAMARA, I NEED to see you in my office before your next ride." Nathan didn't even look at Tamara as he strode past, entering his office and shutting the door with a resounding thud.

As if he doesn't really want me to talk to him.

Since Tamara knew she was in the wrong with Pest, she handed Edie the reins to a very tall, strawberry roan filly named Copper Mercury and entered Nathan's office, fully expecting to be fired.

Nathan sat behind his desk, holding himself very still. That creaky chair of his made no sound.

Tamara eased into one of the tall wooden chairs

that had once belonged to a dining room set. "I knew better than to do what I did. And I could have told you any number of times. I'm sorry that I caved to peer pressure but—"

"I don't want to talk about that."

"But you should. You should tell me off or fire me or curse me five ways from Sunday." Tamara didn't really want him to do any of those things. But his tense stoicism didn't feel right, either.

"We're having five races in the showcase," Nathan continued as if she hadn't spoken. "I need to hire two more jockeys. I need names of jockeys you trust and I need you to help me convince them to ride for us."

"I… Um…" She wanted to tell Nathan about her progress toward conquering her fears, as well as what a joy it was to ride Pest. But now didn't feel like the time. The air vibrated with his anger and upset.

"Kelley's going to cater. Big E and Asher are doing meet and greets. But there will be no showcase if we can't find riders."

"Right. I'll get on that as soon as I'm done with training this morning."

"I'd appreciate it." Nathan propped his elbows on his desk and held his phone practically in front of his face. "You're dismissed."

Tamara didn't budge. "I'm sorry. I—"

"Stop." The phone came crashing down on the desk. "Do you know what it feels like to be played for a fool? To be told you're needed but then be cut out of the loop? To be cast aside as if you're nothing to anyone?"

"No. No. And yes." Tamara got to her feet, spine straightened by anger. "You can yell, moan and gripe at us for twenty-four hours, Nathan. But then, you need to forgive and move on. We've all apologized. We all feel bad. We all thought you'd come around to realize Pest was born to this."

Nathan's expression was closed for business. He'd need more than twenty-four hours to get over this.

As was his right.

But that didn't stop Tamara from trying to broker peace. She pointed at the door she'd come through. "Those people out there love you. Your kids love you. And I..." *Don't go there. That boat has sailed.* She licked her lips. "We all did what we thought was right for Pest and Blackwell Stables. And yes, we went behind your back because..." Tamara drew a ragged breath. "We all agree that you've put blinders on and can't see what a rut you're in."

"I can see just fine," Nathan said stubbornly. "I can even see the knife that's in my back."

He was exasperating, more so because he was right. But Tamara couldn't seem to stop. "You can't see that you limit your world to a teeny tiny corner you believe you can control. But life can't be dictated to. Things happen. Good and bad. And we deal with it."

"I'm not dealing. I'm leaving," he said in a cool voice fractured with hurt.

“Today?” Tamara took another step back.

“No. Not today. I volunteered for something at the kids’ school tonight.” He sounded like he didn’t want to fulfill that commitment. “Tomorrow. We’re leaving first thing tomorrow.”

“But…” *What about me?* “What about Big E and Asher? What about finding the people who doped Pride? What about saving the farm and putting on the showcase?”

“Why should I be a team player?” Nathan gave her an icy look. “Everyone here overlooked what I wanted.”

“You mean…” Tamara leaned forward and lowered her voice. “No, Nathan. You may be stubborn. But you aren’t unwanted.”

His expression broke, only for a moment. But long enough for Tamara to know her words struck home.

He knows we care.

And then his gaze fell to the phone on the desk.

“No one did this out of spite, Nathan.” Tamara softened her words by reaching across the desk to cover his hand with hers.

He didn’t move. Didn’t raise his head. “I need you to go. Now.”

So she did.

“YOU.” NATHAN STOPPED at the refreshment table at Back to School Night and scowled at Patrick Connelly. “What are you doing here?”

What else can go wrong today?

Patrick scowled right back at Nathan. "I got sucked into this the same as you did. By Talia. She's my girlfriend."

Nathan glanced around the auditorium, looking for an out. The place was empty except for adults manning different tables spread around the perimeter. After the day he'd had, Nathan didn't think he could play nice with a family enemy.

"Don't even think about wandering off," Patrick told him. "I know you'd like nothing better than to disappear like you did after high school graduation but that will only annoy Talia. I can't let you do that."

You can't let me leave?

The man bothered Nathan on too many levels. But he came around to the back side of the table, which was filled with paper cups containing red punch and cupcakes provided by Kelley.

"Your boys are in the same class as Talia's Carlton." Patrick smelled of alcohol and bitterness. "Just like old times. Blackwells and Connellys mixing it up together."

Nathan made a mental note to pay more attention to Zeke's complaints about Carlton. "Are you and Talia engaged? You make it sound like you're going to adopt Carlton."

"Talia and I live together. I'm raising Carlton like a Connelly. He's with us all but two weekends a month." Patrick swayed a bit before catching himself on the table. That's when Nathan noticed his eyes were bloodshot.

I wonder how Talia will react to him being drunk at a school event.

Nathan smiled, imagining the fallout with the stalwart Talia. That was worth staying for. "I saw your horse race with Tamara in the saddle."

"Your little jockey surprised me with a win."

Tamara had surprised Nathan, too. With her betrayal with Pest.

That hurt. It cut deep.

"We have a lot of promising two-year-olds," Patrick continued. "From what Tamara said, you have a decent colt, too."

Nathan nodded, content to let Patrick ramble until parents started rolling in.

If only parents would start rolling in now.

"I hear you've got a showcase planned." Patrick's throaty laughter filled the air. "I wouldn't expect too many attendees. I mean, why bother coming to a losing stable? Waste. Of. Time."

Nathan's hands fisted. He needed an outlet for all his frustration.

A woman entered the auditorium. A smiling woman with light brown hair. She reminded him of his mother. Always cheerful. Always rolling with whatever life threw her way.

And suddenly, Nathan was flooded with childhood memories of his mother. Mom coming to sixth grade choir practice with Dad lugging juice and snacks. Mom laughing with Dad at the school ice cream social. Mom and Dad consoling him after a baseball game loss. They were good memories, the kind Asher said he'd find by coming home. But they were also a warning. A warning of how sour Nathan could be in his grief if he followed in his father's misguided footsteps. Something he didn't want to do.

"Waste of time," Patrick repeated, bringing Nathan back to the present.

He's trying to get a rise out of me.

Nathan stared at the round clock on the far wall. The time was going far too slowly. Then he remembered something Big E had referenced. "You were friends with Elliot James." The man caught with the drugs that had doped Pride.

Patrick stared at Nathan as if he'd lost his train of thought.

What's the harm in asking Patrick to admit his guilt?

Nathan pinned Patrick with a hard stare. "Did you pay Elliot to drug our horse?"

"Did I…did I what?" Patrick took a cup of punch and drained it, looking a bit more clear-eyed. "You can't blame me for your bad luck."

"That's not an answer."

"I bet you never find out why Elliot did it." Patrick smiled, taking another cup of punch. "It'll go down in history as one of those unsolved conspiracy theories." He slurped down the drink. Again, looking a bit more sober afterward. Then he smiled snidely at Nathan. "Right now, I bet you're wishing you had something on me… Some type of leverage that would make me admit I was involved."

"Were you involved?"

Patrick waved his question aside. "I think we should race."

"Race what?" Nathan pretended to misunderstand the challenge. "Cars? For pink slips?"

"No." Patrick's laughter grated. "*Horses.*"

"Perhaps you've forgotten that Blackwell Stables is under a ban."

Again, Patrick waved Nathan's comment aside. "We could race at your showcase. That's not a sanctioned event." His smile curled into something unpleasant. "And since you mentioned racing for possession, let's make it a grudge match. I'll race Red Sunset, the two-year-old that Tamara won on, against your two-year-old."

"Tempest Wind?" Everything inside of Nathan went cold. "Not a chance." If his colt fell into the hands of the enemy, he didn't know what he'd do.

"Have it your way." Patrick shrugged. "Once a chicken, always a chicken."

A feral noise escaped Nathan's throat. "And once a thieving fox, always a thieving fox. Why would I race a horse doper? You don't play fair."

"*You don't play fair.*" Patrick's tone begged for Nathan's fist to be put into action. "That's what you said when we were kids. But listen…" Patrick lowered his voice. "As the story goes, your old man built Blackwell Stables by winning a grudge match. If you win, you could be the next Blackwell hero."

And if I lose, I'll remain the family loser. An unwanted man.

"I don't care about being a hero," Nathan said, jaw clenched.

"Good." Patrick reached for another glass of punch. "Then you'll have no problem taking this bet."

CHAPTER EIGHTEEN

"WHAT'S THIS MEETING FOR?" Frannie whispered to Tamara in the break room the next morning. They sat at a table waiting for the rest of the staff to gather.

Tamara shrugged, although she was tense, afraid that Nathan was going to fire them all for training Pest behind his back.

"Probably announcing the place has been sold and we're all out of jobs," Edie said from the other side of Tamara. "All good runs have to end."

Nathan was standing and talking quietly to Asher near the sink.

Owen darted in, claiming a seat next to Frannie. "What did I miss?"

"Nothing." Edie crossed her arms over her chest. "But it isn't looking good. Just take a gander at Asher's expression. It's like someone's died."

Big E strode in, surveyed the table where the staff sat and then took stock of the Blackwell brothers huddled together and whispering. He came over to sit next to Edie. "Why all the long faces?"

"We're getting sacked," Edie told him.

"Nobody's getting let go," Asher said in a loud voice. "At least, not in the immediate future."

Tamara breathed a sigh of relief.

Asher moved to sit at the other table. "Nathan, you tell them."

"First off, I want to apologize for what happened yesterday when I found you training Pest." Nathan rubbed a hand around the back of his neck, still looking as if someone had died. "As most of you know, I've had a hard time getting over Marilee's death. And Frosty's. And because of that, I admit I have tunnel vision when it comes to Pest."

"That's very good of you to admit," Big E said.

"I don't always make the right choice," Nathan went on. "And I understand why you all were training Pest. You had my best interests at heart."

Tamara nodded.

"But that's not all. I...did a thing last night." Nathan stuck his hands in his front jeans pockets, looking humbled. "Something I'm not proud of. I agreed to a grudge race with Patrick Connelly. A race to be held at our showcase."

Big E frowned. "Don't grudge races mean the winner takes ownership of the loser's horse?"

Nathan nodded, looking even more uncomfortable. "But I have full confidence in the horse we're racing." His sorrowful gaze found Tamara's. "And our jockey."

And then Tamara knew.

No. Oh, no.

The fight drained out of Tamara.

I wanted to race Pest but not with these stakes.

"Which horse?" Edie demanded, uncrossing her arms and leaning forward, not having caught on.

"The grudge match will attract more attention for the showcase." Nathan ignored Edie. "And that's what we need to reassure horse owners that we're still an elite training facility."

"Which horse?" Edie demanded again.

"Pest," Tamara whispered.

"Yes." Nathan nodded. "Patrick is running his two-year-old, Red Sunset, against our Pest."

"Didn't you win a race last weekend on Red Sunset?" Big E asked Tamara.

She nodded.

"How do the two stack up?" Asher asked.

"There's no comparison experience-wise," Tamara said in a voice thick with emotion. "Patrick's horse has been racing all year. Pest hasn't raced once. He hasn't even exited the starting gate like he would in a race."

"We have two weeks," Nathan said firmly. "You were all working with him. We can all work together."

"What are you going to tell the twins?" Tamara choked out.

"I'm not going to tell them anything unless I have to." Nathan scuffed his boot on the floor. "I'm relying on you to help me…to help Pest win this race."

The room fell silent.

Tamara kept thinking about how much Zeke and T.J. loved Pest. If the colt didn't win, they'd be devastated.

And it'll be my fault.

All the progress she'd made these past few days… She felt as if she was sliding down a steep hill.

"Tamara, I'd like you to ride Pest in the race," Nathan said, quietly. "We all would."

Everyone in the room agreed.

"Uh…" She was just beginning to regain her confidence in the saddle. And she knew without a doubt that the pressure to win on Pest was going to put cracks in her progress. Maybe even set her back. But she said, "Of course. But that means he needs extra training."

The group spent the next few minutes figuring that out.

Presumably, no one noticed when she slipped out and went upstairs, where she was sick in her toilet. Because according to Zeke, it was against the rules to get sick most anywhere else.

"ARE YOU GOING to be all right?" Nathan asked Tamara as they walked to the hay barn pasture to retrieve Pest and get his training started an hour later.

"I'll be fine." Tamara didn't smile or reassure him in any way.

"I want you to be open with me about your fears. I don't want you riding if you can't ride to win."

"I think I've proven I can win in my current state."

Oh, she was testy.

Nathan cleared his throat. "But there's more at stake here."

"You think I don't know that?" Tamara stopped in the shade cast by the hay barn. "Why did you do it? Why did you let Patrick goad you into a grudge race where the prize is the one horse you've said you couldn't lose?"

Hot shame made him fidgety. "Because… Patrick was just so cocky that I lost all perspective. He always knew how to push my buttons."

"Pride go-eth before the fall."

Nathan reached for Tamara's hand, holding it tenderly, speaking tenderly. "I thought you wanted Pest to race."

"I do." There were tears filling her dark eyes. "But I don't want you to lose Pest. Patrick's horse is experienced. It doesn't matter how fast Pest is. The odds are against us."

"But we all know that Pest loves to run. And when he wins—*when*, not *if*—the Blackwell Stables will be in a better position to survive." Nathan stared toward the pasture where Pest grazed. "I've been thinking about my mother a lot lately and all the sacrifices she made to help my father be successful here."

"Such as…"

"When I was about Zeke and T.J.'s age, Mom sold her miniature horses to help Dad raise capital to invest in a retired stud. She loved those tiny horses." He captured her gaze. "But she loved my father more."

She bit her lip, eyes still teary. "We're talking about a child's horse here. They won't understand if he's taken away."

"I understand what you're saying but I'm being pulled in so many different directions, from Asher wanting me to stay permanently, to you wanting me to come to terms with Marilee being gone, to the betrayal with Pest."

"What do you want to do?" Tamara moved closer, dropping her voice to an intimate level. "There's still time to back out of the race."

"I want…" Nathan smiled wryly, shaking his head. "I want the nice life a good pair of socks promises. No bumps in the road. No blisters on my toes." He stared deeply into Tamara's eyes. "I want happiness and love. But that comes with a high level of trust. The kind of trust that gets a family through the tough stuff." And then Nathan drew her into his arms.

But he didn't kiss her. He just held her close and wished the good things in life were guaranteed.

TRAINING BEGAN IN earnest for Pest.

Within a few days, he was comfortable breaking out of the starting gate. Within a week, he was showing more endurance around the track. But his times were still of the also-ran quality. Tamara had yet to ride him hard, as if they were in a real race. Time was running out.

Every day brought Tamara closer to the showcase and race day. She refused weekend rides from the Connellys and the Richmonds, thinking it would only make her more nervous about the grudge race. But she was nervous.

"I'm so excited that Pest is finally going to race," T.J. said on the last weekend before the showcase. The twins were in Tamara's room eating double-chocolate fudge cake.

"I only wish I could ride him." Zeke fixed Tamara with an assessing stare. "But I guess if someone is going to ride him, it should be you, Tamara."

"You feed a boy enough cake, and he's going to love you someday," Tamara gently teased. "Isn't that right, Zeke?"

"That's not it. Seeing you ride Pest is almost like watching you ride Frosty." Zeke's eyes teared up. "Dad always says I should learn from my mistakes. And I think you've learned from yours, Tamara."

Tamara nodded, throat thick with all sorts of emotions. Awe, regret, guilt and love.

There was a knock on her door.

"I'll get it." T.J. opened the door. "Who are you?"

"I'm Tamara's dad." Her father entered, looking around Tamara's studio apartment as if measuring it against the one he resided in over at Richmond Stables. He was wearing his nicest cowboy attire—pressed shirt, pressed jeans, a black cowboy hat like Big E's.

Tamara introduced the twins, then asked, "You never come to visit. What's up?"

"With this grudge match coming up, I felt the need to check on you." Dad gave her a hug.

"I'm fine."

"Ready to race?" Dad asked.

"Ready to win," Zeke said with complete confidence.

She ruffled the boy's brown hair, grateful for his moral support.

"No pressure. Right, Tammie?" Dad's gaze searched for any weakness in Tamara's demeanor. "It's okay if you're nervous about the race. It's high stakes for all parties involved."

"We have more to lose," Tamara said softly, thinking of the twins.

Something scratched at the door.

T.J. opened it, revealing the gray barn cat. It had something in its jaws. "Luna, you aren't supposed to bring us dead things. Take that to Edie."

"What is it?" Zeke rushed over to the door, dropping to his knees. "That's not a mouse. That's a kitten!" Very gently, he removed the small gray bundle of fluff from Luna's mouth. "I call dibs."

T.J. gasped, joining Zeke on the floor. "Luna, go back and bring me a kitty."

The cat trotted off.

"Why don't you boys follow Luna? Maybe she'll lead you to other kittens." That would give Tamara and her father some privacy. Dad didn't realize the twins hadn't been told their beloved horse was on the line.

The boys didn't need to be asked twice. The twins rushed downstairs to look for Luna.

Tamara shut her apartment door and faced her father. "Who has Patrick hired to ride Red Sunset? No one here has heard."

"Me," Dad said, sheepishly. "Don't hate me. I need the money for something special."

"Oh, Patrick is evil, pitting father versus daughter." Tamara paced the room, a shiver running down her spine. "This is the real reason you came over. To warn me?"

Dad nodded. "I can't take it easy on you. I was offered a significant bonus for winning. And if I win, I'm going to propose to my girlfriend."

Dad has a love interest?

Tamara put that piece of information aside for a moment. "Dad, if you win, those little boys are going to lose their favorite pet. It'll break their hearts."

Her father scoffed. "They're kids. They'll bounce back. Look at how you became resilient when faced with challenges."

Tamara rubbed her arms, trying to ward off the chill. "Dad… I don't want to ride against you."

"You don't want to race against me?" Dad peered at her. "Or you don't want to race? How are you? In here." He tapped his temple.

He may have been her father, but Tamara wasn't going to share her reservations, not now that she knew he was racing against her. "I'll walk you out."

"But… I just got here and I see you have double-chocolate fudge cake." He gave her a winning smile.

"I can't give you cake, Dad." Tamara's smile felt jagged. "I wouldn't want to sabotage your ability to pass the weigh in. I know you always watch your weight before a big race."

"No cake?" Dad staggered back as if struck. "I didn't raise you to be cruel."

"But you did raise me, Dad. And for that, I'm thankful." Tamara led him out of her room, searching for an innocuous topic of conversation. "How do the Blackwell staff quarters compare to Richmond's?"

"Yours are better. Hands down. Caroline has us in tiny rooms that feel more like jail cells." Dad cleared his throat. "You didn't say anything about me preparing to walk down the aisle again."

"I wish you well, Dad. You know that." Tamara bit her lip as she reached the bottom of the stairs, turning to hug her father. "But this race is really important to me, too."

Dad looked suitably chastised. But he didn't offer to back out.

They walked into the filly barn breezeway. The twins had found Luna's kittens in Dandy's old stall. After admiring them, Tamara walked her father out into the sunshine and toward the parking lot.

But she still felt cold.

CHAPTER NINETEEN

THE SUNDAY BEFORE the showcase, they arranged a race between Pest and Slugger. It was the last day they could run Pest full tilt before Friday's showcase.

"I'm nervous," Frannie admitted while they waited for the horses to be brought around to the track gate.

"It's just another ride. Only this time, we'll begin from the starting gate." Tamara fought to project calm. But she was nervous, too. Her father would take advantage of any mistake, any weakness Tamara made on race day.

"Am I supposed to ride to win?" Frannie tucked her short blond hair behind her ears. "Or should I tail Pest?"

"Slugger always runs to win, at least until he runs out of gas." Tamara managed a chuckle. "Pest needs to realize he won't be running alone."

No one knew how he'd react to the challenge of a horse running with him. A lot of horses acted oddly when presented with competition—jagging to the outside rail, refusing to contest for the lead, slowing when they caught sight of a horse behind them instead of speeding up. Horse racing wasn't a science.

Deep breaths. You can only react to what he does.

"Okay." Frannie flashed Tamara a smile. "Game on. Just try and beat me."

"I'll do my best." For Nathan and the twins. For herself and Frosty.

Edie approached them on horseback, leading a saddled Slugger. "He's so ready that he can't get to the track fast enough. He keeps trotting ahead of me."

As if to prove Edie's point, Slugger trotted forward to greet the two jockeys. Then he stopped, turning so his side faced them.

"He wants you to get on, Frannie." Tamara took Frannie's left ankle and boosted her into the saddle.

Without another word, Edie led Slugger onto the track.

Nathan rode up on Blaze while leading Pest, who greeted Tamara with a gentle head butt. Nathan's gaze asked Tamara a silent question—*Are you ready?*—and she gave him a silent answer: *As ready as I'll ever be.*

"I feel like this is a rocket launch," Nathan admitted as Owen joined them, offering Tamara a leg up in the saddle. "And there's one bit of math we haven't worked out."

"You watch too many movies." Tamara gathered

Pest's reins, then stroked his long, gray neck. "We'll be fine. We've taught him everything he needs to know about a race, except how to fight for first." And that, usually, only came from experience.

Nathan blew out a breath. "I hope he has the will to win. If he doesn't—"

"Don't go there," Tamara cut him off, waving to the twins, who were going to watch on the viewing platform.

"Right." Nathan tipped his cowboy hat to his kids. "Let's get Pest warmed up." He cued Blaze into a trot, leading Pest along with him.

They spent the next five minutes trotting back and forth on the straightaway, before moving into a slow gallop.

Tamara patted Pest's shoulder. "He's moving smoothly and he feels warm."

"Let's get him in the gate." Nathan headed toward the starting gate, which Asher had brought out using a tractor. The same tractor he'd use to move it out of the way once the race began.

Frannie and Slugger were entering the second gate, guided by Owen. Slugger was an old pro at racing, having competed all year. He stood quietly in the gate, looking calm compared to Frannie, whose face was pinched in concentration. Owen stood on the side ledge inside the gate talking quietly, although Tamara couldn't tell if he was speaking to Frannie or Slugger.

Asher shut the gate behind Slugger, then turned to Tamara.

"I think Pest should be in the third gate." Edie pointed toward the third position. She came over to guide Pest into the gate. "He needs to get used to horses alongside him."

Nathan unclipped the lead rope on Pest and rode Blaze off the track.

"Aren't you a pretty boy?" Edie crooned, leading Pest into the gate. "And a good boy, too." She climbed onto the ledge, then glanced at Tamara. "Do you think he's too calm?"

Pest shook his head the way he did before he poured on the speed.

"No." Tamara gave the colt a pat on the neck. "He's ready. Aren't you, boy?"

Asher closed the gate at Pest's tail. "We're locked up and ready to go." *Locked up* was the verbal cue to be alert for the bell to sound and the front gates to open.

Tamara flexed her fingers around the reins, drawing a steadying breath.

The bell rang.

The gates flew open.

Pest shook his head before lunging out, immediately a stride behind Slugger. Tamara rose to the martini position.

Frannie took advantage of the space and guided Slugger toward the rail, setting a fast pace.

Tamara kept Pest about half a length back, trying to gauge their speed. Too fast and Pest would burn out coming down the stretch. Too slow and Slugger could outpace him, creating a lead too big to overcome even when he got winded.

Seconds stretched. Time slowed. Hooves pounded a steady pace. Blood roared in her ears.

Tamara was aware of Pest's fluid movements beneath her. He'd found an easy stride. She was aware of how Frannie held Slugger's reins a bit too loosely. She was letting Slugger set the pace.

Maybe Slugger will burn out on the back stretch.

They approached the first turn.

Slugger swung wide—

No, no, no, no.

—nearly bumping into Pest.

Tamara experienced a rush of prickly adrenaline that threatened her riding posture.

Pest didn't like it, either. He lengthened his stride, intent upon passing Slugger.

Or rather, he tried to.

"Not yet. We've got to be smart." Tamara held him in position, his head even with Slugger's saddle.

They reached the back stretch. Slugger and Frannie increased the pace.

And Tamara let them, dropping back until Pest's nose was even with Slugger's haunches.

"Patience," Tamara said as they headed for the far turn.

The far turn. Where Tamara planned to make

her move. Just as soon as she sensed Slugger start to slow.

They began the turn, heading for the apex.

And there it was. Slugger's pace decreased.

"Now!" Tamara cried, giving Pest more rein.

The gray colt surged forward.

Frannie and Slugger felt their lead slipping. Frannie began using her whip. Slugger tried to regain his speed.

But Pest was determined to win this race. He overtook Slugger as they headed into the home stretch. His stride was smooth and fast.

This is fine. Everything is fine.

But Tamara didn't relax. Not mentally. Not physically. The homestretch was where races were most often lost. Horses could slow without another horse to catch. She didn't use her whip but she kept Pest at speed until they crossed the finish line.

And then disaster struck.

Pest stumbled.

NATHAN SAW PEST STUMBLE. He felt a sickening sense of déjà vu.

Frosty. Tamara.

His heart stuttered along with the colt's unsteady steps.

And then Pest recovered.

"I think I just had a heart attack." Asher clutched at his chest.

Big E removed his black cowboy hat and fanned his face. "Me, too."

"Same." Nathan watched Pest, with Tamara, slowly gallop on the far side of the track.

"He slowed down too soon," Edie said, looking just as shaken as the rest of them. "Back hoof clipped the front. Rookie horse mistake."

"I'm guessing he tried to look back to where Slugger was," Nathan said, ruing the fact that they hadn't recorded the race. He wanted to see it again in slow motion.

"We'll put side blinders on his bridle on Friday," Edie promised. "That'll keep his gaze front fixing."

Owen called out Pest's time. And then Slugger's. Frannie and Slugger had finished a length and a half behind Pest.

"That's competitive," Asher said, looking to Nathan, smiling a little.

"But it's slower than Patrick's horse when Tamara ran him to a win." Nathan didn't like that.

"It was a smaller field today. Fewer horses make for a slower result sometimes." Big E chose to look at the bright side. It wasn't his horse or his children's hearts that were at stake here. "I think we have a good chance with Pest one-on-one with Red Sunset."

Not if Tamara refused to use her whip for fear of causing another accident.

In modern day racing, the whip was designed with a softer shaft to reduce the impact when used. It was used to reinforce jockey commands and communicate to the horse that it was time to fly down the homestretch, not to hurt the animal.

Frannie and Tamara brought their horses to the gate, receiving congratulations. Owen took hold of Slugger's reins while Nathan took hold of Pest's.

"I ran Slugger too fast, didn't I?" Frannie asked Tamara. "He was tired at the end."

"Slugger is a sprinter. He needs to have you ride him a bit slower at first." Tamara sounded odd. Her words were stilted. Her face was pale and her hands shook on the reins. "What happened to him on the first turn when you swung wide?"

Frannie frowned. "I don't think he liked Pest that close. He broke stride and lost his balance."

Nathan let Owen move ahead. He glanced up at Tamara. "Are you okay? That stumble at the end was scary."

Tamara's dark eyes were watery and her nose red. "Can we talk about this later?"

"No. You can tell me. You can tell me anything."

Tamara drew a deep breath. "Let's talk after dinner."

"Tamara..."

"*Please.*" Her plea tugged at his heart. She was hurting and rebuffing his offers to listen, problem solve and comfort. "Let's focus on Pest. Make sure he didn't hurt himself."

She was right, of course. Pest was supposed to be a top priority for Nathan. And the colt would have been had Tamara not been visibly shaken by the ride.

They reached the hot-walker station. Tamara leaped out of the saddle, landed on both feet, then crumpled to the ground. And passed out.

Kind of like Nathan had after riding in the showcase as a ten-year-old.

"Owen, take Pest." Nathan released the colt's reins and knelt next to Tamara, gathering her into his arms. "Wake up, honey." He removed her helmet and patted her cheek. Her skin was clammy. "It's okay. Everything's okay."

Her eyelids fluttered. She stared into his eyes. And then, she started to cry.

NATHAN AND THE twins brought Tamara's dinner to her room. A plate of lasagna with fresh green beans and garlic bread. It smelled delicious, like a warm hug, but Tamara wasn't hungry.

Nathan set the tray on her small desk.

"I was just about to come down," Tamara protested, sitting up in bed. She hated herself for passing out, hated that she felt the punch and shiver of fear every time she relived Pest's brief stumble. "You didn't need to do that."

Nathan sat at the foot of her bed, looking grim. "Yeah, we did."

"Dad said you fell asleep in the saddle." T.J. studied her in wonder. "I don't think that's a good thing."

"It's not," Tamara confirmed. "But I'm fine now."

"Do you have any cake?" Zeke asked, opening the small refrigerator.

"I don't. Sorry." Tamara bit her lower lip, fighting the urge to cry again.

There are no tears in horse racing.

Not even if your father wanted to take first place and you feared riding a horse to death.

"It's not for me." Zeke took a slow 360 inventory of her room. "You look like you need some."

"Aw. That's sweet of you, Zeke." Her eyes teared up again.

"Dad, we should go get some cake for Tamara." Zeke stared at her, a worried quirk to his brow. "Or chocolate."

"A kitten cuddle might help," T.J suggested. "Or Zeke's alligator stuffy."

"Boys, why don't you go downstairs and eat dinner?" Nathan got to his feet, herding the boys toward the door. "I'll be there in a minute."

The boys didn't budge.

"You can bring me ice cream later," Tamara suggested. Kelley kept ice cream in the break room freezer.

"Okay!" The pair headed out the door, promising to be back after eating.

Nathan sat on the edge of Tamara's bed again. "You look…no better than you did after the race."

"I think I held too much in after Frosty died," Tamara admitted, fingers knotting in the blanket.

"After the scare at the finish line today, it just became too much to lock inside me." It was time for some hard truths. Both for Nathan and herself. "But this was cleansing. I'm sure I'll be fine by morning."

Nathan shook his head. "I don't think you will be. I don't think you're in shape to ride. Not mentally. I don't blame you, but I didn't realize the extent of the scars you're carrying from Frosty's accident. I can't let you race Pest, or any of our animals during the showcase. What if you pass out during a race? Don't tell me the bump Slugger gave you didn't get your blood pumping."

She wasn't going to admit anything. "You're… you're firing me?"

Again?

"No. I'm…moving you to stable hand duty." Nathan looked pained. But he didn't shy away from her gaze.

"You're demoting me?" Tamara couldn't believe it. Disbelief chased her fears away. "Nathan, I can win that race. Pest and I are just starting to get to know one another."

"I can't risk your safety." His voice was pitched low. His expression unyielding.

"That's not your call to make. I know what I'm capable of. If we weren't…*involved*, you wouldn't even know anything was wrong with me."

"Can't you see that I'm doing this to keep you

safe?" He laid a hand on her calf, currently covered with a blanket.

Tamara wiped away a stray tear. "Why can't you trust me?"

"I guess for the same reason you didn't trust me enough to include me in the decision to ride Pest in the first place." She knew what he was saying was from his heart.

But it was a heart she didn't own.

And Nathan was adamant. She wasn't going to ride Pest. He didn't trust her.

Faced with that wall, Tamara declined the demotion and kicked him out.

It didn't take long to pack up and load her SUV.

But by Tamara's reckoning, it would take longer to pack up the remains of her heart.

CHAPTER TWENTY

"WHAT DO YOU mean Tamara left?" Edie practically shouted the question at Nathan when he returned from driving the boys to school on Monday morning. "I thought she was sleeping in. We need her."

"What have you done, Nathan?" Asher asked, cradling his coffee mug close to his chest.

"She's still going to ride Pest at the showcase though, right?" Big E said, giving no time for Nathan to answer. "We have to keep our eyes on the ball."

Nathan shook his head, not trusting himself to speak, to explain. If he opened his mouth, he'd start talking about how Tamara had broken his heart by leaving.

All I wanted to do was protect her. I can't lose anyone else.

"Look, we need another jockey," Nathan managed to say, forcing the words past a throat clogged with heartache. "A good one."

All eyes swiveled toward Frannie.

"Don't look at me." Frannie dropped her fork on

the table. "I'm not ready. I only ran my first race yesterday."

"No offense, Frannie, but you're our last option," Nathan assured her.

And the green jockey looked fine with that.

"It's my understanding that a jockey is the strategist of the race," Big E said in the deep voice of his. "We need a wily rider in the saddle."

Asher gestured for Nathan to follow him into the filly barn breezeway. "What are you doing? We need Tamara every day, not just on race day. And *you* need Tamara. You love her."

"Well, I…" Nathan ran a hand around his neck, too heartsick to argue the love part. "She passed out after the ride. I told her it wasn't safe for her to race."

"Is she pregnant?" Big E joined them.

"*No.*" Nathan scowled.

"Did she have low blood sugar?" Asher demanded.

"*No.*" Nathan reluctantly explained about Tamara's struggle with her confidence since Frosty's accident.

"She rode fine," Asher pointed out. "If Pest hadn't stumbled, she probably wouldn't have fainted."

"How do you know Slugger nearly bumping her wouldn't have had the same effect?" Nathan certainly didn't. "I can't… I can't risk losing her." He sank to the floor. "I can't risk losing anyone else."

"Except Pest," Asher reminded him.

Nathan washed a hand over his face. "Can't

you see? I'm trying not to be like Dad, putting the horses ahead of family."

It was quiet for a moment. And then Asher sat down next to Nathan, draping his arm over his shoulder. "You don't have to say another word."

"We'll do whatever you decide about Pest racing," Big E said, softly.

"I just want to do the right thing," Nathan said, feeling miserable about letting everyone down.

"I think you are," Asher said, quietly.

"How do you know?" Nathan whispered.

"Because you're miserable," Big E said.

Luna trotted over and deposited a kitten in his lap.

But it would take more than a kitten cuddle to make everything right again.

"DAD." TAMARA FOUND HER father at Richmond Stables after spending the night in a cheap motel in town, drowning in her own tears. She was still feeling drained and weepy. "I've come to say goodbye."

"You can't be serious." Dad looked at her funny, removing his riding helmet. "There's a showcase on Friday. Have you forgotten? Owners will see how good you are and want to hire you."

Tamara shook her head and slowly explained about Pest's practice race, how she passed out afterward and how Nathan had demoted her to stable hand. "I won't be racing you, Dad. I've got to find a place to start over. Don't forget to send me a wedding invitation, okay?"

"Oh, my sweet little girl." Dad hugged her. It was a stiff hug given he still wore his riding safety vest. And when he released her, he held Tamara at arm's length. "Do you remember that car accident we were in when you were a little girl?"

That was easy. There'd only been one. "The one where the guy T-boned us because he didn't stop at the red light?"

"That's it." Dad nodded. "You wouldn't get back in a car for a week."

"I don't remember that part." Funny…in an odd way…that Nathan had been saying that phrase every time anyone referenced his rocky childhood.

Dad paid no attention to her poor memory. "But you did get back in. You'll land on your feet, Tammie. You always do."

Tamara wasn't so sure.

"This is a surprise." Caroline Richmond approached Tamara, looking put together in slim jeans and a plain, pressed red T-shirt. But she also looked curious. "What brings you here?"

"She's no longer at Blackwell Stables," Dad said before Tamara could.

"Is that so?" Caroline's smile curled into something deeply satisfying. For her, anyway. "We're always looking for competent, winning jockeys."

Tamara took a step back. "Oh, I—"

"She'd love to come work for you," Dad said quickly.

Tamara tried again. "Oh, I—"

"And we'd love to have her. Consider yourself hired." While Tamara tried to process what had just happened, Caroline called someone on her cell phone. "Jimmy, we're hiring a new exercise jockey. I'm sending her over to fill out the paperwork."

"I don't know," Tamara said when Caroline had ended the call. "I think I might need to take some time off. Get my head on straight. You know?"

"Walk with me." Caroline didn't wait for Tamara to agree. She just charged off toward the racetrack, stretching her long, jean-clad legs. "Hurry up. Time's a-wasting."

"Caroline..." Tamara scurried after her, trying to find her backbone. "I haven't accepted your offer."

Caroline whirled around, as nimble as a barrel racer at speed. And then she bore down on Tamara. "People don't turn down Caroline Richmond. Especially people who don't want it to be known that they're struggling with their confidence in the saddle."

The way she spoke, so sharp and heated, tested Tamara's tattered resolve.

"We're at a disadvantage, you and I." Caroline pointed from herself to Tamara. "This industry is dominated by men and we women need to stick together."

"I… I know," Tamara stammered, having said much the same thing to Frannie. "But—"

"My offer to help you is a one-time deal, Tamara." Caroline took Tamara's measure in one quick swath of a look. "You'll have a better chance of success with me on your side."

That's a little cocky.

But Caroline could pull off cocky.

"Well?" The Richmond Stables owner raised her brows. "Are you in? Or out?"

"She's in!" Dad said, riding past on a fine-looking dun.

Tamara smiled, if only a little. "I appreciate the solidarity. But I have to know, Caroline. Was anyone at the Richmond Stables involved in the doping of that Blackwell horse? Because if they were…"

"WHAT'S THIS?" ZEKE entered the break room after school later that day. He approached the table where Nathan had set out a cake. "Double-chocolate fudge?"

T.J. glanced around. "Where's Tamara?"

"She's…uh…" Nathan had just picked them up from school and knew he couldn't keep the secret of the grudge race from them anymore. "She left today."

The boys stared at him in open-mouthed disbelief.

"She left because I wouldn't let her ride Pest in

the showcase," Nathan admitted. "Let's have some cake and talk about it."

The twins glanced from Nathan to the cake and back again.

"We don't want cake," T.J. said.

"Yeah, not without Tamara," Zeke said.

Me, either.

"I'm going to cut some slices." Nathan moved to the table where he'd gathered a knife, forks and plates.

The boys scrambled behind him, their boots striking the floor.

But their footsteps receded. They didn't come for cake. The twins ran up the stairs. The sound of their footsteps was demoralizing, along with their shouts of "*Tamara!*"

If they were this upset by Tamara leaving, how would they take the news of Pest being the possible prize as part of the showcase's featured race?

Nathan trudged upstairs, needing to find out.

"DID YOU GIVE me Fire to exercise on my first day out of spite?" Tamara asked Caroline when the trainer came to give her instructions only a few hours after she'd been hired.

The afternoon was overcast and cooler than it had been recently. Caroline had deemed it all right to exercise the horses later than usual. The groom that had led Fire out from the colt barn had unclipped his lead rope and had presumably returned to his other duties, leaving Tamara and Fire a few feet from the track gate.

Fire stomped his front hoof, eager to run.

Tamara held him on a tight rein.

"You can do hard things." Caroline spouted that cliché as if it was her own personal mantra. "You've proven that. I only give jockeys horses I think they can handle."

I can do hard things. Like defeat my fears.

Just being around Caroline for a few hours almost made Tamara believe it was true.

Caroline gave her a hard look, but Tamara felt the woman's bark was stronger than her bite. "Are you going to give me attitude every day? Or just today?"

"Since you didn't answer my question about your involvement with the doping of Pride, I'm going to bring attitude every day until you fire me." There was something about Caroline that rubbed Tamara the wrong way, women backing each other and respect for the owner's training skill aside. And there was probably a bit of anger building inside her over Nathan's desire to keep her from riding.

Whatever it was, Tamara wasn't up to taking anybody's guff.

"Stubborn," Caroline scoffed. "I can tell this isn't going to be a long and cherished relationship." Then she gave Tamara ride instructions and strutted away.

"I see why you're cranky all the time, Fire." Tamara patted his neck.

Fire snorted and tried to bolt onto the track.

"Careful, fella." Tamara pulled back on the reins. "You don't want to test my last nerve today."

But he did anyway.

"ASHER, I NEED HELP." Nathan entered the break room while Kelley was preparing to serve dinner, feet dragging. "I explained what a grudge race is to the twins."

"They know they might lose Pest?" Asher grimaced. "Not fun."

Nathan nodded. "They ran off about twenty minutes ago." And he'd let them, sitting in Tamara's empty apartment doing some serious soul searching. "They aren't with Pest or in the tree house." The one Asher had repaired. "Can you help me look for them?"

"You want to divide and conquer?" Big E had come in behind Nathan.

"No. I… I want family around me." Needed them, in fact. His life had unraveled so quickly. He didn't think he could weave the parts back together without assistance and moral support.

Big E beamed at Nathan. "We're here for you."

"I'll drive." Asher went to kiss Kelley. "We'll be late for dinner, sorry."

"I'll keep it warm," she promised.

The three Blackwells trekked out to the available ATVs.

"Where do you want to start?" Asher asked, sliding behind the wheel.

Nathan sat in the passenger seat, leaving Big E the back. "Let's go to the creek behind the far pasture."

"The one with Pride?" Big E sounded alarmed.

"The one and the same." Nathan only hoped they used the same path to get safely to the creek bed as before and stayed out of the water. He'd repeated that nonstop after their last adventure.

Asher put the quad into gear and off they went.

"I know I let everyone down," Nathan admitted, clasping his hands in his lap. "It isn't just Tamara and the boys. Not even Edie will talk to me."

"Would you do anything different?" Asher asked. "You know, with Tamara?"

"If I'd have known sooner she was struggling—"

"Don't play the what-if game," Big E said from the back seat. "You can't change the past. You can only shape your future."

Asher gave Nathan a significant look. "Big E is loaded with greeting card sayings, just like Dad was."

You can't win them all.

Those were his father's words after that baseball game loss when Nathan was a kid.

Nathan allowed himself a little chuckle. "What was it Dad used to say after we lost a big race?"

"'Losing is a learning opportunity.'" Asher

leaned his forearms on the steering wheel, using them to steer the slow-moving vehicle.

Big E's laughter rippled through the air. "Walter and I are definitely related." His phone chimed with a video call. "Darling, what's up?"

"I missed you, you old codger."

That had Big E laughing again. "I meant to call but there have been some emergencies here I've been dealing with. The loss of a very important jockey. Little boys wandering off unsupervised."

"When are you coming home, my love?"

"Soon!" Asher and Nathan chimed in, exchanging smiles.

"You and I are definitely related," Asher said, heading around the turn and engaging in conversation, possibly to give Big E and his wife privacy.

"I'm glad of that." Nathan's hands were clasped so tight his fingers were turning white. "I've been a bad father."

"Because your kids ran off?" Asher scoffed. "Wait until they're teenagers."

"I'm serious. The last two years were hard on me and I wasn't fully present." He flexed his fingers, scanning the bushes for socks. "I should have recovered sooner."

"They're five. They won't remember."

"Says the single man with no kids."

"Says the single dad who blocked out most memories of his childhood, both good and bad."

"There is that." Nathan slumped in his seat.

"What if they don't want to remember these early years? What if they hate me because of Pest?"

"You're assuming you've lost the race before it's ever begun," Big E said, having finished his video chat. "I've been trying to tell you that it's not too late to make amends. To your kids. And to Tamara."

Nathan didn't think Tamara would ever talk to him again. "I think my goal should be to do Marilee and my mom proud."

"And win back Tamara," Asher said, pointedly.

"Perhaps by approaching Patrick with a different kind of bet," Big E suggested.

"You know he won't accept." Nathan rolled his shoulders back, still looking for socks cast aside along the path.

"I don't know," Big E replied. "And you won't know, either, until you ask."

"Dad would never..." Nathan began.

"But that's the point, brother." Asher spared a hand from the wheel to nudge Nathan's shoulder. "This is our time to run Blackwell Stables. We can run it any way we want."

Before Nathan could process that statement, the yearling colt pasture came into view.

"Look!" Nathan pointed. "There they are."

His kids were mingling with the yearlings.

Probably picking out Pest's replacement.

Nathan's jaw clenched. He couldn't let that happen.

CHAPTER TWENTY-ONE

NATHAN AND ASHER tracked down Patrick at the Galloping Fork Diner after they dropped the boys off at school on Thursday morning. They'd spent the past few days exercising the horses Tamara would have ridden, including Pest, and planning this confrontation.

Patrick was eating breakfast alone, something they'd heard he did every Thursday. The two Blackwells slid into his booth, sitting across from him.

"Waitress, I need a refill." Patrick held up his coffee cup. "And bring these Blackwells some strong coffee. They look like they need it."

The coffee was delivered. The men stared each other down. Nobody drank coffee.

"Patrick," Nathan began. "I need to change the prize structure of our race tomorrow."

Patrick laughed, long and gratingly loud.

"I'd like to propose a cash buy-in," Nathan continued. "You put up five thousand dollars and I'll put up five thousand dollars. Winner takes all."

"Sounds fair to me," Asher said.

Patrick rested his arm across the back of the

booth and smirked at them. "It would have sounded fair last week before we shook hands on the conditions of the race."

"Renegotiations happen all the time in business," Asher pointed out.

"But not in the horse business," Patrick snapped back. "Besides, I don't have the money. That's why I suggested we put up horses."

"Perhaps we can run a different horse." Nathan searched his mind for a suitable two-year-old. "Copper Mercury is a promising filly."

Patrick rolled his eyes. "I prefer Tempest Wind. I'm not budging on this."

Asher and Nathan exchanged glances.

"The racing commission frowns on grudge races," Nathan said, reaching for straws. If Patrick had been involved in bribing Elliot to dope Pride, he wouldn't care about the governing body of horse racing.

"It's a private showcase," Patrick said, firm in his position.

"And if we refuse to race on our private property?" Asher asked, brows arching.

"Then everyone will know that the Blackwells are liars. If there was one thing you stood for, it was the honesty of your father's word."

Asher and Nathan exchanged another long look.

Without a word, they got up and left the diner.

Nathan got into Asher's truck. It had been their father's truck. Just thinking about Dad reminded

Nathan that Patrick's words were correct. His father had been a man of his word. "I can't back out. I shook Patrick's hand and agreed to the terms of the grudge race."

"Agreed. Although it was worth a shot to try to change the terms." Asher didn't start the truck. Instead, he gave Nathan a direct gaze. "Dad would say that you've made your bed and now you have to lie in it."

"He didn't think I added value to the business." And didn't this just prove it?

Asher scowled. "Dad could be a fool."

"Right now…so am I." Nathan recalled Tamara's tearful face when he'd told her he wouldn't let her ride. "What it comes down to was my lack of trust. Not just in Tamara but in Pest."

"You're saying…" Asher peered at Nathan's face. "You're saying you believe they can win."

Nathan nodded. "When Dad ran the stables, he knew which horses to choose to run in which races. He knew which jockeys to choose given the horse, the competition and the track conditions." Nathan removed his cowboy hat and ran a hand through his hair. "I've never had to make those calls."

"You need to trust your gut." Asher reached over his shoulder for his seat belt.

"And Tamara's." Nathan fit his cowboy hat back on his head.

"See?" Asher backed the truck out of the parking space. "I told you the good memories would start coming back."

Nathan nodded once more. They had. "There's one thing I'd forgotten about our childhood." Something Big E spouted like a mantra. "Words to live by, I think."

"What's that?"

"Blackwells always pull together."

And more than anything…

Nathan stared at his wedding ring. He wanted Tamara to be a Blackwell.

"WHAT DID YOU do with Dandy?" Caroline walked down from the viewing platform at Richmond Stables' track after Tamara had taken the filly for an exercise ride.

A groom came over to take hold of Dandy's reins, silently waiting for permission to lead the horse to the hot-walker station.

"She's running differently." Tamara didn't hop off the horse, addressing Caroline from the saddle. She gave Dandy a pat on the neck. "The question is…do you like the way she's running?"

Caroline leaned over the rail. "Yes. There's something different about you this morning, I think." She stared long and hard at Tamara. "Besides your judicious use of the whip as a performance cue, that is."

Tamara preferred not to answer. The truth was that Tamara was riding differently. More confidently. And using her whip. Something she hadn't been able to bring herself to do since the accident.

Caroline is pushing me in the right direction.

But admitting that to her brash, egotistical boss was something Tamara wasn't going to do. Give Caroline Richmond an inch, and she'd hold it over your head for a mile.

Dandy shifted her weight on her feet, turning her head toward Caroline. The groom that held Dandy's reins pretended to study something on the ground.

"Do you have a retirement plan?" Caroline asked out of the blue.

"You mean an investment portfolio?" Tamara laughed. "Not a chance."

"I meant…" Caroline's tone took on an edge, the way it did when she felt she had something important to say and didn't think whoever she spoke to was taking her seriously. "I meant, what are you going to do when you can no longer race, Tamara?" The Richmond Stables owner and trainer was impatient. But then again, she was always impatient, having a short fuse. "Have you thought about it?"

"No." Tamara rolled her shoulders back. It was the same question Nathan had asked her recently. "If you're saying I should retire—"

"I'm saying you can't coast through life, Tamara," Caroline snapped. "You have to have a plan for this year, for five years from now, and a contingency plan in case it all crashes down on you tomorrow." She crossed her arms over her chest.

"I don't know why I take an interest in you. You're a mess."

It was on the tip of Tamara's tongue to feed Caroline's ego by thanking her for taking the time to push Tamara harder than she'd been pushed before. But they were interrupted.

"Tamara." That familiar voice. So deep. So soulful.

Tamara looked up to see Nathan purposefully striding toward her. He looked different, as if something had changed since she'd seen him last. He stood head and shoulders above most of the crowd, brown cowboy hat shading his strong features and darkening his blue eyes.

"What's a Blackwell doing here?" Caroline spit. "Our security guard needs to be reprimanded."

Nathan tipped his cowboy hat brim up and stared at Caroline. "You don't have a security guard."

"Well, we should get one." Caroline waved him off. "Whatever you have to say to Tamara, you have five minutes. Then she's got another ride. We keep to a tight schedule here." She stomped back up to the observation platform.

Tamara dismounted. The stable hand led Dandy away.

And then she was facing Nathan, head held high. "Why are you here?"

To ask me how I'm doing? To rehire me as your race jockey? To tell me you love me and can't live without me?

Tamara contained an eye roll. Her heart would never learn that Nathan was out of reach.

"How are you?" Nathan fidgeted, suddenly looking unsure. "We've…uh…missed you at the stables the last few days."

She smirked. That was highly unlikely.

"The boys and I… Edie and the rest." Nathan stepped out of the way of another exercise jockey taking a horse onto the track. "It's the showcase today."

"I know." Her father had left early to get there. Tamara had no intention of attending.

"Big race for Pest."

"I know."

Nathan eased closer, staring at Tamara's face with a soft smile and a tender look in his eyes. "Your father tells me you're riding better than ever."

I think so.

But she wasn't cocky enough to say that.

Nathan moved closer still. "I'm sorry."

That was a blanket apology. "For what?"

"For not trusting you when you said you could ride Pest in the grudge match." He took hold of her right hand in his larger, stronger, warmer one. "You know yourself best."

She nodded. She did.

"Tamara!" That was T.J. He ran up to join them, followed by Zeke. Both boys had on their Sunday-best cowboy outfits. "We just saw a newborn colt."

Zeke looked blissful, on cloud nine. "He was so cute that I just wanted to give him a squeeze."

"But I wouldn't let him." T.J. gave Tamara a side hug. "It's my job to keep Zeke out of trouble."

"He actually does keep me out of trouble every once in a while," Zeke allowed, giving Tamara a side hug, too. Then he stared up at her with big blue eyes. "When are you coming home?"

"She's not coming back," Caroline shouted from the observation platform. "Two minutes, Tamara. And then I'll expect you in the saddle."

Tamara sighed, gaze dropping from her boss to Nathan's hand holding hers. Catching. Her fingers convulsed around his because… "You took off your wedding ring."

"It was time," Nathan said, quietly. "After my mother died, my father clung to the past and became a bitter man who couldn't find the love that once existed for his sons. I didn't want to become like that. But I was headed down that path. That is, until you made it clear that I need to move on with my life before the chance at love passes me by." He stared at Tamara with such obvious love in his eyes that she wanted to cry. "I'll always love Marilee. But there's room in my heart—lots and lots of room—to love you, too."

Tamara's breath caught.

"We want to keep you," Zeke said.

"*Marry* you," T.J. corrected, elbowing his brother.

"I love you, Tamara," Nathan repeated. "I'm not

going to fight this feeling anymore. I want you with us, both on a personal and a professional level. Because family… *Blackwells*…pull together."

"That sounds like something Big E would say," Tamara noted with a small smile. She loved Nathan but she was too afraid to say the words out loud. Being with Nathan while he worked through tangled emotions had been a roller-coaster ride. He'd taken off his wedding ring, and he'd come here, but—

"We like Big E," T.J. told her.

"Just not as much as we like you," Zeke said firmly.

Tamara blinked back sudden tears.

"We want you to ride Pest in the showcase," Nathan said in that soft voice. "You're ready. He's ready. Together, we can win."

"Pest loves you," T.J. said. "That's why you'll win."

"And you love Pest," Zeke said. "*That's* why you'll win."

Tamara lifted her gaze to Nathan's face. "But what if—"

"Whatever happens, Tamara, it'll happen to us as a couple," Nathan said sincerely. "As a *family*."

As a Blackwell.

"You… You believe in me?" Tamara didn't dare believe it.

The three Blackwells nodded.

"We love you," Nathan stated, plainly. "We believe in you. No matter what happens today, we'll still love you."

The boys gave her big, sweeping nods.

They love me. How can I refuse?

"All right. I'll do it."

The twins hooted and tossed their cowboy hats in the air and Nathan swept her into a spinning hug. And when he set her down, Nathan stared expectantly into her eyes. Waiting.

For me to tell him I love him?

But even with Nathan's confession of love, Tamara couldn't say the words back, not just yet. Because she'd been let down before. By her mother. By Nathan. Even by her father.

Can he really mean it? Win or lose, we'll be together either way?

"Fine," Caroline called down to them. "Take her away to ride in that grudge match. But Tamara needs to be back at work on Monday."

"Caroline, when Tamara wins this race, she's not going to want to return to you," Nathan promised, leading Tamara and the boys away. And then, he spoke only to Tamara. "Because we're going to shower you with love and support, always. We even bought you a new pair of racing socks."

CHAPTER TWENTY-TWO

HOURS LATER, TAMARA was at the Blackwell Stables and wearing the Blackwell silks.

Nathan's silks for Frosty had been black-and white striped. But the Blackwell Stables colors were black-and-white checkerboard. She looked at herself in the mirror in what used to be her tiny studio apartment, unable to believe all the changes that had occurred in the past week—in her, in Nathan, in Pest.

The last of the "regular" showcase races had just finished. It was Tamara's turn to ride. She came down the filly barn stairs, expecting to hurry outside where Owen would be holding Pest.

Instead, a crowd awaited her on the landing.

"Good luck." Asher patted her shoulder.

"I made double-chocolate fudge cake for later." Kelley hugged her.

"It hasn't been the same since you've been gone." Still wearing dirt-splattered silks, Frannie hugged her. "Slugger and I won the last race. I'm dedicating my first win to you."

"Thanks." Tamara moved toward the door, feeling the burning pressure to win build in her chest. It crowded her lungs, making each breath quick and shallow.

Another crowd awaited her outside.

"Win or lose," Big E said, encompassing Tamara in a bear hug. "You'll always be top dog to me."

"Sentimental nonsense," Edie muttered, giving Tamara a quick side hug. "Run the race the way you see fit." She entered the filly stable. "No regrets."

"Where are you going?" Tamara asked.

"I can't watch," Edie replied, disappearing inside.

No pressure.

Nathan was waiting for her next, holding Blaze's reins. The chestnut's bright coat gleamed in the sun.

"Did you put on the new socks?" Nathan asked, smiling as if Pest's ownership wasn't going to be decided in the next few minutes. "A good pair of socks is the best platform for success."

Tamara nodded. He wasn't wrong. Foot comfort was important for any athlete.

Nathan leaned over and kissed her cheek. "I know this is all happening fast. But I need to say it again. We win as a family and we lose as a family."

Tamara gave a brisk nod, very much aware that Nathan was showering her with love but not the romantic kind.

Nathan swung into Blaze's saddle. He was going to lead her and Pest through their warm-up on the track.

A few feet away, the twins were showering Pest with affection, saying their goodbyes.

Tamara almost broke down in tears then.

Nathan eased Blaze up to her side with a timely reminder for everyone. "We win as a family and we lose as a family."

Zeke and T.J. nodded and backed away from their beloved colt.

Owen handed Nathan the lead rope attached to Pest, then moved to the colt's left side, holding his hand down low. "Leg up, Tamara?"

"Yes, sir." He grabbed hold of Tamara's calf and tossed her high in the air. So high that Tamara was nearly launched over Pest. "*Hey.*" She tightened her hold on the saddle, laughing a little. "I don't think you know your own strength, Owen."

"Nerves." The ginger blushed.

Frannie came to stand beside him, taking hold of his hand.

Someone's gotten their happy-ever-after.

Tamara still wasn't confident she'd secure hers today.

Nathan cued Blaze into a walk, drawing Pest in his wake.

"How've you been, fella?" Tamara patted Pest's smooth gray neck. "Are you ready for this?"

The twins ran past, shouting "Good luck!" and heading toward the grandstand.

A familiar, unexpected figure stepped into their path ahead.

"*Caroline?*" Tamara couldn't believe it. "What are you doing here?"

"I came to wish you luck." Caroline tossed her hair as if this should be something Tamara knew. "Obviously. That's what mentors do."

Mentor? They'd only been working together regularly for less than a week. But Tamara smiled anyway, understanding that was Caroline's way of supporting her.

"Are you wishing Tamara luck out of guilt over drugging a different gray Blackwell horse?" Nathan asked with an edge that matched Caroline's in his tone.

She smirked and turned away, heading for the grandstand.

"I can't believe she showed up here." Nathan shook his head.

"I like her," Tamara surprised herself by saying. "If a Richmond is responsible for what happened to Pride, I don't think it was her."

Nathan stared at Tamara a moment before nodding. "Okay. If you say so."

For some reason, that made Tamara feel better.

"And here comes today's loser." That was Patrick Connelly. He stood at the racetrack gate, having just sent off Tamara's father atop Red Sunset. "Have you ever beat your father in a race, Tamara?"

"Why do I think he knows the answer to this question?" Nathan muttered, steering the horses away from Patrick, giving their rival a wide berth.

"I've beaten him once," Tamara said, trying to sound defiant. "You saw that race, Patrick." She'd won on Red Sunset. The same horse she was now racing against.

"But I think your father's still got the statistical advantage," Patrick said, smacking his lips. "Given you've only beaten him in one race."

"Don't listen to him," Nathan advised as they entered the racetrack. He cued Blaze into a trot. "You've got this."

Pest trotted smoothly.

As she began posting up, Tamara's body was consumed by a prickly wave of adrenaline mixed with anxiety. She didn't want to let anyone down.

Dad and a rider Tamara didn't recognize were warming up on the back stretch of the track. She and her father had spent more time together in the past few days than they had since they'd lived together when Tamara was a kid. But her father was cocky about this race, confident that he was going to win.

"Stop thinking about all the bad that can happen," Nathan told her, sitting firm in his Western saddle. "Focus on the race. On Pest. On your father's idiosyncrasies when he races."

He's right.

"Do your best." Nathan gave Tamara a supportive smile. "That's all I'm asking."

"That's all anyone can ask for on race day," Tamara murmured.

Nathan cued Blaze into a slow gallop. Pest transitioned easily. Clearly, he was looser than Tamara was, loose enough to consider the race fun.

I used to think of racing as fun.

But Frosty's accident had stolen that from her, the same way that Marilee's accident had stolen Nathan's joy for life.

I want that joy back.

They finished their warm-up and returned to the starting gate. Patrick's horse was loaded first. Then it was Pest's turn.

"I love you no matter what," Nathan told Tamara before unclipping Pest's lead rope and letting Owen take hold of the colt's reins.

I love you, too.

But Tamara still couldn't bring herself to say the words. To trust that love was real and lasting.

"Tammie!" Dad gave her a wide smile when she and Pest entered the gate. "Patrick told me you were back in the saddle today. What made the Blackwells change their minds about you riding?"

"Love," she told him, no holds barred. She shifted her grip on the reins. "Sometimes, that's all you need."

Before Dad could reply, the bell rang, the gates opened and Pest gave his head a good shake before launching himself out onto the track. Out of habit, Tamara rose out of the saddle and into the martini position.

The medium-sized crowd let out a cheer.

But Tamara had no time for that. Her father was already a half length ahead of them.

Oh, no. We're going to lose.

That's when Nathan's words came back to her: *Focus on the race. On Pride. On your father's idiosyncrasies when he races.*

Pest was easily keeping up with Red Sunset as they passed the grandstand proper.

What are Dad's racing quirks?

He liked to hug the rail. He'd already moved there.

He liked to gab while he rode. He turned his head back toward Tamara. "Now, you're riding, Tammie!"

But she was riding half a horse length behind him as they approached the first turn.

And Red Sunset? That colt had the endurance of a marathon runner. And one speed. Fast.

I'm not going to win thinking about them.

"It's just you and me, Pest." Tamara shifted her weight forward and focused on herself and her own horse.

And suddenly, Tamara felt connected to Pest—his breath, his stride, his desire to win. It was the same way she felt connected to Nathan—his concern for everyone's safety, his level head, his strong sense of responsibility. It was the same way she loved and appreciated the twins' zest for life.

It's love that binds us all. Unconditional love.

Win or lose, Tamara was suddenly certain Nathan's love for her would remain. But more than anything, she wanted to win.

They came out of the far turn and Tamara tapped Pest with the whip, just once. Telling him it was time to make their move.

Pest surged forward smoothly, inching past Red Sunset and her father.

"Too soon, Tammie," Dad told her as they strode ahead now.

It wasn't too soon. Pest liked to take the lead. And so did Tamara.

PEST WON THE race by a length. It was a decisive win. A team win.

So many had helped Tamara regain her confidence, which had allowed her to give her all to Pest.

It was a moment she'd never forget.

"You beat me fair and square, Tammie," Dad said as they slowed their horses to a gallop.

Tamara kept patting Pest's sweat-dampened neck. He'd run a strong race, as if he knew the stakes and wanted to make a statement—that he was a Blackwell, too, and always would be. Tamara spared her father a glance. "I love you, Dad."

"But you don't need me." He shook his head, sounding rueful. "I used to tell you that you'd be fine on your own. And look at you. You finally proved me right."

They both turned their horses around, heading

back toward the grandstand, and the pomp and ceremony awaiting Pest and the Blackwells.

"Hey." Tamara caught her father's attention. "I'll always need you, Dad. And if you love someone, you should keep them in your life." The way she intended to keep in contact with him from now on.

Dad looked like he might cry. He slowed his horse and hopped off, handing over the reins to a very angry looking Patrick. "He didn't have it today."

Tamara rode Pest to the small winner's circle so she didn't hear what Patrick had to say. She assumed it was what sore losers always said, casting the blame elsewhere. There was applause and congratulatory shouts. But they floated over her head.

Because there was Nathan and there were the twins. Waiting for them.

As soon as Owen took hold of Pest's reins, Tamara leaped off and into Nathan's arms. "I love you, Nathan."

"I know," he said, softly, before kissing her deeply, exactly how she'd wanted him to since that first tentative kiss they'd shared in his apartment. And after he'd thoroughly kissed her, Nathan said, "You didn't have to wait to run the race to tell me."

"I did. I needed that ride. It was a long time coming." But she'd tell him all about her experience on the ride later. She turned to Zeke and T.J., who'd just finished loving on their winner of a horse. Still in the shelter of Nathan's arms, Tamara called them over. "I love you, boys. I love you so much."

"More than double-chocolate fudge cake?" Zeke asked, eyeing her suspiciously.

"More than life itself." Tamara hugged him, thrilled when he hugged her back.

"When you and Dad get married, can I call you Mom?" T.J. asked, eliciting *aws* from those close enough to hear.

And although Tamara was touched by the sentiment, she didn't want to usurp Marilee's place in their hearts.

"Why don't you save 'Mom' for your mother. I can be your…" Tamara searched her brain for what she wanted to be called.

"We'll call you Mama T," Zeke said firmly, solving her dilemma.

"That's brilliant." Tamara hugged Zeke once more.

And then she was swept into the winner's ceremony, congratulated by her coworkers and Nathan's family. Pest held himself very still when the band of roses was placed across his withers. He looked so proud, as did Nathan and the twins.

Tamara spared a glance up to heaven.

Thank you, Marilee. I'll take good care of them for you.

THAT EVENING WAS unexpectedly cool.

There'd been a break in the hot weather. A strong breeze swept across the blue grass. It almost felt as if that same breeze swept the cares away from Nathan's heart.

He and Tamara stood at the hay barn pasture, leaning on the rail while the twins played in the tree house and three horses, Blaze, Red Sunset and Pest, grazed contentedly a few feet away. "It was a good day."

"The best day," Tamara murmured, snuggling closer to him. "Love makes everything right."

"Love and socks," Nathan reminded her with a gentle tease. He glanced back toward the stables proper, imagining his father striding between the colt and filly barns, a broad smile on his face after a successful day at the track.

Oh, yeah. I forgot a lot of the good memories.

And with any luck, they'd keep coming back to mind.

"I've been thinking," he told Tamara.

She glanced up at Nathan with those dark eyes, a smile on those tempting lips. "About what?"

"About the future and life not passing me… *us*…by." He curled his arm around her. "I'd like to sell the farm in Paducah and start a new operation here."

"You don't need my permission," Tamara gently pointed out.

"But I want you to have a say." He tipped his cowboy hat back with his free hand and then kissed the top of her head. "Your feelings count, too."

"I like Gold Finch." She smiled at him in return.

"And I like that you aren't going to let life pass you by anymore. It's always best to keep reaching for a dream."

A life with Tamara was his new dream, an outline colored in and made richer by making a life at his childhood home.

Who'd have thought?

"We should race two-year-olds before the local season ends." Tamara slipped her arm around his waist.

"Whatever you say." They'd garnered contracts to train some new two-year-olds after the showcase.

"Whatever your trainer says," Tamara qualified.

"I'd like to promote *you* to head trainer." Nathan had discussed it with Big E and Asher earlier. They'd all been in agreement. "You have the ability to evaluate our horses and put them through the training they need."

Tamara backed away. "I'm not touching Pride."

"No," he agreed. "Pride doesn't need a trainer. He needs a horse whisperer to modify his behavior." And his brother Caleb was just the man for the job.

"Whew." Tamara took Nathan's brown cowboy hat and plopped it on her head. "Of course, I still want to be a race jockey and I'll step aside as trainer if one of your brothers is better suited because right now, riding and being with you and the boys is what I love. But..." She chuckled. "Caroline had words with me before she left." Tamara's dark eyes sparkled with amusement. “She told me to dream bigger and to insist that the Blackwells make me their horse trainer of record.”

Nathan’s eyes narrowed. He had a distrust of Caroline Richmond. Of all the Richmonds. But he couldn’t find fault with Caroline’s words when she’d come to the same conclusion he had.

Nathan adjusted the set of his cowboy hat on Tamara’s head. “I guess we need to look around the property and find a good place to build a house.”

“A wondrous place,” Tamara murmured, nodding with enthusiasm.

Nathan couldn’t believe his luck. Most people never found true love. But he…he’d been able to find love not once in a lifetime but twice.

“Blackwell Stables in Gold Finch, Kentucky,” Tamara was saying. “It sounds like the perfect place to make a home, one filled with love and amazing people, places and things.”

“Including socks,” Nathan quipped, wrapping his arms around her. “Socks are very important to a good life.”

Tamara grinned. “Including socks, my love. Now kiss me.”

Nathan’s answering grin felt deep and lasting. “Whatever you want, my love.”

For now and always.

EPILOGUE

"I SHOULD HAVE KNOWN." Big E set down his cell phone.

He'd just arrived home in Falcon Creek, Montana, kissed his wife hello, hugged his grandchildren and great-grandchildren and then just settled into his favorite recliner, when the call came in from an inquiry that he'd made about the EPO drug.

Big E picked up his phone again and called Asher. "You're not going to believe this," he said before Asher had time to say hello. "Do you know Julia Eisler?"

"Of course I know her. She's our veterinarian."

Big E bit back a curse. He knew he remembered her name from somewhere but he'd been too tired after the drive from Gold Finch to recall. "Your veterinarian is the one who purchased a lot of EPO. I mean, the same batch that Elliot had in his apartment when he died."

"Julia is the drug supplier?" Asher seemed aghast. And then he seemed to repeat what he'd heard for the benefit of someone with him. "Dr. Julia Eisler bought the drugs that doped Pride."

"Call the sheriff!" That sounded like Kelley's voice. "Make a citizen's arrest."

"Julia has no motive for drugging him," Big E reminded Asher.

"But she's involved," Asher said. "She has to be. She was paid to be part of this."

"It seems so, but we need someone with the right medical experience to consult on this. There are a lot of laws and policies surrounding medication that I'm not familiar with. Isn't one of your brothers a veterinarian? Ridge, I think you said." Big E's grandson Ethan was also a vet but he had a wife and young children to keep him busy. Big E couldn't ask him to take an indefinite trip to Gold Finch.

"Ridge is a vet. I'll call him tonight to lay the groundwork for him to help."

"Good idea." Because like all of Walter's children, there was a reluctance to come home. "Let me know if I need to pay Ridge a visit."

Because when it came to family, Big E wasn't going to sit idle for long.

* * * * *

Don't miss the next romance in
The Bluegrass Blackwells miniseries,
coming next month—

A Cowboy To Come Home To *by Carol Ross!*